FORSAKEN

DAUGHTERS ✦ OF ✦ THE ✦ SEA ✦ SERIES

KRISTEN DAY

Edited by: Stacy Sanford
Formatting and Cover Art: Daydream Designs

This is a work of fiction.

All of the characters, organizations and events portrayed in this novel are a product of the author's imagination. Any resemblance to persons, living or dead, actual events or organizations is entirely coincidental.

To Mom and Stacy - thank you for believing in my dreams and catching me when I fall.

Praise for Forsaken Daughters of the Sea #1

"I can't remember the last time I thoroughly enjoyed a book this much! It was inspiring, attention getting, and had romance, mythological creatures, adventure, suspense, and paranormal aspects."   - Reading in the Window Seat

"Truly entertaining and also kudos for being a true YA book. It is clean and smut free enough for me to recommend to the teens I know without question. Forsaken brings to light a world of sea gods and goddess that I can't wait to delve deeper into."   - SupaGurl Books

"Forsaken is a passionate and beautiful book, encompassing a lovely heroine, her hilarious and grounded friends, and a seductive and mysterious lover all uncovering a destiny more grand than any of them could've imagined."
- Between the Bind

"This book caught my attention immediately and it never left. It was a very quick and enjoyable read! The story really came alive in my mind and totally swept me into it. And there was a definitely swoon worthy male character in this one, oh my!"   - My Miscellaneous Bookshelf

"I am a fan, of Kristen Day, of the Daughters of the Sea series, of Stasia and her friends. Fresh ideas, a main character with a fun voice and unusual abilities, a love story and more make Forsaken an enchanting YA novel."
- Reader Girls

"I found myself sitting on the edge of my seats with some of the twists and turns the book took too. Those are the kinds of books I love too when I never know what may happen next. The author has a phenomenal writing style that makes you get into this world and never want to leave."

- Doctor's Notes

"The author did such a great job with the setting of The House of Lorelei that I pictured it very clearly in my mind. I immediately wanted to hop on an airplane and go visit, it was so vivid in detail. In terms of plot, all I can say is wow. This series is ideal for students who love mythology but are looking for some great romance with it."

- Geo Librarian

the fifty nereids

THETIS	leader, spawning	GALATEIA	white sea foam
KETO	sea monsters	GALENE	calm seas
PSAMATHE	sand	GLAUKE	blue grey waters
LANEIRA	healing waters	GLAUKONOME	gray seas
AMPHITRITE	queen of the sea	HALIA	brine
KALYPSO	the concealed one	HIPPOTHOE	swift waves
OREITHYIA	raging waves	CLYMENE	fame
AGAUE	The illustrious	KYMO	wave
ACTAEA	sea shells	KYMODOKE	steadying waves
AMATHEIA	fish eggs	KYMOTHOE	running waves
AMPHITHOE	sea currents	LIMNOREIA	salt-marsh
AUTONOE	tidal pools	MELITE	calm seas
DEXAMENE	swimming	NAUSITHOE	swift ships
DIONE	the divine	NEMERTIS	unerring counsel
DORIS	sea's bounty	NESO	islands
DOTO	generous catch	PANOPEIA	panorama
DYNAMENE	the sea's power	PASITHEA	all divine
EIONE	beach strand	PLEXAURE	twisting breeze
ERATO	the lovely	PLOTO	sailing winds
EUAGORE	good assemblage	PONTOPOREIA	crossing the sea
EUDORA	fine gifts	POULYNOE	rich of mind
EUKRANTE	successful voyage	SAO	safe passage
EULIMENE	good harborage	SPEIO	sea caves
EUMOLPE	the fine singer	THALIA	blooming sea
EUNIKE	fine victory	THEMISTO	customary law

descendant traces

stasia

finn

phoebe

willow

carmen

kira

sirens

tritons

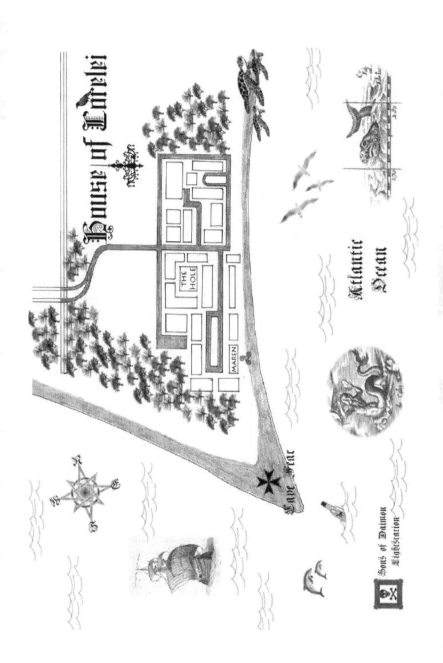

Prologue

"I don't know if I can do this, my love."

Peering down at her, he fought to muster the same strength within himself he saw shining in her wise, beautiful eyes. She was so strong, so poised. Only someone who'd spent a lifetime with her could discern the depth of pain in the slight lines framing her eyes.

"It is for the best – this is the only way," she whispered as she lowered the extravagant basket onto the wooden porch. Then louder, with a resolve coming from deep within she proclaimed, "It shall come to pass."

She took a small step back from the front door of the town police station with what seemed to be a great deal of effort. Her eyes closed and her head bent forward as a single tear escaped and rolled down her cheek.

He observed silently as the night air swirled through her hair; lifting it from her shoulders as if to caress her sorrow away. With the silver moon high in the clear sky, the rest of the town was fast asleep. The two o'clock hour was approaching fast and even the stars seemed to shine with urgency. Time was almost up.

Glancing back down at their precious delivery, he took a deep breath and inhaled the rich aroma of the sweet grass woven into the intricately crafted basket. He hoped in vain it would be successful in warding off evil. Kneeling down carefully, he unfolded the overflowing layers of silk and velvet blankets. The piercing blue eyes that gazed back up at him took his breath away. Swirling with all the colors of a Caribbean lagoon, they watched him intently. As if guessing what had to happen next.

His words caught in his throat as hot tears threatened to spill over. He swallowed and tried again to say the words he needed to say. "My precious baby girl. You are my moon, my stars and my sky. You are the very breath that gives me life. One day an understanding will come. But for now, we must say goodbye."

She reached for him and gave him the brightest toothless grin he'd ever seen. His heart slowly ripped apart and shattered into a million jagged pieces that would never be whole again. Remembering the braided seaweed bracelet he'd been holding in his hand, he carefully secured it around her tiny left wrist.

"This is not goodbye forever, my sweet girl, only for now. We love you with all our hearts...." His tears finally spilled over and he felt a hand softly touch his shoulder. She nodded in understanding as he stood up and walked down the steps, unable to stop the overwhelming wave of complete and utter heartbreak.

He looked on as she whispered something into the basket, and then kissed their little girl's cheek with such tenderness it broke his heart all over again. She folded the soft layers of fabric back to protect their baby from the crisp wind blowing off the ocean, and then slowly stood. She turned, met his eyes and walked down the steps to stand by him. His rock. His everything. They would do this together. Hand in hand, they took one last look at their miracle and walked into the shadows; leaving no trace they were ever there.

I registered the icy cold first – a slow, painstaking ache felt all the way down to my soul. The realization that I was swimming at a dangerous depth came next, followed by an absolute and suffocating panic. The pressure surrounding my body had become utterly relentless and my lungs screamed for oxygen. Suspended in the darkness, I couldn't see anything except for a thin ribbon of silver appearing in my line of sight. Slithering side to side, twisting and turning, it taunted me. I froze when it slowly wrapped around my neck and left a trail of icy pinpricks across my bare skin. It continued down my body; encasing me in fear. Suddenly, it tightened with such force that the small amount of air I had been clutching in my lungs was forced out. As I heard the sickening crack of bones and felt a paralyzing pain searing through my body, I knew no amount of struggling would help.

Unable to do anything but watch the last of my oxygen bubble up to the surface above, I tried to come to terms with what was about to happen. I was going to die. Completely alone and scared, I was going to drown in this darkness.

Unbelievably, just as quickly as it had locked around me, I was released. I looked around frantically and braced myself for another attack, only to find a pair of piercing blue eyes watching me. The same deep blue eyes I'd seen in so many other dreams glared back at me with something that resembled rage.

"Why are you here?" I barely heard his next words as my lungs began to burn and my vision blurred. "Your soul will never survive."

He turned abruptly and my vision cleared just enough to catch a glimpse of the horrors lurking behind him. Hundreds of silver ribbons quickly morphed and twisted into shadowy human forms. They turned in my direction in unison and descended upon me.

I bolted upright; my heart hammering relentlessly against my chest. Warm water surrounded me, but it was of the bubbly, lavender-scented variety, not the cold, murky darkness I just came from. I was still in my bathtub. No wonder I dreamed I was drowning. Shaking my head, I tried to erase the vivid memory of it. Unfortunately those eyes - his eyes - never faded. They had haunted my dreams for years.

I rolled my eyes at my own unruly imagination and slid down into the tub so that my head and shoulders were the only things showing above the thick layer of bubbles. My heart rate eventually slowed and I began to think straight again. I closed my eyes and tried to relax…

"Hannah Elizabeth Whitman!!!" So much for the slow heart rate. I rocketed back into a sitting position and covered myself with my hands.

"You scared the crap out of me, Dee!" Doris Whitman stepped all the way into the steamy bathroom, and the smell of baby powder and freesia followed her in. She shook her head at me. "You've been in there so long, I swear I can hear your fingers and toes wrinklin' up. Now get washed up and get dressed – we're gonna be late!"

"I'm hurrying, I'm hurrying," I mumbled as she turned on her heel and marched back downstairs, already giving out orders to the rest of the family.

I decided I'd rather hide under the blanket of soapy bubbles and try really hard to disappear into an alternate universe instead. Submerging my body completely underwater, a smile crept across my face as the sound of the outside world became instantly muted. All I heard was the faint lapping of water on the sides of the tub, my own beating heart, and a faint melody tickling at my ear drums. It reminded me of wind chimes blowing in the wind....wait. Wind chimes? I listened harder and heard them again, this time louder, and something else... like someone singing...

With ninja-like speed, I jumped out of the claw foot tub in one swift movement and stared down at the water in shock. I tried to convince myself I was just hearing things. There were no wind chimes hiding in my bathtub. I'd just add that to the long list of weird things that had happened to me over the last couple of years. That list was getting way too long for my taste.

"I hope all that racket up there is you jumping into your clothes!" That woman must have sonar for ears or something.

"I'm almost ready!" I wrapped a fluffy blue towel around me, padded into my bedroom and did a quick search of my closet to find something to wear. The Hartfords had been planning this party for months, and according to Dee, 'everybody who's anybody' would be in attendance. Living in the Deep South, Georgia to be exact, I'd become accustomed to Atlanta's Society and all the trappings - I mean opportunities! - that came along with it. But I hadn't always lived there. The Whitmans had adopted me when I was thirteen years old. They had high hopes I would turn out to be a perfect southern debutante like their own well-bred, silver spoon daughter. Little did they know I was damaged goods from the very beginning, and no amount of grooming or etiquette classes would ever change that. Bouncing around from family to family in the Georgia foster care system, I experienced and witnessed things that would make a grown man cry. I learned the hard way that once you've seen evil, it brands you for life. Your heart becomes hardened and you are never, ever the same.

Don't get me wrong, I tried to live up to my adoptive mother's expectations, but it had been a futile effort. I'd love to be like the girls I knew who had always known the security of a loving family. Who spent their nights dreaming of debutante balls, parties and the perfect wedding. Unfortunately my dreams...or more accurately, my nightmares...were much, much different.

After deciding on a strapless, blue seersucker dress, I threw on a pair of strappy white sandals, a mother of pearl necklace and matching earrings. I fixed my hair and makeup and then glanced in the mirror to make sure my look would pass Dee's inspection. My long blonde hair was naturally straight, but a curling iron gave it instant bounce. I could have used a couple more trips to the tanning bed, but the blue of the dress brought out my blue eyes. Which reminded me of another pair of dark blue eyes staring daggers into me. I really could get lost in those eyes. I shook my head to rid myself of my most recent nightmare. I grabbed my Coach bag that Dee had insisted on buying me last Christmas, a pearl bracelet, and added a quick swipe of light pink lip gloss to complete the ensemble. I almost looked like I belonged there. Almost.

Taking the stairs two at a time, I made it to the foyer just in time to crash into my sister, Laura Beth as she came around the corner. After shooting me a look that could wither plants, she marched past me into the formal living room; a cloud of pretension following in her wake.

"You really shouldn't run in heels, it scuffs the floors," she threw at me over her shoulder. I wanted to scuff up her face, but I settled for a dramatic eye roll instead.

The fitted canary yellow dress she wore offset her dark brown curly hair perfectly, which she'd pulled back into a low ponytail secured with a navy blue ribbon. Being the same age, you would have thought we'd be closer, but she'd decided a while back that she saw me strictly as competition. I believe the first words she spoke to me were 'I hope you don't think you're sleeping in my room'. Nothing says 'Welcome to our home!' like a loaded threat and an icy glare. Dee looked up from her freshly painted toenails as we entered the room.

"Ready?" She quickly inspected us with intense scrutiny, decided she approved, and then shooed us towards the front door. The heady scent of cigars and old books surrounded Charles Whitman as we collected him from his study on the way out. We piled into the car and headed to the Hartford Estate.

I saw the cars before I saw the house. Row after row of shining Mercedes, Jaguars, Range Rovers and BMWs greeted us as we turned up the Hartford driveway. After several twists and turns, the house finally came into view. The word house didn't quite do it justice, however. The Hartfords lived on an old plantation that had been in their family for generations. The long, winding drive looped through the manicured lawn lined with cherry blossom trees, and eventually circled in front of the house. One hundred year old oak trees dwarfed the home on both sides, skirted by a beautiful garden bursting with tulips, lilies and lush vegetation. Large white columns lined the front of the house, which allowed you to take in its truly massive size. Every inch of the estate oozed history and reverence. It looked like a scene straight out of Gone with the Wind. Absolutely breathtaking. After Dee handed the keys to the valet, we made our way up the wide stone steps. Two stately doormen promptly swung open the ornate French doors for us and we were swept inside.

I did a quick sweep of my surroundings, from the maple hardwood floors to the overbearing crystal chandelier hanging above our heads. A stuffy looking gentleman was playing a grand piano nearby, as sophisticated women in brightly colored dresses paraded around the sitting area in small groups. The men could always be found congregating outside on the veranda or in the library smoking; discussing the latest political debate or recent corporate mergers. I noticed Charles had already disappeared and Dee was making her way toward several older women wearing large brimmed hats and tight smiles.

"Laura Beth! I'm so glad you're here!" A dazzling brunette in a pink and white polka dotted sundress skipped over to us. Meredith Hartford was drop-dead gorgeous and famous for buying a brand new wardrobe every weekend. Only problem was...she knew it. She glanced in my direction and seemingly noticed me for the first time.

"Oh, hey Hannah, how are you?" She plastered on her best 'now that I've made eye contact I have to speak to you' smile, then clutched Laura Beth's arm with excitement.

"I can't wait to tell you what happened last night with Spencer...." As they scurried away whispering and squealing, I spotted a familiar face in the crowd. I made my way to the other side of the room where Sarah Lawson stood with her mom near an open bay window. She caught a runaway strand of auburn hair as the wind blew it across her face, and her mossy green eyes brightened when her eyes met mine.

"Hannah! How are you?" When Laura Beth made it her mission in life to explain to everyone at school how her family had saved me from a lifetime of poverty and how I'd be going to a therapist for the rest of my life, I was instantly shunned and forever stalked by looks of pity. With 'charity case' branded on my forehead from the very start, only a select few treated me like a human being. Sarah was one of those select few.

"Hey Sarah! Hello, Mrs. Braddock." Sarah's mother picked me apart with her eyes, gave me a disapproving smile, and found someone better to talk to across the room.

"Sorry 'bout that," Sarah whispered as her mom stalked away.

"It's okay." Her mom's obvious aversion to me stung, but I shrugged my shoulders and smiled anyway.

"So how's your summer going?" Sarah asked. "Been on any vacations? We just got back from London a couple weeks ago. You would not believe the shopping over there...."

I continued to listen diligently as she described the details of their extensive trip to England and Scotland, and made sure to add in a few head nods at the appropriate times. My attention had been drawn to my adopted mother, who was now making a beeline for us. The heavy makeup she wore couldn't hide the irritation tightening her features.

"May I have a word?" she asked me with one raised eyebrow.

"I'll be right back," I assured Sarah, and grudgingly followed Dee out onto the back balcony. Overlooking a massive meadow below, I was struck by the beauty of the plantation all over again before Dee proceeded to shatter it with crude and obvious condemnation.

"How many times do I have to tell you to cover up that tattoo?!" She literally spit out the last word in disgrace.

"What? You're kidding, right?"

"Wrists. Now. And mind your manners," she hissed. I sighed and held out my wrists as if waiting to be handcuffed. The metaphor wasn't too far off. She unclasped my bracelet and switched it from my right wrist to my left.

"We can't have all these people seeing that thing on your wrist, now can we?" Heaven forbid.

"Dee, no one is paying attention to my wrists."

"That isn't the point, young lady." I hated when she called me that.

"I don't care what people think."

"Hannah, you represent this family and I will not have you parading around like some homeless person with tattoos all over her body!" Well at least she wasn't overreacting.

"It's only one tattoo, and it's not even that big. Honestly, Dee…"

Interrupting me with a harsh look, she continued hastily, "As of this weekend, I'll be looking into the process of getting it removed permanently."

I glanced down at the intricate design on the inside of my left wrist. My 'tattoo', as I had called it my whole life, consisted of a small upside down triangle with one spiral extending out of each corner. The lines of the spirals appeared to be made up of a single vine of ivy. It had been there for as long as I could remember, and if you looked closely, you could tell it wasn't even a tattoo – more like a part of my body, resembling a freckle or a birthmark. I cherished it. Out of habit, I traced the vines with my finger. It seemed to shimmer beneath my touch. The world shifted unexpectedly and I quickly lost my balance. Reaching for the sturdy balcony railing, I caught it just in time to see a look of embarrassment and horror cross Dee's face. Then everything went black.

'Anastasia…Anastasia…' The name was spoken like a prayer, whispered within my mind. The intense longing laced with heavy sadness in the woman's voice squeezed my heart. 'Anastasia…' My thoughts rushed to catch up with what was happening. My breath hitched as I took in a magnificent white sand beach with crystal blue waters lapping gently at the water's edge. The sun shone high above, but I couldn't feel its heat. The wind blew, but didn't touch me. The waves crashed just off shore, but I couldn't hear the roar.

"Anastasia…." This time it was said aloud. Concerned and a little more than confused, I whipped around and tried to find who the velvety voice belonged to. All that lay behind me was dense jungle – wild, exotic plants stretching upward toward the giant palm trees that gracefully swayed in the elusive ocean breeze. Where was the voice coming from? Turning back to face the water, she materialized in front of me. Her feet were hidden by the incoming tide and she stood frozen, as if in a trance. Long blonde hair cascaded around her delicate shoulders. The white dress that hugged her slender figure had threads of silver interwoven; creating a sparkling effect. Her immense beauty was astonishing. She lifted her arms to the sky and proclaimed, "It shall come to pass." She closed her eyes and my already upturned world exploded.

After what felt like days, I opened my eyes, disoriented and baffled by what had just transpired. I sat up carefully and tried to find my bearings. This time I was the one in the water. I stood, just in time to miss a wave crashing over me. Bright red streaked across my peripheral vision and my eyes followed it to the beach. A couple argued in front of me, several yards away on the white sand. The flash of red was the woman's hair. Waves of deep burgundy fell all the way down to her waist; making her look more petite than she already was. A struggle began and she was thrown to the ground by her much larger attacker. I caught a glimpse of something silver in his hand. I ran in their direction, unsure of what I intended to do once I got there, but before I could even step foot on the sand I hit something. Or someone. As I regained my balance, my eyes washed over his well-defined chest, broad shoulders and kiss-worthy lips. His dark hair swept down onto his furrowed brow and was lightly ruffled by the ocean breeze. Overwhelming temptation hit me, but the threatening way his square jaw flexed as he stared down at me brought reality crashing back. Anger sparked in his deep blue eyes and I was reminded of storm clouds gathering; dark swirling hues of blue and gray.

"Turn around and leave," he demanded, as my attention shifted back to the scene unfolding on the beach.

"But I have to help her! He's hurting her!" I tried to plead with him. I attempted to push him aside, but he grasped my shoulders and easily held me captive.

"What do you think you can do for her? Get yourself killed?" he retorted with a slight smirk.

"I have to at least try! Look at what he's....!" I gestured toward the beach and realized the fight had abruptly ended. The man had vanished. Lying on her side, the woman's body was being overcome by the incoming tide. A puddle of deep red formed around her and slowly absorbed into the wet sand beneath.

I finally charged past him and sprinted to her side. I felt for a pulse but found only stillness. With agitation, my eyes flitted upward to see why he wasn't helping me, but he was gone. When I looked back down, the woman had disappeared as well. All of my energy drained and I collapsed onto the sand in defeat.

"I should have helped.... I should have helped..." I repeated uselessly, as if it would have changed what I'd just witnessed.

"Hannah! Hannah, look at me! Answer me, Hannah!" frantic voices shouted incessantly at me. I was sitting right there for goodness sake! There was no need to scream. Unlike the voices around me, my own voice wouldn't cooperate. Instead, I squeezed my eyes shut and tried to stop the shrill ringing in my ears.

"Wake up, Hannah! Open your eyes!" I felt myself being shaken, so I peeked out from under my droopy eyelids. A swarm of people were crowded around me. Each face reflected a mixture of panic and concern, except for Dee, who was frowning down at me with indignation.

"I'm okay, I'm okay," I mumbled, just as the memory of my dream slammed into me once more. "Where did she go!?" I tried my best to sit up, but unknown hands kept my body from moving.

"Where did who go? Who were you talking to?" I recognized Dee's voice amidst my stupor.

"The woman – she was killed...." I stumbled over each word, realizing how farfetched it sounded even to my own ears.

"You're talking nonsense, Hannah. We need to get you home." I felt myself being picked up and carried back through the house, down the front steps, and into the backseat of our car. Someone got in beside me, doors closed, and I heard the faint sounds of people talking outside. That's when the person beside me piped up.

"I can't believe this. You ruined my whole night!" Laura Beth's voice echoed in my ears. I could always count on her to make every situation about her. "Why do I have to have the sister who's crazy?" she wailed. "You are soooo gonna pay for this!"

She slumped down in her seat and I desperately hoped she was done with her little temper tantrum. I heard two more doors shut as Dee and Charles got into the car. More hushed conversation followed, and then we were finally on our way home.

The next time I was awakened, I found myself back in my spacious bedroom lying under the covers of my four poster bed. At some point my dress had been replaced with sweatpants and a tank top. I tried unsuccessfully to sit up on my elbows. My head was two seconds away from exploding, so I lay back down and rubbed my temples.

"You have an appointment tomorrow morning with your new therapist." After jumping out of my skin, I painstakingly turned my head to the side. Dee was perched beside the bed in a chair from the breakfast table downstairs. She tapped her fingers on my nightstand, anger still evident in her grim tone.

"She comes highly recommended, and I'm sure she'll get you fixed right up." She kissed my forehead with unrestrained obligation and closed the door behind her as she left the room.

She made it sound like I had a broken arm that simply needed to be set. I didn't need to be 'fixed up' any more than I needed a new therapist. If I had to explain what I'd been through with my multiple foster homes one more time to someone who smiled sympathetically and patted my knee, I was going to poke my eyes out. I already knew what happened – I was there. How could I get past it if I constantly had to relive it? What I really needed was to run far away from everything and everyone who only saw me as crazy and disturbed – start anew. Where my past didn't define me and pity wasn't lurking around every corner. Unfortunately at seventeen, I didn't have that luxury. What I wanted was rarely taken into consideration. I sighed and eventually fell back asleep to the steady sound of my pounding head.

The next morning brought warm sunlight that washed over the back of my eyelids, but from the pain it unleashed, it might as well have been the flash from an atomic bomb. Okay, so maybe that was a slight exaggeration, but my tender head wouldn't have disagreed with the comparison. Squinting in agony, I rolled over and pulled the covers back over my head. I was in no hurry to get up. The only thing tempting me was the distinct smell of chocolate chip pancakes wafting up the stairs. Dee definitely did that on purpose. She knew I couldn't resist those. My stomach gurgled loudly, reminding me I wasn't getting any pancakes hiding under the covers, so I groaned and made myself get up.

"Well, look at you up and at 'em so early this morning!" Dee's smile was a little too wide and she looked much too cheery for seven a.m. How someone could be dressed, with impeccable hair and makeup, and be so full of energy that early in the morning was beyond my comprehension. I became aware of my own hair, momentarily posing as a rat's nest, and pulled it into a messy bun on top of my head. I didn't have to try very hard at the messy part.

"Mornin." I gave her my best effort at a grin and plopped down at the breakfast table.

She set a plate overflowing with plump pancakes dripping with sticky, sweet syrup down in front of me, along with two extra strength Excedrin tablets. "I expect you can get yourself to the therapist on time? I've left directions for you on the counter. Your appointment isn't until eight-thirty, but you need to get there a little early for paperwork."

"Mmhmm," I answered between mouthfuls. There was no time for chit-chat when there were chocolate chip pancakes to be eaten.

"I've got some errands to run, then I'm meeting Suzanne for lunch, and I'm due for a game of bridge with the girls at the club after that. Do me a favor and tell your sister her room better be spotless by the time I get home. That goes for you too."

"Mmhmm," I replied again as I kept chewing. As if Laura Beth would listen to anything I had to say.

Once Dee left and my stomach was completely stuffed with pancakes, I went upstairs to get ready with the urgency of a sloth. My headache had dulled slightly, but it was still vehemently fighting for its life. It wasn't going to give in that easy. By the time I threw on my favorite skinny jeans, flats, and a tank top, I had about fifteen minutes to make it to the therapist's office. I rushed downstairs, collected the directions off of the counter, and slid into the white convertible BMW I shared with Laura Beth. It was way too pretentious for me, but Laura Beth insisted her reputation would only survive if she drove a BMW or Lexus.

Two wrong turns and one almost fender bender later, I pulled into the parking lot of a bland-looking brick office building. I took the elevator to the third floor and found suite thirty-one-A just in time.

"Hannah?" After a brief wait in a lobby smelling of stale lemons, a petite middle-aged woman poked her head around the corner and motioned for me to follow her. I stood reluctantly and complied.

"I'm Dr. Hansen. How are you today?" Her short, black hair bounced around as she spoke.

"Pretty good, I guess," ...for being in a therapist's office.

Her thin lips curved up sympathetically, and she directed me into a small office with large windows that covered one entire wall. The room was painted a light blue, probably in an attempt to create a calming ambience for her patients. Black and white photographs of lighthouses decorated the walls, and an imposing oak desk sat in one corner. As she took her seat behind the oak monstrosity and began to sort through papers, she motioned for me to sit as well. Looking at my options, I noticed a plush corduroy couch against one wall, two brown leather recliners, and a wooden chair facing her desk. I chose the wooden chair. No sense in getting comfortable.

"I hear you had quite an experience last night," she prodded me delicately, and took a sip from a coffee mug that read 'World's Best Therapist'. Seriously?

"It was...um...interesting." I clasped my hands in my lap and looked out of the windows; trying to feign boredom.

"Do you want to tell me what happened?" she questioned me further.

"I just fainted. That's honestly all that happened."

"I hear there was a little more to it than that." Maybe she should tell me what happened, since she seemed to know so much! I felt a familiar frustration bubble up in my chest.

I pulled my eyes off of the trees outside and glanced in her direction, already planning my escape route. My eyes slid past her and landed on an oversized fish tank in the corner. Bright orange, yellow, and red fish swam lazily back and forth. I was pretty sure one in particular was staring at me, but it swam off with a flip of its fin. Crazy fish. I'd go nuts if I were stuck in a glass tank all day, too.

Realizing she was still patiently waiting for me to elaborate, I figured the quicker I got this over with, the quicker I'd get out of there.

"I was just arguing with Dee about my tattoo when I got dizzy and fell. I blacked out and had a really weird dream. Then I woke up. The end," I finished matter-of-factly; daring her to ask me more questions.

She just grinned back at me smugly like we'd shared an inside joke. "What kind of tattoo do you have?"

"I'm not sure what it is, but I've had it forever." I held up my wrist for her. A confused look crossed her features for an instant, but just as quickly she was calm and collected once more.

"You were adopted, correct?" Her tone changed from casual conversation to skeptic detective in a millisecond. She tapped her chin with her silver pen.

"Yes." I tried to catch up with the sudden change of topic. She shifted in her seat and scratched her head. After a minute or so, I started to get a little uncomfortable with her intrusive stare.

"If you want, I can tell you who my last therapist was. I'm sure they can send over my records..." I offered with slight irritation.

"No, no, that's not necessary," she replied a little too quickly. "Tell me more about this dream you had when you blacked out." I explained the dream to her in detail and waited for her to prescribe me Prozac. Instead, she sat back and stared at me once more.

"Hannah, I'm going to refer you to one of my colleagues." She smiled and sat up straighter in her chair, apparently proud of herself. "I think she'd like to talk to you." Wonderful. Just wonderful.

"If you'll excuse me, I'm going to make a quick phone call." She stood and walked out of the office; closing the door behind her. I turned my attention to the exotic fish swimming laps within their rectangular glass prison. I got the urge to feed them, or maybe release them back into the ocean where I was sure they had been stolen from. Seeing a jar of fish food perched beneath the tank, I ambled over and peered through the thick glass.

"Anybody hungry?" I questioned them in a ridiculous baby voice usually reserved for puppies. They immediately stopped doing laps and darted up toward the surface. "I guess that's a yes." I lifted the lid and shook some of the multi-colored flakes into the water.

"What are you doing?" I dropped the lid with a loud bang and raced back to my chair. Dr. Hansen watched me curiously.

"I'm sorry, I thought they might be hungry, so…." I trailed off; feeling foolish.

"From the looks of it, I'd say you were right." Her smile was full of understanding. I glanced back at the tank to see that the flakes had already been gobbled up. The fish followed my every movement,; obviously hoping for more.

"They would probably eat all day long if I'd let them." She gazed at the fish with tenderness before sitting back down. "Well, I just spoke to Dr. Campbell and I'm happy to tell you she has an opening later this afternoon!"

I wasn't sure if she was expecting me to celebrate with her, so I just replied, "Okay."

"You'll need to tell Dee right away because it takes 4 hours to get down there, and I can't imagine she'd want you to drive that far by yourself."

"Four hours?" Why couldn't she have a colleague in Atlanta?

"Dr. Campbell's office is located down in Savannah. Have you ever been there? It's a beautiful city."

She was probably still talking, but I had already stopped listening. She was sending me all the way to Savannah? Today? To talk to another doctor? This couldn't possibly get any worse.

THREE

"Savannah?! Today?!" I moved my cell phone back from my ear several inches so Dee's voice wouldn't break my ear drum.

"That's what she said." I read over Dr. Hansen's note scrawled on a sticky note again. "My appointment is scheduled for four o'clock p.m."

She sighed and took a deliberate, deep breath. I could tell her blood pressure had increased in the five minutes we'd been talking. "Okay, I'll cancel my plans and be home as soon as I can."

"Thanks Dee, I'll see you soon." I didn't want to go to Savannah any more than she did, but it didn't look like we had a choice. Apparently my issues were that severe. The dream was odd, sure, but I didn't expect them to slap me with a psych ward bracelet just yet. Or maybe that's where she was sending me. Maybe 'Dr. Campbell' was code for a straight jacket and white padded walls. It might not be too bad. Instead of pity and sympathetic looks, they would just give me a shot of something strong to knock me out for a few hours. I could live with that.

Five hours later we pulled into the bustling city of Savannah. I'd only been there twice before. Once when I was fourteen for a St. Patrick's Day family trip, and once before that when I was too young to remember. From what I'd been told, I was left on the porch of the Police Station on Skidaway Island, which was located several miles southeast of Savannah. Unfortunately they didn't know where I had been born or who had dropped me off, just that I was discovered when I was approximately 8 months old. I tried not to think about what could drive a person to abandon their own flesh and blood. Thankfully the Sheriff had found me when he arrived at work that morning. I was turned over to the state, put into foster care, and the rest was history. Any time I thought about it I was overcome with so many emotions, I had no choice but to push those thoughts out of my mind. Even if I had wanted to find my real parents, it would have been impossible. There were no records of my birth, so there was no way to track them down. Even my birthday, April seventeenth, was a guesstimate based on how old I appeared to be when they found me.

"Looks like we made it!" Dee wove through the already heavy traffic towards downtown Savannah. On the outskirts of the city, it could have been any other place in America with gas stations, McDonalds, and a Starbucks on every corner. But once we entered the city in earnest, the history and beauty were hard to ignore. As we passed beneath the canopies of the mangled live oak trees, I gawked at the nineteenth century buildings and cobblestone streets of the historic district. Finding somewhere to park near the River Walk was no simple task, however. We found a small spot between a massive truck and an even larger SUV, and finally found the door to Dr Campbell's office on River Street.

"Go have a seat and I'll take care of everything," Dee assured me. The receptionist area had a simplistic beach theme with wooden pelicans and bright seashells adorning the white wicker tables, while potted palm trees stood watch in the corners of the room. I took a seat on one of the wicker chairs and picked up a magazine to read. I got no further than the first page when a swinging door opened and a young woman with golden skin and jet black hair came out to greet us. She appeared to glide across the floor in her long, flowing cream-colored dress. I caught a glimpse of purple toenail polish and several toe rings, and realized she was barefoot. Her arms and hands were covered with silver bangles and rings of turquoise. Nothing about her resembled my vision of straight jackets and padded rooms, which I'll admit was instantly reassuring.

"You must be Hannah!" She stepped around Dee and shook my hand with enthusiasm. "I've been looking forward to our visit ever since I got the call from Diane." Still grasping my hand, she led me back through the swinging door and into a large office. Dee trailed behind us, watching her with skepticism. Her office reminded me more of a small apartment, with one large room sectioned off into smaller areas. To our left was a sitting area dominated by a ceiling-to-floor bookcase overflowing with old books. The aroma of hazelnut and cedar warmed my soul, and I tried to imagine the depth of knowledge stored in that one bookcase. Toward the windows in the back was a small area full of toys for younger patients. The only thing missing was a big official desk that would look out of place anyway. I found a fluffy circular chair to fall into, and began to wonder how I'd gone my whole life without sitting in something this comfortable. Dee took a seat on an elegant arm chair across from me. Dr. Campbell gracefully sat in the other chair next to Dee and smiled at both us.

"Would you girls like some water or maybe a cup of coffee?" she asked politely. The genuine personality she portrayed continued to contradict every shrink stereotype ingrained in my mind.

Dee instantly perked up. "I would love a cup of coffee."

"How about a cappuccino?"

"That would be lovely!" With that one peace offering, Dee's demeanor had taken a one hundred and eighty degree turn for the better.

"And for you, Hannah?"

"Nothing for me, thank you." I was anxious to get the session started and, more importantly, over with. Coffee would only prolong the inevitable.

Dr. Campbell floated over to a slight kitchenette on the right side of the room and began punching buttons on what looked to be a very impressive cappuccino maker. I could tell Dee was beginning to like her too, or at least her taste in coffee.

After gingerly handing Dee a steaming cup, Dr. Campbell sat back down.

"Mrs. Whitman, I'm sure you're aware as to how important patient/doctor confidentiality is, so I'm afraid I'm going to have to ask you to wait outside for a little bit while Hannah and I talk."

Dee seemed surprised at first, then gathered her purse, thanked her for the coffee and walked back out into the lobby. Once she was out of sight, Dr Campbell turned her undivided attention on me.

"So, Hannah," she began leisurely, "tell me how old you are."

"Seventeen."

"And when did you start having nightmares and blackouts?" she asked; writing furiously on her notepad.

"How'd you know about my nightmares?" I couldn't help feeling paranoid.

"Just a guess." She smiled encouragingly at me, but I felt there was something she wasn't telling me.

"I used to have nightmares about normal stuff – people chasing me or falling. But then about three years ago they started changing and becoming more…um…real? And harder to forget." I shrugged my shoulders, hoping to convince her it wasn't a big deal.

"And the blackouts?" she prompted without looking up.

"I've never had them before last night. That was the first time. But it didn't feel like a dream, it seemed like something more. I don't really know how to explain it."

"Your answer is perfectly fine." She covered my hand and squeezed it reassuringly. Peering down, she eyed the design on my wrist.

"How do you…?" She leaned in closer to get a better look. "I mean, how long have you had this?"

"For as long as I can remember. It's just always been there," I explained.

"You don't remember getting it? Seems like something you'd remember." I started to feel like she was trying to catch me in a lie, so I decided she wasn't going to get any more answers no matter what she asked.

Giving my hand another squeeze, she sat back in her chair in deep thought. "I'm going to step out for a minute and speak with Dee, alright?"

"Okay…" I retorted with hesitation. The visit really wasn't making much sense to me so far.

She gracefully rose from her chair and disappeared to find Dee. A couple of minutes later, they both strode back in and sat down with serious faces. I had a bad feeling I wasn't going to like what she had to say next.

"After careful consideration, Dee and I believe it would be in your best interest to be enrolled in a special boarding school for young people very much like yourself."

My mouth dropped open. Did she really just say what I thought she said? A boarding school? And I thought it couldn't get any worse. Boy, was I wrong. And what careful consideration? She had only asked me four questions!

I looked wide-eyed at Dee and wondered how she had been brainwashed in such a short amount of time. I opened my mouth to speak, but nothing seemed to come out right. "But I….how can….I don't….because of nightmares…the occasional fainting spell…?"

Dee just shot me a loving smile. "You're going to love it, Hannah! It's called the House of Lorelei and it's on an island up in North Carolina. This is perfect timing, because the new school year there starts next Monday! It's a year-round school, so you won't miss a beat!" She clapped her hands together happily as if this was a good thing. "You'll be able to come home during the holidays and on breaks. And the best part is that Dr. Campbell has made all the preparations for you to move in immediately! Isn't that wonderful?" No. It wasn't. And I found it hard to believe that she'd made all of those 'preparations' in the three minutes she left to talk to Dee.

I cast an accusing glare at the doctor and stood up, ready to argue. "What do you mean, 'people like me'? You can't just up and move me to a different state because you think it's a good idea! I don't belong there! You don't even know me!" I felt my face growing hot as my anger spilled over.

Slowly inching closer to me, the doctor placed a gentle hand on my shoulder and spoke softly. "But do you really belong here?" she asked cryptically. "Trust me, Hannah. I promise you won't regret this. Please trust me." I narrowed my eyes at her, instinctively looking for an ulterior motive, but found only genuine concern and a small gleam of excitement in her eyes. For some reason I wanted to trust her. Well, crap.

I sat back down and tried to sort out the confusion clouding my mind. What could it hurt, really? A new school - new people who knew nothing about me or my past. A new start. Wasn't that what I'd been wanting? A new beginning? I felt the fight go out of me and a brand new emotion took hold. It felt a lot like....hope.

FOUR

Friday. The day my life would change forever. I was embarking on a new journey - a completely different direction - and I had no idea what to expect. It was as unsettling as it was exciting. I sank into seat twelve-C on the plane and said a quick goodbye to Atlanta, as well as the life I was leaving behind. I'd gotten pretty good at goodbyes. Maybe a little too good. I had lived with five different foster families before being adopted at the age of thirteen, and I made sure never to allow myself to get attached to anyone or any place. I never knew when I'd be picking up and moving on to the next place, so it was just easier that way. My current situation was a good example of that.

Unfortunately, by the time I arrived at the Whitman's home three years ago, that self-defense mechanism had stuck and no matter how hard they tried, those walls had been built too tall and too thick to break through. I had so many barriers around my heart, it would take an entire army to break them down. Until that army came, I was perfectly content with my walls. I'd gotten used to the security, albeit dysfunctional, they had provided through the years.

I watched the Atlanta skyline shrink below me as the plane gained altitude. I reminded myself, once again, that a person was more likely to die in a car crash than a plane crash. I closed my eyes and tried my best to get comfortable. The sound of heavy footsteps had my eyes flying open in confusion. Smoke swirled in the slanted rays of sunlight streaming in through the windows, and the smell of old cigarettes mixed with stale liquor filled my senses. I wasn't on the plane anymore.

Suddenly, I was lifted to my feet. Glaring at me through bloodshot eyes, he held me up with one hand and shook an empty ice cube tray in the other.

"Why's there not any ice cubes?" he slurred. The stench of his breath in my face made me gag. "The water ain't gonna jump out the sink and freeze its damn self!"

He threw me back onto the couch and tossed the empty ice cube tray in my lap. "Go make me a drink," he demanded through yellowed teeth. I stared up at him and hoped I didn't sound as scared as I felt.

"No," I whispered.

"No!? Is that what you just said?" His oversized hand gripped my scraggly arm and dragged me into the kitchen. Before I could regain my footing, he pushed me against the cabinets. One of the blunt, metal drawer knobs pressed into my back.

"Make. me. a. drink." He loomed over me with bloodshot eyes.

I immediately crouched down to hide my face, hoping he'd just give up and leave me alone. Instead, he found an empty beer bottle on the counter and threw it at my head. His aim was surprisingly good for being so drunk. It shattered against the side of my face and shards of brown glass stuck into my skin. The pain was sharp and immediate. I scrambled to my feet and ran down the short hallway, while he stumbled after me laughing. I made it to my bedroom first; shutting myself inside the small closet opposite my twin bed. My breath came quick as fear constricted my throat. I placed my hand over my mouth. I didn't know if I was going to scream or cry, but I couldn't afford to give away my hiding spot. The ringing of the phone in the living room stopped his black boots from breaking the threshold of my small room. He mumbled something inaudible and stumbled back down the hallway.

As soon as he was gone, I let the sobs building in my throat spill out. Hot tears instantly mixed with the fresh blood running down my cheek, while my head pounded from the newly formed welt on my face.

The closet door creaked as I peeked out cautiously, making sure he was really gone. Expecting to see my bedroom, I was shocked to find the scene before me had shifted. As I climbed to my unsteady feet, it became apparent to me that I wasn't the younger version of myself anymore, either. I lightly touched a shaky finger to my eyebrow and noticed the absence of blood. The welt on my cheek had also disappeared. As I tiptoed out into the foreign room, carpet gave way to wooden floor beneath my bare feet. Soft evening light cast long shadows across the room, and I was taken aback by its size and opulence. I could barely make out the shadowy figure of a woman sitting across the room in a rocking chair, softly crying as she gazed out the window. She didn't stir at my entrance, only continued to cry one word over and over with such agony and longing, it broke my heart. "Anastasia…. Anastasia…"

My eyes jerked open and I instantly whirled around, trying to figure out where I had been transported this time. Thankfully I was still seated in twelve-C amongst the other passengers. I felt the frenzied pumping of my heartbeat as I tried to calm my breathing. It was just a dream. Just a dream. If only it could have been a dream all those many years ago. I touched my eyebrow and rubbed the tiny scar I'd carried with me since I was nine.

"Hannah Whitman?"

"Yes?"

"Hi, I'm Kira. I'll be your personal escort for the next couple of hours." She swept her slender arm down and bowed dramatically. Wearing short white shorts, a light pink blouse that had fallen off one very tan shoulder, and Rainbow flip flops, she couldn't have been a day over twenty-one. Bright green eyes sparkled as a wide smile lit up her face and she straightened. She tucked a piece of sun-bleached blonde hair behind her ear and took my carry-on. "So, how was your flight?"

Probably not the best time to bring up my nightmares. "It was pretty uneventful, I guess."

"That's definitely a good thing when all you have between you and the ground is several miles of air," she chuckled. A nervous laugh escaped my lips as we began navigating through the airport. Glancing sideways at her, I couldn't help but think about how normal she seemed. What exactly did Dr. Campbell mean when she'd said 'young people like me'? Was everyone there going to be blacking out randomly during the day and screaming through nightmares at night? That didn't seem very likely.

"I was thinking we'd grab something to eat and talk a little bit before getting to the island. How do you feel about pizza?" she asked with a smile. She appeared very at ease in her own body and acknowledged each person we passed with a nod or smile. She had a glow of happiness that reached out to others, making them smile with her.

"That sounds wonderful," I admitted. "I haven't had anything to eat since breakfast." It was almost dinnertime and my stomach was growling loudly. I would have been surprised if she couldn't hear it.

My eyebrows shot up when we stepped outside and Kira gestured towards a white Jeep Wrangler with oversized tires waiting at the curb. I don't know what I expected. Maybe a taxi? Or a van?

"Your chariot awaits, madame." She tossed my carry-on into the back seat and I realized we hadn't picked up the rest of my luggage. I glanced back towards the doors and turned to say something to Kira.

"The rest of your bags are being taken care of. They'll be waiting on you when you get to the school." I had tried not to bring every piece of clothing I owned, but it was difficult. After stuffing four bags full of clothes and shoes, I wasn't looking forward to carrying them all over Wilmington, so the fact that I wouldn't have to was wonderful.

I literally climbed up into the passenger seat while Kira slid on a pair of silver aviator sunglasses and grinned at me. She started the Jeep and we bounced onto the streets of Wilmington. Several minutes later, we parked in the lot of a small pizza shop. We found a vintage-looking wrought iron table outside and Kira ordered peach flavored sweet tea. I decided to give it a try too.

Even though I couldn't tell how close we were to the beach, I smelled the hint of salt water in the air. It was just as humid as Georgia, but much more bearable thanks to a light breeze blowing. I took a deep breath and felt myself relax for the first time in what felt like years. I could get used to the leisurely pace of the beach. Everyone who meandered by on the sidewalk was sun-kissed and smiling without a care in the world. A sizzle of excitement ran through me as I thought about the new chapter in my life I was about to begin.

"So what do you do at the school?" I questioned. She looked too young to be a teacher or administrator.

"I'm considered something like a graduate student, and we get credits for mentoring incoming students. I definitely got lucky with my first assignment," she clarified, winking at me.

"How long do you mentor me?"

"For as long as you need me," she answered simply. "So, how much do you know about the House of Lorelei?"

"Honestly, not a whole lot. All I know is that it's year round, on an island, and the kids there are....like me?" I hoped she could shed some light on that last part. A part of me sighed in relief knowing Kira would be my mentor. Feeling a little vulnerable for some reason, I absently looked down at my hands...and gasped. My 'tattoo' was...shimmering? I twisted my wrist back and forth; squinting to make sure I wasn't seeing things. Yep, it was definitely doing something weird. Just then, the waitress came back with our drinks. I instinctively placed my other hand over it to hide it momentarily. The waitress gave me a weird look, but kept walking to the next table.

"Can I see?" Kira's eyes danced with excitement.

"Uh...it usually doesn't...do...that." I held out my arm for her to see my tri-spiral 'tattoo'.

"Oh, it's beautiful! Mine only does that when I'm in the ocean," she said nonchalantly.

"Yours?" There was no way she had the same tattoo. She must be trying to make me feel better about hallucinating.

"Yep, but my trace is on the back of my neck." She swiveled in her chair and lifted her hair to show me. "See?"

I stood with wobbly legs and walked around the table. Sure enough, right there on the back of her neck were two birds mid-flight. I leaned in to get a better look. It did look like mine – not a tattoo, but more like a part of her body.

"What kind of birds are they?" I couldn't hide my amazement.

"Seagulls. Unfortunately they have a bad reputation for stealing your Cheetos when you're lying out at the beach, or for hanging out in grocery store parking lots, but they're so much more. Seagulls represent freedom and vitality. They spend their lives riding the energy above the waves," she explained with pride.

"It's amazing." I took one last glance and then remembered what she'd called it. "You said it's a...trace?"

"That's right, we all have one," she replied breezily, as if that cleared everything up. "Although I've never seen a design like yours." She looked like she wanted to say something more, but just then a large, steaming pizza was set down in front of us, overflowing with ooey, gooey cheese.

"So, do you surf?" she asked between bites. I noticed she ate her pizza backwards, starting with the crust first. I made a mental note to try that out next time.

"I took swimming lessons back in Atlanta and swam at the club pool all the time, but I've never been in the ocean," I explained through bites. She almost choked. Once she was done coughing, she stared at me wide-eyed.

"Seriously? Not at all? Not even your feet?" She eventually picked her chin up off the ground.

"Nope, not one toe."

She smiled wickedly. "That's definitely going to change."

After devouring an entire twelve-inch pizza, we jumped back into the Jeep and continued the journey to the House of Lorelei. Bald Head Island was south of Wilmington, but there were no bridges or roads leading to the island. When I read that in the pamphlet Dr. Campbell had given us, a picture of Alcatraz popped in my head and had remained there ever since. Something seemed a little too final about a place you couldn't drive away from.

About thirty miles later we arrived in the small town of Southport. Small boutiques and coffee shops lined the main road as tourists wove in and out of the stores. I tried to rein in my hair that was continually smacking me in the face, as Kira took the right turn toward the Deep Point Marina. The ferry that would take us to the island ran every hour during the day and even at night. From what the pamphlet said it was about two miles from Southport to Bald Head Island, which amounted to a twenty minute ferry ride. We parked the Jeep, bought our tickets and got in line. Waiting with us were families weighed down with beach toys and luggage, couples standing close or holding hands, and several younger girls wearing matching t-shirts with Ebb & Flo's Oyster Bar and Restaurant written on the back. A bar for just oysters? If my memory served me right, oysters were slimy, salty little aliens that came in their original shells. I remembered trying one when we went to Savannah for St. Patrick's Day. It only lasted about two seconds in my mouth before I spit it out in my napkin. From then on, I vowed to stick to fish and shrimp.

A horn blared and the ferry slowly docked beside the boardwalk. Workers jumped to action as they removed luggage and trunks; sending them down a ramp and onto a moving belt. The ferry itself was bigger than I expected and packed with visitors leaving the island for the night. They were all windblown and giddy, and I couldn't help smiling at them as they filed off the boat. A little boy walked by with his dad and waved shyly at us. He held a stuffed sea turtle tightly in his arms, but what I noticed first was the red beach bucket he wore as a hat. It was in the shape of a sandcastle and sat lopsided atop his head. I waved back and silently mourned my own childhood void of happy memories.

"Time to go!" Kira clutched my hand with anticipation. We traversed the skinny ramp onto the deck and found seats at the open-air back of the boat. Never having been on a boat I was apprehensive, but still excited about the new experience. The ferry gently swayed back and forth as the rest of the passengers boarded. I watched a lanky crane glide above and land on one of the pylons nearby. It stood perfectly still on one leg looking for fish to snag up out of the water. Several minutes later, the ferry's engine roared to life and a nervous shiver ran down my spine. We inched forward, turned left gradually and made our way past the two pylons; exiting the marina. As the ferry passed by the crane's perch, I watched in awe as it extended its massive wings and took to the sky.

"Look!" Kira called above the engine and the wind. "That's Southport over there to our right."

A small wooden pier stretched out into the water, while the same shops and boutiques I'd seen before were visible farther back. A couple of minutes later we made a slow left turn and she pointed again.

"And that's Fort Caswell on the very end of Oak Island," she informed me. The walls of the fort were overgrown with hungry vines and moss, but it was still a majestic sight. As we rounded the point, the full grandeur of the sun setting over the Atlantic Ocean came into view. I carefully stood up on the rocking deck and made my way to the side of the ferry to get a better view. Striking shades of orange, red and yellow lit up the sky and reflected off the water. It was magnificent.

"You know, if you look over the side sometimes you can see dolphins swimming next to the ferry." Kira came over to stand beside me.

"Really?" I leaned over the side precariously, holding on tightly to the railing...just in time for the ferry to run over the wake from a passing boat. A wall of salt water sprayed up and hit me square in the face. I tumbled backwards and fell against Kira.

"Aren't the dolphins just beautiful?!" She doubled over with laughter while I tried to dry my face. I crossed my arms over my chest and tapped my foot at her. Finally she got a hold of herself and looked up at me, but then another bout of laughter shook her body as she held onto the railing to keep her balance.

"That was so not funny!" I giggled and gave her shoulder a little shove. "You did that on purpose!" My hair and face were completely soaked. She moved towards me in an attempt to console me, so I took that opportunity to shake my hair out and spray her with pellets of water. She shrieked and took off towards the back of the boat. We fell into our seats laughing and wiping water off of our bodies. I wasn't usually this gullible, so I decided to keep a watchful eye on Kira. It did feel good to have a little fun without being reminded I needed to 'act like a lady'. My wet hair and clothes would have given Dee a coronary.

Eventually another piece of land came into view up ahead. I looked at Kira and she promptly announced, "There she is! Old Baldy!"

"Old Baldy?" I raised an eyebrow.

"The lighthouse! It's called Old Baldy." I spotted a weathered, stone lighthouse rising up over the sprawling vacation homes and scraggly trees. The ferry maneuvered into a small marina dotted with sailboats, fishing boats, and one very large yacht. We sidled up to the boardwalk, and I felt the ferry crawl to a stop.

The horn sounded again and we descended the exit ramp, following the rest of the passengers along the boardwalk. Up ahead, Ebb and Flo's Oyster Bar and Restaurant welcomed the newcomers, as well as several other buildings housing souvenir shops and golf cart rentals.

"So there are no cars on the island at all?" I asked Kira, even though I already knew the answer.

"Nope, only golf carts – even the roads are golf cart size! But we aren't renting one. We need to go this way." She ushered me down a sidewalk and through a small chain link fence. "The school has its own fleet. They keep some here, and the rest are back on school grounds."

One long row of golf carts stretched out before us. They weren't your normal golf carts, however…these were black, sleek and sitting on fat beach tires. The emblem for the House of Lorelei was on each side. It was made up of a simple circle containing a swooping letter 'L'. We climbed into the first cart in the row and Kira stomped on the gas pedal; throwing me against the back of the seat. I searched around for a seat belt. The absence of doors, in addition to Kira's questionable driving skills, didn't do much for my quickly building anxiety.

We zipped down the road heading east, and families riding bikes and vacationers in other golf carts waved as we passed. Bald Head Island sat between the Cape Fear River and the Atlantic Ocean. The island's western side housed the marina, shops and the lighthouse, while the southern side was the most populated; boasting sprawling vacation homes and beautiful beaches. The northern section of the island was made up of marshland and largely uninhabitable.

The House of Lorelei was located on the eastern side, facing the Atlantic Ocean. The entire island was full of lush trees and plant life, with the most prevalent being the live oak tree. Many years of constant wind had twisted and mangled their branches; forging works of art that stretched over the road and created an enchanting canopy of green.

The skin on my wrist began tingling and I glanced down to see if there was something crawling on me. Instead I noticed my trace was not only still shimmering, it had started to change colors as well. The once black lines were now a silvery blue. Fortunately my bewilderment was quickly interrupted by the huge, ornate iron gate we were stopped in front of. Unless you were directly in front of it, you could easily miss the school's entrance. Ivy and moss twisted around and over the gate, which made it look as much a part of the landscape as the live oaks. Beneath the overgrowth, the House of Lorelei emblem adorned both sides of the iron bars. My stomach began doing flip-flops in anticipation. Ever so slowly, the gate swung inward and we drove onto the school grounds.

Once we were clear of the gate, Kira hit the gas again and I held on for dear life for another half mile or so. Gray stone walls lined the road, weathered by wind and time. The campus of the House of Lorelei unfolded before us as we rounded a sharp corner. Buildings made of the same weathered gray stone stood on every side of us; appearing very gothic in the hooded light of the setting sun. We came to an abrupt halt in front of a two story building, and Kira motioned for me to follow her in.

"Before I take you to Maren Hall where you'll be living, we need to take care of a couple minor details," she explained. Once inside, we entered a modest office labeled 'Kira Baylor'.

"Okay. Let's see, let's see…" She shuffled through some papers on her desk. "Here's your meal card. It works all over the island, not just on campus. And here's the key to the suite you'll be sharing with your new roommates." She handed me a black debit card and a small manila envelope with a key inside. She produced several blank forms and began to fill them out.

"The name 'Hannah Elizabeth Whitman' was given to you by the state of Georgia, correct?"

"Just the 'Hannah Elizabeth' part. 'Whitman' came from my adoptive family," I clarified. As she continued filling out more information, I got an idea. If I was going to have a new beginning, I might as well make it official.

"So, if a person wanted to change their name now that they were beginning a new school and had the rare opportunity to recreate themselves…as it were…would that be an option?" I asked hesitantly.

She looked up and smiled knowingly. "And what would said person want to change their name to?" Only one name came to mind.

"Anastasia."

She gave me an odd look and quickly directed her gaze back down to the paper. "Okay, Anastasia." She put emphasis on my new first name and scribbled something down on the form. "Name officially changed. Now let's go introduce you to your new suitemates!"

Back in the golf cart, we passed several more gray stone buildings and veered onto a cobblestone street lined with beach shops on either side. The golf cart's large beach tires had us bouncing around like a demented carnival ride. By the time the shops ran out and the road changed back to smooth pavement, we were both laughing hysterically.

"Normally we don't drive down that section," Kira explained sheepishly as she wiped a couple of happy tears from her cheek. "But sometimes it's just fun to do." Several looming buildings to my right caught my attention.

"Here we are!" I looked up in wonder at a seven story building that resembled a medieval beach resort. The constant roar of the ocean greeted me as we walked up the stone steps of Maren Hall. The strong smell of sea grass filled my nose and the warm nighttime air tickled my skin as it swirled around me. The gothic feel of the exterior stopped abruptly at the front doors. The extensive lobby was filled with large, overflowing brown leather couches and chairs. Flat screen TV's hung on several of the walls, and an enormous fish tank was set into the wall on my left; exotic-looking fish cruising along its length. Straight ahead, more doors led out to blackness. Kira's eyes followed mine.

"Maren is one of the two oceanfront halls. The other is Rostrum Hall next door, which is one of the guy's halls." This was too good to believe. My new home would be oceanfront? I could count on one hand the number of times I'd been to the beach, and now I'd be living on it!

We rode a sleek elevator to the third floor and came to a stop at a normal-looking door labeled three-twenty-seven. Kira knocked three times and I heard a pair of feet running towards us.

The door flew open and a petite girl with chunky layers of red, blonde and brown hair stood before us.

"Hey Kira!" Not waiting on an answer, she turned her attention to me. "And you must be our new roomie! Willow! Carmen! She's here!" She wrapped me in a bear hug and then motioned for us to come inside. Two more girls walked into the room.

"Look guys, she's here!" She was practically jumping up and down with excitement.

"You'll have to excuse Phoebe. She forgot to take her meds today," the dark haired girl joked as she collapsed dramatically onto the couch and took a big gulp of Gatorade.

Phoebe shot her a look and rolled her eyes. "That's Carmen. She's just mad 'cause I beat her at tennis on the Wii today." Then she whispered loudly enough for everyone to still hear, "I've got a wicked back hand." Glancing over at the girl on the couch, she stuck out her tongue.

"I'm Willow." The third girl gave me a genuine smile.

"I'm Anastasia. It's nice to meet you," I returned the sentiment. The second I said my name, the other two girls quit arguing and looked at me the same way Kira had earlier. Feeling extremely awkward, I continued, "But you can call me Stasia."

Willow recovered first. "Welcome to Lorelei, Stasia. We're really happy you're here."

Kira squeezed my shoulder and turned towards the door. "You girls help Stasia get settled in and I'll stop by tomorrow to see how things are going, okay?" She gave me a wink. After she left, I turned and looked at my new suitemates. They couldn't have been more different.

Phoebe was no taller than five feet, one inch, and her tri-colored hair matched the rest of her rocker girl style. She wore gray skinny jeans, red Converse sneakers and a vintage AC/DC t-shirt. Her hunter green eyes were on the smaller side, and they crinkled up when she laughed. Her smile was infectious and could brighten an entire room. Willow lived up to her name as she floated into the kitchen in a white strapless sundress with lace trim, bare feet, and unruly, wavy blonde hair braided down her back. Wisps of hair feathered out around her round face; framing her full lips and big blue eyes. Her demeanor was very calming and put you at ease right away. Carmen's Brazilian descent was evident in her dark features and long legs. Her deep brown eyes shone with confidence and her mouth seemed to be stuck in a permanent smirk. She gave off a distinct aura of attitude. Her dark chestnut hair was piled on top of her head in a loose bun, and she was still lounging on the couch in yoga pants and a tank top.

Phoebe's slender hand slid into mine. "Come on, I'll show you your room! You get to share a bathroom with me!" She pulled me farther into my new home. The common room was like an apartment, with a small galley kitchen on the right that opened up to the rest of the room via a bar with four wooden stools. A small table sat in the space between the kitchen and living room, but I could tell they never used it by the amount of books and papers piled on top of it. The living room had a comfortable-looking, cream couch decorated with fluffy turquoise pillows, a cream and turquoise striped love seat and two recliners, which all encircled a wooden coffee table. A flat screen TV like the ones downstairs hung on the wall and glass French doors led out to a balcony facing the ocean. There were four bedrooms; two on each side of the common room. Phoebe opened one of the doors and my jaw dropped.

"We did a little decorating," Phoebe said sheepishly. She launched herself onto the bed in a flurry of giggles, sat criss-cross-applesauce and waited for my reaction. The queen size bed was covered by a white down comforter and at least ten pillows of different sizes and shapes. A long wooden dresser with a mirror stood opposite the bed and an armoire towered in the corner. A big blue shag carpet rug decorated the floor. Behind the bed hung three large picture frames with the words Live, Love, and Laugh written in swirling letters. Everything was decorated in light blue, silver, and white. There was a small closet and another door that led into the bathroom I'd be sharing with Phoebe.

"So what do you think?" I could tell the suspense was literally killing her.

"I absolutely love it!" She jumped off the bed and gave me another quick hug. Over her shoulder I spotted my luggage in the corner, waiting to be unpacked. I couldn't believe how amazing my new home was. I had expected a cramped dorm room with maybe a mini fridge. This rocked.

"I picked out the comforter!" Carmen yelled from the other room. I could tell her attitude was really just a cover for the very caring, sweet person she really was on the inside. It made me wonder what happened in her life to cause her to build walls around her heart, too.

"You guys are too much! Honestly, this is amazing," I addressed all of them with gratitude. Phoebe beamed with pride. I looked at her, slightly perplexed by how very normal she seemed as well.

"Everybody here seems so normal. So…what brought you here?" I hoped the question wasn't too personal, but she gave me an equally perplexed look and frowned.

"The same thing that brings everybody here, silly," she replied. Before she could continue, she sniffed the air and her green eyes lit up with mischief. I did the same, hoping I remembered my deodorant this morning, but the rich, sweet smell of cake filled my nose instead.

"Hey Carmen, what time is it?" Phoebe shouted into the other room. I heard the delightful anticipation in her tone.

"Smells like....cupcake thirty!" Carmen called back to her. Willow snickered from the kitchen.

"Cupcake thirty?" I questioned Phoebe, but she just licked her lips and dragged me up to the bar.

"Willow's our baker and cook all in one," she announced proudly, and pulled out a stool for both of us.

"Same thing, Phoebs." Carmen dragged up a stool for herself, and then pulled her hair back like she was preparing for an eating contest. Phoebe unfolded a napkin and tucked it in the collar of her shirt; creating a make shift bib. I was half expecting them to grab their forks next and start beating them on the counter chanting, 'We want cupcakes'. I could tell I was going to enjoy living with these girls. If nothing else, they were entertaining.

"No they aren't. A baker bakes things, a cook cooks things. Duh." Phoebe and Carmen started arguing and I peeked up at Willow, who was in the process of taking the cupcakes out of the pan and spreading on icing. She shook her head at the other two with a disapproving frown and handed me the first cupcake.

"Go ahead and add referee to that list," she said warily, then spoke up to interrupt Phoebe and Carmen. "I'm gonna give these cupcakes to our best friends next door if you two don't stop," she threatened, and by the way she said it, I could tell best friends meant the complete opposite. Carmen and Phoebe shot Willow mock looks of horror, then grinned and stole a couple of cupcakes each.

Phoebe bit down into one. "No way am I letting any of these cupcakes get wasted on those hateful be-yotches," she huffed through a mouthful.

"These are really good," I complimented Willow as I took another bite of the red velvet cupcake with cream cheese icing. "So I take it I won't be getting a welcome basket from our neighbors?"

"Not unless it has poison in it." Phoebe made a face normally reserved for spiders or snakes. "I swear they are pure evil."

"Definitely evil," Carmen agreed. "But it was pretty funny when Olivia got pinched by that crab yesterday. It's bad when the wildlife don't even like you." She giggled and raised her dark eyebrows at Phoebe.

Phoebe put her icing-covered hands up in defense. "I promise I had nothing to do with it. Seriously!"

Willow grinned and showed her dimples. "Uh huh, likely story, Phoebs."

Before I could figure out how in the world Phoebe would be able to make a crab attack someone, a yawn fought its way out of me and I felt the exhaustion of the day hit me like a sledgehammer.

"Oh Stasia, I bet you're exhausted!" Phoebe said sympathetically. "Plus you need to get your sleep. We're going out to the beach tomorrow. Only two more days until classes start, so we have to take advantage of every minute of freedom."

I said goodnight to my new roommates and headed to my unbelievably awesome bedroom. I shut the door and smiled as a renewed sense of hope filled my heart. The House of Lorelei already felt like home.

The next morning I awakened to the aroma of sizzling bacon and singing. I don't know if I'd really call it singing, however, more like nails on a chalkboard. I threw on some sweats and peeked out of my bedroom door. Phoebe was sitting on the couch listening to an IPod with her hands in what could only be described as a portable sandbox. I saw that it was some sort of pottery shaped in a square, completely filled with sand. Maybe everyone there was two fries short of a Happy Meal, after all.

I walked out into the living room and noticed Willow working her magic in the kitchen. The sight of scrambled eggs, bacon, and cheese grits cooking on the stove had my mouth watering. I was going to get spoiled if she kept this up. Right when I sat down at the bar, a very irritated looking Carmen came out of her room and scowled at Phoebe.

"Somebody find that dying animal and put it out of its misery before I jump off the balcony." She took one of the ear buds out of Phoebe's ear. "Hey Taylor Swift, give it a rest." Instead of a witty comeback, Phoebe put the ear bud back in, blew a kiss at her and started singing even louder. Deciding it wasn't worth it, Carmen took a seat beside me. A couple of minutes and one song later, Phoebe snuck up behind us, planted a kiss on each of our cheeks, and then hopped up onto the stool on my other side. She still had a thin layer of sand coating her small hands.

"Man, I'm starving! Shaping sand really works up an appetite." She sighed dramatically and propped her elbows up on the bar. Yep, definitely a couple fries short.

After filling my stomach with a five star breakfast a-la-Willow, I was sporting a light pink bikini beneath a white cotton cover up, and we were on our way down to the beach. I was a little nervous, knowing the whole school would probably be out there too. But at least I had three new friends to lessen the anxiety...three very tan and very in-shape new friends, to be exact. Seeing Phoebe's perfectly sculpted figure in a silver Roxy bikini, I decided I definitely needed to do some shopping. Glancing at Carmen, who resembled a Hawaiian tropic model in her red bikini, I decided some sit ups wouldn't hurt either.

Outside the sun was shining and the breeze picked up the smells of the beach as it swirled around us. The aroma of tanning lotion and saltwater assaulted my senses; making me smile. There were people playing beach volleyball, groups of girls laying out, and groups of guys watching the groups of girls laying out. The tide was on the way in and the waves were dotted with surfers. We found a clear spot on the sand and put down a soft cotton blanket that held all four of us.

"It doesn't get any better than this," Willow breathed, and slathered some SPF 30 on her pale skin. I was about to agree when a group of guys ran by us carrying surfboards; throwing up sand with their feet on the way to the ocean.

"Hey! Watch where you're going!" Carmen shouted and wiped sand out of her dark eyes. They just kept running and I couldn't help but admire the view. Tan and shirtless, with swim trunks hanging low on their hips, they made it to the water and immediately jumped on their surfboards and started paddling out. They all had very dark hair. Not one of them had light brown or blond hair, and idly I wondered if they were all related somehow.

"I'd like to watch where they're going for sure," Phoebe told Carmen, and winked a green eye at me. "Carmen, on the other hand, only has eyes for Logan." She started making kissing noises and Carmen threw a stray seashell at her.

"Is that your boyfriend?" I asked Carmen.

"She wishes," teased Phoebe.

"Whatever, Logan can't stop drooling over Cassie long enough to notice anybody else," Carmen sighed and laid back down. "I'm so over it."

"You're imagining things. He's definitely into you, not Cassie," Willow commented, as she put on white Wayfarer sunglasses and a straw hat.

"Yeah, it's just hard to tell because Cassie throws herself at anything that walks," agreed Phoebe. She turned her attention to me. "Don't worry, I'm sure you'll get to meet Cassie soon enough. We have the pleasure of living beside her, Olivia and the other two evil queens."

I laughed at her dry tone. "I can't wait."

An hour later, we flipped onto our stomachs and ate the ham sandwiches Willow had brought down. Carmen lost herself in a People magazine and Phoebe absently stared at the sand in front of her. I looked on with curiosity when she flattened her palm just above the sand and moved it back and forth slowly. The sand started swirling around beneath her hand. Her fingers wiggled and the sand swirled faster and faster. Mesmerized, I jumped when she smacked her hand down, bounced up and smiled down at me.

"I need to cool off. Wanna go in the water?" A little confused by what I had just seen, all I could do was nod my head and stand up. Not until we took several steps towards the ocean did the feeling of unease twist my stomach. I shouldn't be afraid. I mean, it was just water. Not as clear as a swimming pool, but there couldn't be anything too dangerous in there, right? Once we reached the water's edge, the surf raced up the sand and rolled over my feet. I felt like it was teasing me, daring me to venture out farther out into its seductive grip.

"What are you waiting for? Come on!" Phoebe called to me, as she ran ahead and dove into a cresting wave. Wishing the entire school wasn't behind me on the beach watching, I forced my feet forward. I jumped and let out a tiny squeal each time a wave hit me. Eventually the water was up to my waist and I was used to the chilly temperature. It was now or never. Phoebe bobbed effortlessly about fifty feet away from me. I took a deep breath and dove in.

I kept my eyes squeezed shut and fought against the movement of the water. I kicked harder and dove a little deeper. My skin started tingling all over, and a surge of adrenaline flowed out from my chest. About to float back up to the surface, I froze when something slimy rubbed against my leg. Another slimy something wrapped around my ankle. Something else started bumping into my back, arms and stomach. I opened my eyes in alarm. An entire school of tiny silver fish had completely surrounded my body; blocking my vision. When I looked down at my legs, all I could make out were green blurs swaying against them. My eyes began to burn with a searing pain like I'd never experienced before, and I desperately needed oxygen. I wiggled my legs to get them out of the slimy fingers, all to no avail. All of the kicking in the world couldn't free me. As mind numbing panic took over in earnest, the fish darted away suddenly and a pair of eyes swimming towards me took their place. Deep blue eyes. Everything turned fuzzy and I assumed I was hallucinating. I closed my eyes.

Strong, warm arms that smelled incredibly good carried me with ease. I opened my eyes hesitantly as I was laid softly on the sand. The blinding sunlight instantly sent more pain pulsing through my already burning eyes. Casting a shadow over my face and restoring my vision, he leaned over me. Time slowed and my heart stopped. He was so close I saw the swirls of gray in his stormy eyes. Those tantalizing blue eyes, only inches away, were gazing down into mine with what looked like wonder. Droplets of water ran down his handsome face, and with the sun shining brightly behind him, he resembled a dark angel. His chiseled jaw was doing that flexing thing I'd seen in my dreams and his wet, dark hair clung to his brow. He was mysterious, dangerous and beautiful all at once. I willed myself to say something but I couldn't breathe, nonetheless speak. Suddenly his features hardened and I was blinded by sunlight once again. A shiver went through me as if a part of my soul had left with him. I managed to sit up as a crowd of people swarmed around me.

"Stasia! Are you okay?! Oh my God!" Phoebe hugged me. "What happened?!"

"Are you hurt?" Willow looked me over intently; searching for scrapes or bruises.

"Move back you guys, and let the girl breathe." I looked over at Carmen and silently thanked her. Phoebe and Willow moved back all of a millimeter, but continued watching me with concern.

"I'm okay, I promise," I reassured them. "I just got...caught on something." They stared blankly at me. Carmen raised a skeptical eyebrow and, taking a silent queue, pushed past the other two. She helped me to my feet while maintaining a supportive arm around my waist.

"Alright people, show's over," she announced to the crowd that congregated around us. She half-carried, half-dragged me back to Maren as Willow and Phoebe gathered our stuff from the beach. I was busy looking over my shoulder to find where my rescuer had disappeared to.

"You sure you're okay?"

"Yeah, I promise. I think my legs got stuck in some seaweed or something. It was weird." She gave me another skeptical look and gasped.

"Stasia, your eyes!"

"What about them?"

"Wow," she whispered.

"Wow, what? What's wrong with them?" She was really starting to freak me out.

"They've....changed colors."

"What?" Not exactly what I was expecting to hear.

"They were regular blue before, but now they're like a bright teal or turquoise." She looked closer. "It looks like you have those colored contacts in or something." Grand. That was excellent news.

Back upstairs, I made a beeline for the bathroom mirror. I just stood there and stared in disbelief until Phoebe materialized behind me.

"Wow – look how pretty they are!" she exclaimed; smiling wide.

"Yeah, if by pretty you mean freakishly weird." My eyes had in fact changed colors. They were a striking aquamarine hue, which contrasted starkly against my pale blonde hair. This was going to take some getting used to.

"I bet it has something to do with your abilities," she surmised. My abilities?

"What are you talking about?" I turned to face her.

"You know, your Tyde abilities." She looked at me with confusion, which quickly turned to shock. "Oh my God, you don't know, do you? Kira didn't say anything to you?"

Now I was the one confused. "About what? What's a 'tide ability'?"

"Um, you might want to sit down."

We gathered in the living room and waited while Willow fixed us some lemonade, and I wondered if things could get any weirder. Unfortunately for me, things could always get weirder.

My roommates seemed to have trouble beginning the conversation. After a few false starts, Carmen came up with a solution.

"Phoebs, why don't you show her your sandbox?" She shrugged her shoulders.

Phoebe vanished into her room and came back with the bowl I'd seen her playing with earlier that morning.

"Okay. Watch closely," she instructed me. I leaned forward, not sure what I was watching for. She placed her pointer finger in the sand and slowly started making circles. She peeked up at me to make sure I was still paying attention, and then gently lifted her finger. The sand followed. Higher and higher it went, still swirling. I couldn't believe what I was seeing! She had created a mini sand tornado…with her finger. I inspected her face and saw total concentration as she stared down at the sand. She glanced up again, flashed a mischievous grin in my direction and then quickly flattened out her hand. The sand stopped spinning and neatly dropped back down into the box. Everyone looked at me expectantly.

As they stared holes in to my head, I could actually feel my entire belief system shift and morph as it widened and made room for things like mini sand tornadoes commanded by a single finger.

"That is the coolest thing I have ever seen," I said slowly. "I might need to see that again." Phoebe's face lit up in a bright smile and Carmen wrapped an arm around my shoulder.

"You haven't seen the half of it." Her brown eyes danced with excitement.

"So, what is this place? I thought I was being sent here for blackouts and nightmares?"

"Maybe that's just the reason they gave your parents, but things like blackouts wouldn't really be considered unusual here at Lorelei," Willow insisted. A sense of relief washed over me, but it was quickly followed by disbelief.

"So…does everybody here have…" I couldn't believe what was about to come out of my mouth, "powers?"

Carmen snickered at my word choice. "Every person at Lorelei is a descendant of a sea God or Goddess, including you. We're part human and," she paused for dramatic effect, "part sea nymph."

"Okay, whoa." I put a hand up to stop her. "Sea nymphs? If you tell me I'm going to grow a tail and start brushing my hair with a fork, I'm walking out of here right now." Scenes from The Little Mermaid movie popped into my head.

Phoebe collapsed into a fit of giggles and Willow shook her head and laughed. "No, dear. No forks and no tails. But we all have sea nymph blood running through our veins, which means we have a very special connection with the ocean and marine life. We also have abilities that I guess you could call powers, but they're different depending on which sea God or Goddess you're descended from. We...," she swept her arm in a circle; encompassing all four of us, "...are Tydes, which means we're descended from one of the fifty Nereids." Her eyes held mine, probably hoping I wasn't about to go screaming from the room.

"Nereids?" I wrinkled my nose, not sure if I wanted to know the answer.

"The Nereids are the fifty Goddesses of the sea, also known as the fifty daughters of the sea." Willow nodded toward Phoebe. "For example, Phoebe's descended from the sea Goddess Psamanthe. She's the Goddess of sand, hence Phoebe's abilities to control sand."

"I also have a connection with the creatures of the sand, which is pretty cool," Phoebe told me with pride. I remembered the conversation that morning about the crab, and it clicked into place. "But our abilities don't reach their full capacity until we turn eighteen. So while we're here, we learn how to control and use them."

"So what about you guys?" I looked at Willow and Carmen. "Who are you descended from? What are your abilities?"

"I'm descended from Laneira, so I have the ability to heal," Willow divulged.

"Heal?" I asked, surprised. "You mean, you can heal people?"

"Yep." She smiled.

"Wow." This was getting more unbelievable by the minute.

63

Carmen leaned forward. "I'm descended from Oreithyia, which is Latin for 'raging waves'." She grinned wickedly. "So I can control the waves."

"Uh, more like the waves control you." Phoebe laughed. "She hasn't quite gotten the hang of it yet."

"Yes I have! I just need to…practice more." She glared at Phoebe and continued with slightly less confidence, "At the moment I can only do it when I get mad, but it's still pretty cool."

"We try to stay out of the water when she's practicing. You never know when a whirlpool will form and swallow you whole," Willow teased, and Carmen threw a pillow at her. I felt myself getting a little jealous of their amazing abilities, when I realized she had included me in that whole 'We are Tydes' comment.

"You wouldn't happen to know who I'm descended from, would you?" It was worth a shot, but they just shook their heads. I looked down at my hands. "I don't know what my abilities are, or if I even have any." I rubbed my thumb over my trace. If Kira had one that meant…

"So do you guys have one of these like Kira? Does that mean she's a Tyde too?" I held up my wrist and more questions than I could ask in one conversation began popping into my head. Carmen took my arm and they all dissected my trace with curiosity.

"Yep, she's a Tyde too. Wow! I've never seen one like that!" Phoebe squealed.

"We learned about the different traces in class, but I don't remember seeing this one in the book." Willow leaned back in deep thought.

"So, what do your traces look like?" My eyes did a quick search of Willow's pale skin.

"Mine's an hourglass," Phoebe piped up, and threw her short leg up on the coffee table; showing me the design that decorated her ankle. "The sand of an hourglass represents continual change and growth."

"Mine represents the power of health." Willow held up her left palm. I didn't know why I hadn't noticed it before. It was a single swirl with a line going through it that hooked at the top. I'd never seen a symbol like that, so I decided to take her word for it.

"See if you can guess what mine is." Carmen frowned with contempt, lifted her hair and pointed. Right below the hairline, behind her left ear, was a little swirl with a tail.

"A wave?" I guessed.

"Ding, ding, ding! Tell her what she's won, Alex." She laughed darkly. "Not very original, huh?"

"I think it's pretty cool, actually. At least you know what yours means. I've got no clue about mine. I mean, I'm one big, fat mystery. I don't know who I'm descended from, I have a trace no one's ever seen before, and my eyes randomly changed to turquoise." I shook my head at the ridiculousness of it all.

"So you don't know who your real parents are?" asked Willow. I launched into the story about how I was found as a baby, grew up in the foster care system, and then was adopted by the Whitmans. They were silent for a minute and my questions started flying again.

"So, is everyone here a Tyde?" I asked them.

Carmen stood up and stretched lazily. "Now that's a loaded question. I think we might need to discuss that can of worms over a certain massive cinnamon roll."

"Mmmm…that's exactly what we need! Cinnabon, here we come!" Phoebe flew off the couch in search of her flip flops. Willow came to sit next to me.

"We'll get it all figured out, I promise. At least now you're where you belong." I started to tear up at her words, but blinked them away and squeezed her hand.

"I couldn't agree more."

EIGHT

"Oh my God, I can already smell it." Phoebe leaned her head back and quickened her pace. I recognized the street from when Kira and I had bounced down it the night before. We passed by eclectic beach shops and restaurants, but I was too distracted to pay attention. Even though I told myself not to, I couldn't help scanning the crowds of people for a particular guy with dark hair and blue eyes. I never thought he was...real. But sure enough, he was there. And he saved my life. I got a shiver when I thought about his blue eyes looking into mine and the water dripping off of his golden skin...

"Evil queen alert..." Phoebe interrupted my thoughts with a warning. I followed her gaze to the two girls currently on a collision course with us. If I had to guess, I'd say these were the be-yotches. They stopped in front of us and blocked our path.

"So who's your new friend?" one of the girls purred. She had hair blacker than night, dark smoky eyes, and appeared to have Puerto Rican or Dominican blood in her. Her skin was the color of dark caramel and she reminded me of a panther watching its prey before it pounced.

"This is Anastasia, our new roommate," Willow proudly announced. "Stasia, this is Olivia and Cassie." She gestured to the other girl, who paled in comparison to Olivia. She had a slight figure and light brown hair cut into a long bob. She gave me a tight smile. The panther girl looked me up and down, and then laughed.

"I seriously doubt that," she smirked at me. "From what I could see this morning, you seriously need swimming lessons." I felt my cheeks getting hot, but Carmen stepped forward so she was face-to-face with Olivia.

"Don't you have some puppies to slaughter or something?" She put her hands on her hips and raised an eyebrow.

"Isn't she just delightful, Cassie?" A sarcastic smile slithered its way onto Olivia's face. "Now if you don't mind, we have more important things to do than waste our time talking to you." Carmen and Phoebe glared at their backs as they purposefully strode past us.

"Come on, you guys, let 'em go – it's not worth it," Willow insisted; ushering us forward. They turned around reluctantly, still scowling.

Once we arrived at Cinnabon, we ordered as many delicious, fattening things as possible and claimed a table near the window. In the middle of one supersized cinnamon roll, I caught sight of Kira walking through the door. I waved her down and she pulled up a chair.

"How's your first day going so far?" she asked me.

"Well besides my eyes changing to a freakish color and the entire school watching as I almost drowned in the ocean, I can't complain," I snickered.

"I thought your eyes looked different." She leaned in for a better look. "And please tell me you're joking about that last part."

"I wish I was. It was so embarrassing, Kira. Everyone was watching! So much for making a good first impression." I looked down at my hands and ran my finger over my trace.

"Everyone will forget about it by tomorrow, don't worry," she said sympathetically.

"I could hold Phoebe under water and then pretend I'm saving her life?" Carmen suggested. "Then we'll be the talk of the school." She cut her eyes at Phoebe. "But I'm not doing mouth to mouth."

"Oh, no you don't. If anybody's pretending to save a life, it's gonna be me," Phoebe retorted. She pointed at Carmen with an icing-covered finger. "Besides, I have a camera ready face." She batted her eyelashes and we all erupted with laughter.

I turned to face Kira. "So why didn't you tell me about being a Tyde? The girls told me some stuff, but now I've got a million questions. I mean, I watched Phoebe create a little sandstorm with one finger. Talk about a wake-up call."

"I thought it would be better if you witnessed a couple of abilities first. Would you have believed me if I had tried to explain it yesterday?" she asked.

"I would have checked to see if your drink was spiked."

"Exactly, so don't worry - we'll have plenty of time for questions. That's why you have a mentor. And I must say…I'm one of the best." She tossed her blond hair over one shoulder dramatically and posed for us.

"She was asking us if everyone here is a Tyde. Maybe you could explain instead?" Willow asked Kira.

"Well that's easy enough." She turned her attention towards me again, while I sat on the edge of my seat in anticipation. "There are four different Orders: Tydes, Sirens, Tritons and the Sons of Daimon."

"Tritons are usually pretty nice to look at." Phoebe grinned. "Just ask Carmen."

"I can't help it if I'm attracted to the knight in shining armor type. Plus, I'm just good at being a damsel in distress." Carmen fanned herself and pretended to faint.

Kira just rolled her eyes and continued. "Anyway, Tydes can be male or female. Sirens are only female, and the Tritons and Sons of Daimon are only male. That's where the 'Sons' part comes in." She grinned at her own corny joke. "We're all descendants of different sea Gods and Goddesses. Tydes are descendants of the fifty Nereids, and we each have varying abilities. Like Phoebe's sand manipulation. Or Willow's healing ability," she explained. I remembered her seagull trace.

"So what are your abilities? Something to do with seagulls?" I guessed.

"Actually yes, but that's a conversation for another day." She smiled like she was hiding a secret she couldn't wait to tell.

"Now, Sirens are also descendants of the Nereids, but only one of them. They're all related to the Nereid named Keto, who had a bad reputation for trickery. Long story short, they broke away from the rest of the Tydes centuries ago. When they broke away and created their own Order, they lost most of their abilities. All except for influencing through their beauty, as well as the ability to cantillate in order to get what they want, which is a lot like singing but much more beautiful. Experienced Sirens can be very dangerous."

Willow nodded and continued where Kira left off. "Tritons are descendants of the sea God Poseidon. You've heard of him, right? Well, they have immense strength, therefore they usually end up as defenders and guardians, or knights in shining armor." She winked at Carmen, who shrugged her shoulders innocently. "They also have affinities toward certain weapons."

Kira began again. "The Sons of Daimon are all descended from the Underworld God Charon."

"Underworld?" Fear crept up my spine. "A God name Sharon?"

"Yes, but it's spelled with a C," she corrected. "They are the most recognizable, because they all look alike with dark hair and dark skin. Only their eye color varies." A particular pair of deep blue eyes flashed in my mind and I couldn't help but wonder if that would be the order he

69

belonged to. "Sons can be very dangerous as well. But that's why we have schools like Lorelei all over the world, to educate each generation about the other Orders. We find the relationships that are built early on help keep the peace. For the most part, anyway." She got a faraway look in her eyes and shook her head like she was trying to erase her thoughts.

"Wow." That's all I could manage to say as everything slowly sunk in.

"So that's the Cliff notes version," Kira assured me with a smile. "I know it's a lot to digest."

"It's just so crazy. I mean, it's an entirely different world that I never knew existed. I always felt like I was different, but I never dreamed just how different that was. The good news is that this craziness is a far cry from the 'normal' world I used to live in." I smiled at my mentor and friends and my heart swelled. "I never really liked normal anyway."

Later that night I snuggled into my bed and tried to sort through the mountain of new information that had been thrown at me. Sea nymphs? Abilities? Gods and Goddesses? It was all so hard to believe, but it did explain a lot. The weird dreams, the blackouts, hearing singing in the bathtub. Well, okay maybe it explained absolutely nothing. But at least now there was a general reason for all the weirdness in my life. The only thing I would change would be to go back and come to Lorelei earlier. One year wasn't long enough to figure out an entirely new world, not to mention an entirely new life. All of a sudden I wasn't the person I thought I was.

This was the trifecta of identity crises. A brand new school, new friends, and a new me. Once I figured out who my parents were, I'd be able to add another one to the list. What would that make it? A quatrofecta? Anyway, I wasn't sure where I needed to start to figure any of this out. Was Dr. Campbell from Lorelei? Is that how she knew I needed to transfer here? And if I was descended from a sea Goddess, where were my real parents? Why did they abandon me in a world where I didn't belong? All I had were questions and no answers. I wanted someone to tell me what my abilities were. Explain why my eyes changed colors. Why the ocean attacked me if I was supposed to have a special bond with it. And why I couldn't get a certain blue eyed dark angel out of my head. Where was he? What was his name? Did he dream of me too?

I woke up to distant thunder rolling in off the ocean and rain spattering against my bedroom window. It was almost dawn so I threw on some sweatpants, snuck out to the living room and looked through the curtains. I had been terrified of storms when I was younger, yet completely fascinated at the same time. I would hide under a blanket with only my eyes peeking out as lightening lit up the world and thunder rumbled so loud my insides vibrated. As scared as I was, I loved every second of it. Now that I was older, I wished I could get even closer. I wanted to sit up in the clouds and look down as the rain dampened the earth and the strength of the wind moved trees. When the pure power of nature's energy was channeled it could move mountains. Being so close to that intense energy would be exhilarating.

I gingerly opened the French doors and stepped out onto the balcony. Even being up on the third floor, I could see miles out to sea. The dark storm clouds were still building as they rained down on the ocean, and the wall of water looked like a gray curtain strung from the billowing clouds. Lightning danced across the sky and I felt like I was witnessing a light show created just for me. I curled up on one of the lounge chairs and watched as the storm made its way towards land. I got that weird feeling of being watched again, so I glanced around to the neighboring balconies. No one was there, but I couldn't seem to shake the feeling. Gazing out at the ocean, I let the rumbling thunder soothe my soul.

"If you didn't like your bed you could have just said something." I opened my eyes to see Carmen grinning down at me. I must have fallen asleep watching the storm. Good thing I didn't sleep walk! The new day was fifty shades of gray and pretty chilly. Goose bumps rose on my arms as I stood up and headed for the warmth of the living room.

After a unanimous vote we decided to have a movie day spent on the couch, eating as much snack food as our meal cards could buy. After the excitement of yesterday and classes starting tomorrow, I was really looking forward to doing something low-key like watching movies. Willow and I began making pancakes for breakfast, while Phoebe and Carmen ran downstairs to the Red Box to rent movies and buy food. After a chick flick, a comedy and a movie about a girl who took on the entire Russian mafia (Carmen picked that one out), we started to get a little restless. When Phoebe started flinging sand from her box at Carmen with one finger, I told them the idea that had bounced around in my head for several hours.

"You want to do what?" Carmen stared up at me as she playfully tried to smother Phoebe with a pillow.

"It's the perfect time, you guys. Nobody's outside to watch me humiliate myself, and I have you guys to save my life." I gave them my best puppy dog eyes.

"It's kind of cold outside; don't you think the water will be freezing?" Willow stood and looked out the window, doubtful.

Phoebe came to the rescue after finally pushing Carmen off of her. "Well, I do have an extra wet suit that might fit you?"

I ran over to her. "That's perfect, Phoebe! And if you have an extra wet suit that means you have another one you can wear too, right?" I wiggled my eyebrows at her.

"Crap. I guess I walked right into that one, didn't I?" I could tell she was going to give in. "I'll go in with you on one condition."

73

"Name it."

"If I can't save your life, don't come back and haunt me."

I rubbed my chin, contemplating, and then smiled. "Deal!"

It took a good twenty minutes to zip me into Phoebe's wet suit, and I'd already started wondering how in creation I was going to get that thing back off. If nothing else a pair of scissors would do the trick. Carmen and Willow tagged along behind us on the beach wearing rain jackets and holding umbrellas. The rain let up, but a strong mist had blown in; keeping everything damp.

"I cannot believe we are doing this right now," complained Carmen. "My hair and rain do not get along. Frizz is the devil."

"Stop complaining or I'll throw you in the ocean along with them," Willow threatened her, and then handed her a Twix.

"Yes, mother," Carmen retorted. She grabbed the Twix and grinned like a kid in a candy store.

As we walked toward the surf I started to get nervous again. This had seemed like such a great idea in the comfort of our living room, but now I wasn't so sure. I was determined not to let anything get the best of me, especially not some water. If I really was a descendant of a sea Goddess, being afraid of the ocean was not an option. Some sea nymph I was turning out to be.

Fighting past the breakers in a wet suit was much easier than I expected, but being in the ocean without actually feeling it was an odd sensation. It was still chilly, but the wet suit kept my body heat in; warming me. Once we made it past the waves, Phoebe stopped and waited on my next move. I moved past her and dove in head first. I swam as deep as I could and felt that same tingling sensation spread throughout my body. I steeled myself and opened my eyes. This time it didn't burn at all, but what really shocked me was how well I could see. Not only could I see through the murky water for at least twenty meters, it was as if the whole world had suddenly turned to high definition and I'd been watching my life in analog all these years. The amount of detail I saw was overwhelming and everything had a certain surreal quality to it. Sea grass swayed in the current below and flashed at me in a million vibrant shades of green and brown. I never imagined brown and green could be so beautiful. They also appeared translucent; allowing me to see not only the outside, but the inside of the grass as well. Very carefully, I sank down just close enough to skim my hand along the tops of their fronds. As I made contact, a jolt of energy shot up my arm. It could only be described as their life force flowing into me. I yanked my hand back in surprise and realized I was running out of air, so I quickly swam back up to the surface. At least they hadn't attacked me this time.

Taking a big gulp of oxygen, I saw Phoebe a couple of meters away floating on her back. Good thing I didn't need rescuing. I swam over to her, grabbed her ankles and yanked them toward me. She started flailing her arms and wiping water from her face, shrieking. I laughed at her and dove back underwater.

As soon as I did, my stomach plunged to the ocean floor and my body froze. An enormous sea turtle had appeared out of nowhere. I'd never seen one up close, but this one was much bigger than I would have guessed they could get. He watched me with big, black curious eyes. His head was light gray with brown scales that matched the larger ones on his shell. From his size and the scars riddling his body, I surmised he had to be very old. He looked almost regal as he idled closer to me; nodding his head up and down. I got the feeling he was happy to see me, which was a plus, considering his beak looked particularly sharp and was the size of my fist. Not sure what to do, I stayed put and followed him with my eyes as he slowly swam laps around me. He nudged my side with his head and looked up at me, which reminded me of a dog happy to see its owner. He nodded his head one more time and swam away. As he faded into the darkness, I decided swimming may not be the best way to describe it. He resembled a majestic bird of prey flying through the air; graceful and serene. I looked around and found Phoebe a couple of feet away, her eyes wide with shock. I headed back up to the surface for air and she followed me up.

As soon as I broke the surface, I was immediately overcome with a deep aching in my heart to stay underwater. It was almost as if I was more alive down there. I felt more like myself. It was addictive.

"Oh my God, that was amazing! Did you see it? It was so cute! I can't believe it was swimming around you like that!" I didn't even attempt to get a word in. Instead, I took another breath and dove back under one more time. The only greeting I received this time was the seaweed swaying below and tiny silver fish weaving around it searching for food. As I was about to go back up, I heard a faint song. Or melody. No, that wasn't right either. More like several melodies all intertwined into one. I glanced around trying to place the sound, when I noticed my turtle flying back towards me. But this time he wasn't alone. Four more turtles flanked him. All different sizes and colors, they each stopped in front of me, nodded their head, and then began circling around me. The five massive turtles continued their laps, encasing me in somewhat of a whirlpool. I started to spin as the current became stronger, but I didn't try to fight it. Within the turtle tornado, I knew without a doubt that the melody was coming from them. Each had its own tenor; harmonizing with the other turtles to create a thrumming vibration that resonated throughout my entire body. I closed my eyes and just listened.

Once they were done spinning me around, my sea turtle swam up beside me again and nudged my left hand with his head. Very carefully, I reached out and ran my fingers along his shell. Before I could register the stone-like texture, I was instantly berated with images as a slide show of epic proportions took my vision hostage. Completely caught off guard, I panicked and kicked to the surface. Heart racing and gasping for air, I headed toward shore. I noticed Phoebe popping up out of the corner of my eye, but I was already on my way to the beach.

I collapsed onto the sand next to Willow and Carmen and tried to catch my breath. Phoebe wasn't far behind me, and she'd already started calling to Carmen and Willow.

"The sea turtles...swimming...so many...unbelievable!" She was breathing so hard I couldn't understand anything she was saying. Or maybe that was just the ringing in my ears. I closed my eyes and took a few deep breaths. What just happened? The images flashed through my mind so quickly, I couldn't even register what they were of. I think I remembered pictures of other turtles and random beaches, but I couldn't be sure. Did I see into the sea turtle's mind? That shouldn't be possible, right? Someone pulled me to my feet while I struggled to regain my balance.

"You okay, Stasia?" Willow beamed at me. "I'm so proud of you! You dove right in like nothing even happened yesterday!" I tried to smile convincingly and decided to keep the images to myself until I could sort it all out. Somehow I found enough strength to walk back upstairs to our suite before falling in a heap of exhaustion onto the couch.

I was outside of the building Kira had taken me to that first day on campus. Feeling compelled to walk inside, I opened the heavy wooden door and quietly made my way down the main hall. I stopped when I heard voices and pressed my back against the wall. A sliver of light was coming from underneath a door near the end of the hall. I inched my way forward and listened.

"...don't know that for sure though!" someone said.

"But what if she's really who we think she is?" another voice asked.

"We'll just have to take care of it," hissed the first voice; a woman. "We will watch her closely to see if we have reason to worry. In the meantime, I want you to talk to Kira. Get as much information about her as you can. Do whatever it takes. We've come too far to have this orphan girl ruin everything."

My heart jumped into my throat. Orphan girl?

Chairs scraped and I crept back down the long hallway. I was completely out in the open with nowhere to hide when the door opened. Frozen against the wall, I held my breath. Two people exited the room and started down the hallway at a fast pace. One woman had somewhat of a glow about her; the golden hair cascading down her back enhancing the effect. The other woman had long, curly brown hair falling down around her shoulders, bright green eyes and gave off a certain air of status. Even though I was in plain sight, they never so much as looked my way. They continued down the hallway, out the door, and disappeared into the night.

I began to follow them, but the hallway dissolved; effectively halting my progress. I found myself standing on a large platform. Water surrounded me in every direction, but the platform rose high above it. The moon glimpsed in and out of the clouds, but it still provided a good amount of light. I heard something to my left, so I turned and saw two guys circling each other in the center of the platform. Both wore black clothes and easily blended in with the night. I moved slightly closer with soft steps; hoping not to announce my presence.

They continued circling and suddenly lunged forward at the same time. Someone collapsed when one of the punches connected. He was up again in less than a second, picking up the other and slamming him down hard on his back. More punches were thrown and blood splattered around them. One guy recovered slightly faster than the other and was more fluid in his movements. He had strips of leather wrapped tightly around his forearms, wrists and knuckles, which created a kind of glove. Before his opponent realized what was happening, he picked him up and tossed him onto the platform again. He was on top of him immediately; holding his neck with one hand as he reached into a sheath on his back with the other. He pulled out a double-bladed axe and my veins turned to ice as fear paralyzed me. As if he'd done it hundreds of times, he swung the axe around his head and down toward the other guy's neck in one swift movement. I screamed and ran forward in the hope I could prevent what I was about to see. He stopped mid-swing and whipped his head around. He looked directly at me and the pale moonlight was captured in his deep blue eyes; dancing wild with anger. One was beginning to swell and the other had a nasty gash just below it. Recognition hit hard and everything suddenly disappeared.

"Stasia! Wake up, you crazy turtle girl!" Phoebe stood over me with a big, goofy grin on her face. "Good, you're awake! It's brownie-thirty, plus, our class schedules came a little while ago!"

She ran off and I closed my eyes, my head full of confusion from the dream I just had. Was that real? Or was it a really just a dream? It sure felt real. And what if it was? Who were those two women? What were they talking about? My heart rate spiked again as I remembered the second part of my dream and who was a part of it.

The smell of brownies dragged me out of my own thoughts and I sat down clumsily on one of the stools at the bar. Carmen handed me an envelope.

"Happy new school year," she said sarcastically and dug into a fudge brownie. If I didn't know better I'd think Willow was trying to fatten us up. I opened the envelope and took a look at my schedule for this semester.

1st period: Stark Bldg./Rm 232Greek Literature
2nd period: Lassiter Bldg./Rm 134 Geometry II
3rdperiod: Elan Bldg/Rm 220 History of Orders
4th period LUNCH
5th period: Harlow Bldg/Rm 312 Marine Biology II
6th period: Elan Bldg/Rm 126 Oceanic Experience

"What's Oceanic Experience?" I asked whoever might be listening.

"Is that on your schedule?" Carmen ripped the paper out of my hand. "That's an advanced level class! How'd you get that if you just got here?"

"I have no idea," I insisted. "So what is it?" Before she could answer, another hand grabbed my schedule.

"You have Greek Lit with me and Carmen!" Phoebe bounced up and down. "Hey Willow, don't you have History 3rd period?"

"I think so," Willow said as she looked up from her brownie.

"Thank goodness, because I have no idea how to find these buildings." I had secretly hoped my roommates would be in some of my classes for that very reason.

Phoebe put an arm around my shoulder reassuringly. "Don't worry; we won't let you get too lost."

"Just a little bit lost, right?" I teased her.

"Right. I take no responsibility for rogue hot guys who may cause me to veer off course, or the occasional stampede in stairwells. In those cases, you're on your own." She gave a salute and went back to her brownie.

"Comforting." I smiled and shook my head.

I tried on half of my wardrobe the next morning, hoping to find the perfect outfit for the first day of classes. I finally settled on a pair of navy blue shorts, a flowing white silk top and some silver gladiator sandals. I added some jewelry, took one last look in the mirror and met the other girls in the living room.

Carmen, Phoebe and I walked toward our first class, while Willow headed off in another direction. They tried to map everything out for me last night, and said we'd meet after classes and at lunch. Hopefully by the next day I'd be self-sufficient. I had an uncanny ability for getting lost, so I wasn't getting my hopes up. I only prayed my other 'abilities' were more useful.

The first three classes went off without a hitch, with just the normal first day technicalities. With my roommates in some of my classes I felt a little more at ease. But I was still slightly distracted as I tried to guess which Order every person I came into contact with belonged. The Sons of Daimon and some of the Tritons were obvious, but the others were more difficult to pinpoint. When fourth period came around and it was time for lunch, Willow and I strolled over to a place called The Hole. Not until we reached our destination did I understand the name. It was a sunken rectangular area in the middle of campus, with two more recesses acting as steps. It was about the size of a football field with different sized tables for eating, each with an umbrella to shield its inhabitants from the summer sun. There were beautiful stone planters that carved out walkways throughout the entire area, overflowing with orchids, calla lilies and hydrangeas. Surrounding The Hole were small shops with different food vendors - pizza, sandwiches, Chinese food, sushi, salads…you name it, they had it. The smells alone made my mouth water. After grabbing some sandwiches, we spotted Carmen and Phoebe sitting at a table next to a stone fountain that housed a small pond with brightly colored fish.

"Hey you guys!" Phoebe tore her eyes away from her pizza long enough to acknowledge us. "What do you think of The Hole, Stasia?" We took a seat opposite her and Carmen.

"Definitely an upgrade from a high school cafeteria," I answered. And that was an understatement.

"Definitely an upgrade," Carmen agreed.

"Why, thank you," replied a guy's deep voice. "I have on a new shirt and got a haircut yesterday, so I know I'm looking good, but 'upgrade' is quite a compliment."

We all looked up in surprise at the two guys standing beside our table. From the horrified look on Carmen's face I made the assumption that the guy who'd spoken up was her crush, Logan. He had light brown hair that was styled in that just-ran-my fingers-through-my-hair look that was actually a spent-thirty-minutes-in-the-mirror-styling-my-hair look. He was tall, built like a quarterback and good looking in a pretty boy kind of way.

"Got room for two more?" asked the second guy. He was a little more rugged, with brown hair and a trace of stubble on his face as if shaving was too much of an effort that morning. Sleepy green eyes and dimples made him look younger than he really was. His faded green t-shirt showed off the muscles in his arms as he and Logan took a seat. I immediately filed them away into the Triton category.

"I'm Noah," the green shirt guy said as he shook my hand. It was strong and warm around my much smaller one.

He grinned and his dimples deepened. A nervous tickle ran through me.

"I'm Stasia."

"And I'm afraid ya'll weren't the upgrade we were talking about," Carmen threw out at them playfully. "It's gonna take more than a new shirt and a haircut to impress us."

"Clearly," Noah commented, eyes still on me.

Logan cleared his throat. "You must be Stasia."

"That's me." I belatedly realized he hadn't told me his name. "And you are....?"

"Incredibly annoying," filled in Carmen, while Logan gave her a playful pinch on the arm. "See? Proves my point." She grinned back at him.

"I'm Logan," he said to me, confirming my suspicions, then went back to pinching Carmen's arm. Willow was right, he was definitely into her. All of a sudden I got that feeling of being watched again, and my eyes locked in on the culprit sitting about three tables away with two other dark haired guys. The world stopped mid-spin and everyone else disappeared. He held my gaze with confidence.

Hi, he mouthed.

Hi. I felt my lips move in response, although I didn't remember telling them to do so. I also didn't remember telling my cheeks to grow warm, but that's exactly what they did. His dark features contrasted with the brightness of The Hole; taking my breath away. It was as if he didn't belong in the sun, among the flowers. His face was unreadable except for a slight grin that lifted one corner of his mouth. He had an air of self-assurance and purpose that wouldn't release my attention. I felt myself being sucked into a world where only he and I existed. A world I never wanted to leave. Overwhelmed by his intense gaze and the frenzy of feelings running through my body, I looked down at my food to get a grip on reality.

"Right, Stasia?" I heard Phoebe ask, and everyone looked at me expectantly.

"Uh…what did you say?" I squeaked, feeling shaken.

"That we would see them at the bonfire tomorrow." She winked, and Carmen's eyes were practically begging for me to agree.

"Oh, yeah…sure, we'll be there." I glanced back up at his table, but to my surprise they were gone. I swept The Hole with my eyes but didn't find a trace of them. Then like a wrecking ball another thought occurred to me. His face had been flawless. No bruised eye or deep gashes like I had witnessed last night. So did that mean they really were just dreams? Disappointment wrapped around my heart. Even though they were usually frightening, I'd come to enjoy his nightly appearances. And he saved my life. He seemed to recognize me, too. How did you explain that?

I noticed Willow peering at me with a concerned expression, so I plastered a smile on my face to reassure her I was fine. I hoped it could also reassure me I wasn't losing my mind over a certain dark haired, blue eyed guy. It was almost time for fifth period, so we gathered our stuff and stood.

"I'm glad you got to meet me." Logan smiled at me. "See ya around."

Noah laid a hand on my arm and I retreated from his touch, surprised with his sudden closeness. "I'll see you at the bonfire, Stasia." He gave me a dimpled smile and strode off with Logan.

"Looks like somebody has an admirer." Willow grinned at me.

"He's just being nice, that's all," I brushed off her comment.

Carmen laughed. "Whatever. No guy looks at a girl like that if he's just being nice."

"She's right. He totally wants you. He's probably thinking of ways to get you alone at the bonfire already." Phoebe wiggled her eyebrows at me again.

I rolled my eyes at them and headed to Marine Biology, praying I didn't get lost. After a couple of false attempts, I made it to the right room and took the last seat available. Which also happened to be right beside the evil queen herself. Olivia dissected me with a scrutinizing look and whispered something to the girl in front of her. I had a feeling they weren't discussing how to solve world hunger, especially when they both glanced back at me and kept whispering. What was this, third grade? If it was, I would definitely give her a wet-willy right in the ear. The thought made me smile and I turned my attention to the teacher. I almost fell out of my chair.

"My name is Isadora Dixon." There was an undercurrent of a threat in her introduction. "You will not call me by my first name, you will raise your hand if you have something to say, and I will not tolerate tardiness."

She glared right at me and I shifted restlessly in my seat; fighting the urge to run out of the door as fast as possible. She was one of the women from my dream. Dark, curly hair rested on her shoulders and her green eyes bored into mine. Her left eye seemed to twitch, and then she addressed the rest of the class.

"Is that understood?" she demanded. Mumbles of agreement came from my classmates. I was too shocked to move or say a word, and I remained that way throughout her lecture and the assigning of homework. More groans from the class and finally fifth period was over. I raced out of the room.

I let out a breath I didn't know I was holding as I found the girl's bathroom down the hall. I splashed cold water on my face and looked up to see my bright turquoise eyes staring back at me in the mirror, stricken with panic. Did she know that I heard them talking last night? Could she have seen me? Should I tell Kira? Could I trust Kira? Unfortunately I didn't have long to think about it because a group of girls walked into the bathroom. I made a speedy exit; not wanting an audience. I just needed to get through one more class. I could do this. Then I could freak out in the privacy of my own bedroom.

I made it to Harlow Building and into my next class with time to spare. I had to look at the number on the door twice to make sure I was in the right place. Instead of desks there were ten substantial tables; each holding a large, square container made of glass. Walking down the center aisle, I noticed they were each about a foot deep and completely filled with water. I chose one at random and took a seat behind it. The chairs were tall, cushioned and even twisted back and forth. I settled into mine and watched the water as it gently rolled back and forth within the container. Completely mesmerized, I didn't hear him until he was already sitting in the chair beside me.

"You could cause a flood doing that, you know." Even though I'd heard his voice many times in my dreams, I still wasn't prepared to hear it in real life. My eyes met his, my heartbeat kicked into overdrive and I struggled to keep my voice steady.

"I'm not doing that." Brilliant answer.

"Of course you are." He grinned at me like he knew a secret, whereas I was just trying to remember how to breathe. "Who else do you think is doing it?"

"How do I know you aren't doing it?" Another award-winning answer.

He smiled and twisted in his chair to face me. His dark hair was swept across his forehead; threatening to fall into his blue eyes that currently watched me with amusement. He wore a fitted dark gray t-shirt, jeans that were snug in all the right places, and flip flops. The sun had turned his skin a golden tan that made his eyes look even bluer. I was momentarily distracted by the muscles in his arms as they flexed when he turned toward me. His smile widened and his eyes lit up with mischief. Once again I felt like I'd missed the punch line to a joke I never heard.

"What are you grinning about?" I asked, wondering what could possibly be so entertaining about me.

Instead of answering, he asked me a question of his own. "Did you know that aquamarine represents foresight and courage?"

"Aquamarine?" I asked with confusion.

"The color of your eyes." I froze. He paused and then continued with a suddenly serious tone. "Do you have foresight and courage, Anastasia?" The profound way he looked into my eyes had my palms sweating.

"How do you know my name?" I asked; feeling a little lightheaded.

"Everyone knows your name." Leaning forward, his knee brushed mine and I was all too aware of how close he was. His face darkened.

"Stay away from the light station, Stasia," he whispered. "People get hurt there. It's dangerous." I couldn't tell if it was a warning or a threat, but he searched my face for an answer.

"What light station?" was all I could manage to say under the weight of his stare. So he did see me! This earth shattering revelation almost unraveled me right there in front of him. Did that mean he remembered all the other dreams, too?

His lips formed a slight smirk and his eyes sparkled. I could tell I was amusing him again, which apparently was a new talent of mine. Mrs. Wyatt chose that very moment to begin class so I turned my attention to the front of the room, still a little shaken from his sinister tone.

"For the first week, we will remain indoors and then apply what we've learned in the actual ocean during the second week." I perked up at this while she continued. "Throughout this class, the things we will work on could be

87

potentially dangerous." I thought I heard an ill-timed snicker beside me. "So I expect your full attention at all times. My hope is that you will learn a great deal, as well as have a little fun." She winked at us and I instantly decided I liked her.

She passed around an outline of what we'd cover throughout the semester, but my mind kept wandering to the much more intriguing mystery sitting beside me. He'd been in my dreams for years and I still didn't even know his name. With a sideways glance, a gasp escaped my lips. A black skull and crossbones trace adorned the muscle on his forearm. It moved slightly as he tapped his fingers on the table, making it appear even more menacing. Did every Son of Daimon have the same trace? I assumed that was the order he belonged to. But considering I didn't even know his name, it was hard to assume much of anything.

My eyes moved up to his face and my breath hitched again as I was caught in his piercing gaze. The corner of his mouth turned up in a taunting grin. A small voice in the back of my mind told me I should probably be afraid of him. My dreams were obviously real. And if that was true, it meant I watched him try to kill someone the other night. And he may have finished the job after I disappeared. Besides, there was only one thing a skull and crossbones stood for: death. I felt his presence wrap around me like a warm blanket on a cold night, and found myself unable to look away. Holding my eyes, he reached out and ran a finger over the trace on my wrist. Paralyzed by his touch, I couldn't ignore the heat it sent up my arm. I swallowed hard and tried to control the emotions coursing through me.

"I make you nervous," he whispered. It wasn't a question, but a statement. The smirk on his face told me he knew it was true. I straightened stubbornly in my chair.

"You wish." I raised an eyebrow. Two could play at this game.

His smirk turned into a full blown smile and I felt my heart melt right out of my chest.

"That sounds like a yes to me," he whispered, and I hoped the warmth I felt rise to my cheeks didn't give me away. He smiled again. "Why are you blushing?" Damn.

"I don't know what you're talki-" I started to argue, but a voice interrupted me.

"Ms. Whitman?" Mrs. Wyatt raised her eyebrows at me.

"Yes ma'am?" I immediately turned forward, looking all kinds of guilty.

"Is there something you would like to share with the rest of us?"

"No ma'am." I heard another snicker beside me, so I cut my eyes at him. Getting in trouble on the first day was not the best way to start off the semester. Mrs. Wyatt nodded her head at me with tight lips and continued addressing the class. A piece of paper was pushed towards me.

'Busted' was scrawled in the bottom left-hand corner. I grabbed the paper.

'Your fault' I accused him, and gave him my best pissed off glare that I could tell fell short.

'And you're still blushing' he answered with a smile. I grabbed the paper, balled it up and slipped it into my bag. Then I stared at him with defiance, daring him to keep distracting me. The last thing I needed was to get in trouble twice in one day. It would be a lot easier to follow the rules if I could think straight around him. But he just kept smiling at me and making my insides turn to mush.

Throughout the rest of the class I was hyper-aware of his every movement. Every time he ran his fingers through his hair. Every time he tapped his fingers on the table. Every time he scratched his chin. And I had no idea what Mrs. Wyatt discussed the entire hour. I would need to record her lectures in the future so I could listen to them later. Sitting next to a dark, mysterious, incredibly hot guy was wreaking havoc on my ability to concentrate on anything else. Finally the class ended and I put my things into my bag.

"By the way," his breath tickled the skin on my neck as he leaned down to whisper in my ear, "my name's Finn." My heart skipped a beat and I looked up at him, his face inches from mine. He flashed that breathtaking smile at me once more, straightened confidently and sauntered out of the room.

Eleven

"I'm just saying I think she's graceful. Her steps need some work, but that dress looks amazing on her." Phoebe crossed her arms.

"Their wardrobe isn't part of the score, Phoebs. It's how they dance. And my grandma can dance better than she can." We'd been watching 'Dancing with the Stars', and Phoebe and Carmen had a bad habit of arguing over every contestant.

"For all I know your grandma's a professional ballroom dancer."

"She's in a wheelchair," Carmen retorted smugly.

"Well that doesn't matter. Haven't you seen those guys that play basketball in wheelchairs? That's got to be way harder than normal basketball." Unsure of how the conversation went from dance scores to playing basketball in wheelchairs, I turned back to the bar as Willow handed me a plate of nachos dripping with cheese. I put them on the coffee table and took a seat on the couch beside Carmen.

"I'd like to see you two get up on stage and dance in four inch heels in front of the entire country," I challenged them.

"I'd win for sure." Carmen nodded her head with assuredness.

"I'd have to get some implants," Phoebe frowned down at her chest. "I couldn't fill out those dresses with these sorry excuses for boobs."

"I'd have to get butt implants," Willow said as she patted her backside. We all giggled and she stuck her tongue out at us.

"So I have a question," I began. "I know Tydes have different traces depending on who we're descended from, so does that mean all of the Sons of Daimon have the same one? And what about the Sirens?" I threw the Sirens in there so they wouldn't question my specific interest in the Sons.

"That's right - the Sirens all have a nautical star, the Tritons have a trident and all of the Sons of Daimon have the scepter, which is like a staff or rod with an ornamental top," Willow answered.

But that didn't make sense. Finn's skull and crossbones was definitely a trace. He had to be a Son, though. He didn't fit into any of the other Orders. I guess he could be a Tyde, but it just didn't feel right.

"Is it possible to have two?" I asked carefully.

"I don't know." Willow explained further, "I think it depends on a lot of things. I think if you're a direct descendant or Chosen you could. Or if you have several really strong abilities."

"What do you mean by 'chosen'?" I asked.

"If the Gods or Goddesses have chosen you for a specific journey or destiny," Phoebe explained.

My jaw dropped. "Wow. That sounds absolutely terrifying."

"No doubt," Carmen consented.

"I'd have to ask to be un-Chosen," Phoebe chuckled.

"I think it would be amazing to have that kind of purpose in your life, but you're right, it would be scary," Willow added. While I was asking questions, I might as well throw another one out there.

"So do Tydes have the ability to...." I paused and tried to think of a way to say it, "...go places in their dreams?"

"There are a few rare cases, but it's not very common," Carmen answered; grabbing a handful of nachos. "Instead of a dream it's called a reverie. From what I've heard, it's like leaving your body and going wherever your soul takes you. But that's all I know. Kind of freaky if you ask me." This from the girl who could control waves.

"Did you hear about it in your classes today?" Willow asked, perplexed at my seemingly random question.

"No, I think I, um, might have that ability." I waited for their reaction. All of their eyes grew wide and nothing was said for a full minute.

"Holy shit!" Phoebe exclaimed.

"No way!" Carmen's mouth hung open.

"Have you done it already? What happened?" Willow hid her shock the best. I tried to find a way to sum it up without mentioning hot, mysterious guys and creepy teachers.

"Well, I think I've always been able to do it, but I've just recently figured out that it's actually real and not a dream. I don't think I can control it though. I just sort of...show up places."

"Wow. That's amazing. I've never known anyone who could do that." Carmen looked at me with something like awe.

"Will you guys promise to keep it secret for now, at least?" I pleaded with them. "I just want to figure some things out on my own before I talk to anybody else about it."

They all agreed, but I could tell by the excitement in their eyes that they wanted to know more. Leave it to me to have one of the freaky abilities no one else had.

That night I lay in bed wide awake. Wary of falling asleep, considering I had no idea where I might end up, I stared up at the ceiling as my thoughts raced uncontrollably for the third night in a row. I still didn't understand how Finn didn't have a scratch on him. From what I'd seen, he should at least have a black eye and stitches. None of it made sense. The other thing I didn't understand was how he could obviously see me in the reveries, but why was he the only one? Mrs. Dixon looked right through me, even though I was only standing a couple of feet away. Maybe I was hidden in the shadows, or maybe they were so distracted they weren't paying attention to their surroundings. I also needed to learn how to control them, because I couldn't just be popping up in random places at random times. Could I get hurt? Who was the lady I saw get killed on the beach? Could I really have helped her? And what was Finn doing there?

I'd never felt more confused. At least when I was in foster care I knew I was human; I knew my limitations. This world was one big mystery, and I was just aimlessly wandering around looking for answers that may or may not exist. I knew Kira might be able to help, but could I really trust her? I closed my eyes and my mind spun endlessly until I finally dozed off into a peaceful, dreamless and reverie-less sleep.

The next evening I searched through my closet, hoping to find the ideal outfit for a bonfire. I'd never been to a bonfire on the beach, so I wasn't real sure what to wear. Bathing suit? I would say the chances of us going swimming were pretty slim. Sundress? That could be tricky with the wind. Ripped jeans, tank top, and a hoodie? Perfect.

I didn't even remember the bonfire until second period. It sounded like fun, but I wasn't sure I wanted to hang out with Noah and Logan the whole time. Noah was pretty cute, but I wasn't really interested. And what if a particular dark haired, blue eyed guy showed up? During sixth period when Mrs. Wyatt began her lesson and five minutes turned into fifteen, I realized Finn wasn't coming to class. Disappointed would have been an understatement, but at the same time I'd actually heard her lecture. Now I was wondering if he'd be at the bonfire. To ward off disappointment twice in one day, I tried to convince myself it didn't matter.

The bonfire was at the Cape, which was only a short walk down the beach. The four of us headed that direction. It was a gorgeous night. The silver moon above was completely full, and it lit up the world like a giant disco ball. The sand beneath our feet reflected its light; creating the illusion it had been lit from below. With the ocean glistening around us, it felt like we had been transported to another world. The refuge of night was captured in the ocean breeze ruffling my hair and the enchanted white crabs scurrying around our bare feet.

The warm glow of the bonfire could be seen from miles around, but as we got closer I could make out the individual embers shooting up from the blaze; riding on the wind. Freed from captivity, they flew high in the air before snuffing out. I suddenly understood why ancient man sat around staring at fire. It was a beautiful dance as old as the dawn of time. You could easily become entranced within its flames; stripping away everything except the raw humanity that burned within us all.

We were drawn closer by the heat radiating out from the fire. Large pieces of driftwood were set up around the bonfire as seats, so we claimed a relatively empty one. I stretched my legs out in front of me and scanned the crowd. I saw a couple of kids from my classes, couples sitting closely together in their own world, and a group of guys playing something that looked like lacrosse down towards the water. I also noticed Olivia and Cassie with two other girls sitting on a blanket nearby. They were surrounded by six guys who hung on their every word. The one thing I didn't see were Sons of Daimon. Maybe they weren't the social event type?

"Look who finally made it," Logan spoke up behind us. He was trailed by Noah and two other guys who put The Hulk to shame. They were at least six feet, six inches tall and built like tanks. Noah took a seat in between me and Willow, while Hans and Frans sat on either side of Phoebe. Logan and Carmen snuck off towards the water by themselves.

"How's your first week going?" Noah attempted conversation with me.

"Pretty good so far," I replied politely. He smiled a dimpled smile at me and I noticed he was definitely cute, but he needed a lesson in personal space. I scooted an inch down the driftwood, but he just leaned farther in my direction as he talked.

"It definitely takes some getting used to. Especially if you haven't been around our kind your whole life. That's got to be hard." If he only knew.

"A lot of things have been a shock, but I know things will fall into place with time." I looked down at my trace and tried to turn the conversation back to him. "So you and Logan are Tritons?"

"Logan is, but I'm not," he told me. "I'm a Tyde like you."

"Really? I have a hard time telling the Orders apart, except for the Sons of Daimon." Which sent my thoughts to deep blue eyes.

"Well I'll tell you a secret," he said, and leaned even closer. I thought about asking him if he'd be more comfortable sitting in my lap. "We all have different stones that represent our Orders. The Tyde stone is turquoise, and most of us wear one all the time." He pulled a necklace out from under his shirt. It was a thin leather string with a single turquoise bead flanked by two knots.

"That's amazing!" It dawned on me that maybe the décor in our living room was turquoise and white for that very reason. I'd have to ask Willow about that.

"My mom got me this when I started at Lorelei, but there's a shop near The Hole that sells all kinds of stones." He tucked the necklace back under his shirt. "If you want me to take you some time, just let me know." He looked at me hopefully.

"Thanks, I'll let you know if I decide to go." He smiled and I felt guilty for giving him false hope. If I went with anyone it would be Kira or my roommates.

My mind wanted to ask what the stone was for the Sons of Daimon. Thankfully it didn't come out that way. "What are the other Orders' stones?"

"The Sirens wear sapphires, the Tritons wear obsidian, and the Sons wear the black onyx." Definitely fitting. I'd have to see if I could spot one on Finn the next time I saw him.

"There's so much I don't know." I looked out over the ocean. It was still and calm, which reminded me of an infinity pool, not that I'd seen an infinity pool other than in magazines or on TV.

"You'll learn," he reassured me. "You've only been here a couple of days. You can't expect to learn everything that quickly."

"I'm not the most patient person in the world." I tossed a rogue seashell in to the fire.

"I can see that." He laughed and his dimples showed again. "You wanna go for a walk? The fire's starting to get hot." I glanced over at Willow, who was now talking to Phoebe and the other guys. What could it hurt?

"Sure." We stood and strolled towards the point of the Cape. The sounds of the ocean filled my ears, and I had the strangest urge to run as fast as I could and dive beneath the waves. I also got the feeling of being watched. I looked around but no one was even remotely paying attention to us. I shrugged it off and zipped up my hoodie.

"I don't know if I could ever live anywhere but the beach," Noah proclaimed thoughtfully.

"I like how you can look out over the ocean and see the curvature of the earth." I pointed out toward the horizon to emphasize my point. "It makes you realize just how small and insignificant we really are."

"I don't think you're small and insignificant, Stasia." He was suddenly closer to me. Goose bumps popped up on my arms, but I couldn't tell if it was because of the cool wind or his uninvited nearness. I felt his arm wrap around my shoulders and tensed. I knew I should probably relax and lean into him, but something stopped me. I turned away, towards the bonfire.

"I'm getting chilly, I think we should go back to the fire." He furrowed his brow in confusion but followed me back. I got that feeling of being watched again but still didn't see anyone watching us. The hairs on my arms rose and my chill bumps started growing chill bumps. I started walking faster.

"Hey there, lovebirds," grinned Phoebe. I gave her a look that could kill and Willow elbowed her in the ribs. I sat down beside her, suddenly very comforted by the fire and my friends. Noah and Hans began talking about the upcoming football season and I tried to relax. I should probably have found out what their names were instead of calling them Frans and Hans, but decided against it. After a while I gazed back at the ocean. The urge to be underwater slammed into me again and it became harder to ignore. I could almost feel the water's soothing touch enveloping my body; sweeping me away with the currents to places I'd never been.

Unable to concentrate on anything else, I informed Phoebe and Willow I was going to take a walk. They gave me a strange look but just warned me to be careful. Being that we were on an island not accessible by cars, I figured the chances of something bad happening were pretty slim. A flash of the dead woman lying on the beach entered my mind, but I pushed it away just as quickly. I walked down the beach and out of the fire's light. The darkness of night brought a tender smile to my face. I made it to the water's edge and took in everything around me. The wet sand beneath my feet mirrored the sky above, and the water sparkled with the light of the moon. As the waves rushed up to greet me, I stood mesmerized and fought the urge to join them. My thoughts strayed to Finn. The turbulent water reminded me of his stormy blue eyes. I wanted to get lost in them again. I tried not to think about what it would be like to be close to him.

"You really shouldn't fight it."

Twelve

I jumped as Finn seemingly materialized next to me. I couldn't tell if he was talking about the ocean or my desire to be close to him. I lost all train of thought as he fixed his blue eyes on me.

"What are you doing here?" I said a little too spastically.

"Baking cookies." He smirked at me.

"You shouldn't tease me like that - it's dangerous. I take baked goods very seriously." A slow smile formed on his lips.

"Dangerous happens to be my specialty," he said in a low voice; taking a step closer to me. My entire body warmed. He was like my own personal bonfire. "Being afraid reminds us how alive we are. What makes you afraid, Stasia?" I felt my legs get wobbly.

"Nothing scares me," I said with as much confidence as I could muster. He definitely terrified me, but only because I didn't trust my body to function correctly around him.

"Nothing at all?" His gaze intensified.

"Nothing at all." I straightened and held my chin slightly higher to prove it.

"You're not a good liar." He leaned in closer and I felt his breath on my cheeks.

"What makes you afraid?" I whispered. I was having trouble breathing. His answer was another slow smile. If I moved forward even an inch, his mouth would be on mine. Trying not to hyperventilate, I noticed when his eyes glanced down at my lips. His smile disappeared abruptly and he took a step back. As he turned his attention to the water, I tried to figure out what had just happened. My entire body hummed with electricity and was instantly cooled by the distance he'd put between us.

"Come with me." He took my hand in his and led me down to the water. It fit perfectly in mine, and warmth spread up my arm and into my chest. We stopped once the waves hit our ankles. "Don't move your feet." He grinned down at me as I rolled up my jeans. He raked his fingers through his dark hair and the skull and crossbones trace on his forearm shimmered at me. In the pale light of the moon, it was dangerously alluring.

"I used to do this all the time when I was younger," he explained with obvious nostalgia. My feet disappeared farther into the wet sand, locking me in place, while the water rushed onto the shore and then back out again.

"What happens if we need to go somewhere?" I asked. I could be buried up to my knees in no time at this rate.

"Who says we're going anywhere?" He held my eyes and put a hand on my shoulder. Before I could come to grips with the tingling sensation his touch created on my skin, he lightly pushed backward. Too late, it dawned on me. Once set in motion however, I had no way of preventing it. My knees bent and I fell right on my butt onto the wet sand. The water crashed over my knees and soaked my jeans. I tried to stand back up and failed miserably. I glared up at my assailant.

"What are you doing way down there?" He looked down at me with mock surprise. I scooted forward and pushed behind his knees with my hand as hard as I could, and he came crashing down beside me. "What was that for?" he asked innocently.

"I told you I can be dangerous. Bad things happen to people who try to push me around." If he only knew how true that was. I shook the thought and smiled at him. A piece of leather peeking out of the sand caught my attention. Wrapped around his ankle, it held four small black beads shining in the moonlight. I had a good guess as to which type of stones they were.

"If that's all you've got, I'm not too worried," he taunted me. I dipped my hand in the wet sand and grabbed a handful. I slowly raised it above his head; threatening to release it. Before I even noticed, he caught my wrist and pulled it back down. Holding my eyes, he delicately threaded his fingers through mine while wet sand squished out. The gesture was somehow very intimate and a shiver ran down my spine. The wet sand ran down my arm but I didn't even notice. We stayed like that, hand in hand, and faced the ocean for what seemed like hours.

I had a million more questions waiting in the wings, but decided this wasn't the time to open up that can of worms. So I settled for the least complicated one.

"Why weren't you in class today?"

"There was somewhere I had to be," he answered simply.

"You missed a very important lesson. It was life altering," I teased him.

"The only thing I really missed was sitting next to one very extraordinary girl." I didn't think I was breathing anymore.

"She sounds wonderful." I tried some humor to shake off my nervousness.

"You have no idea."

Someone laughed in the distance and I pulled my eyes away from his. I realized my roommates were probably getting worried about me.

"I should be getting back to the bonfire. They're going to think I've been kidnapped." He pulled me toward him in one quick motion.

"Kidnapped insinuates some sort of struggle," he purred in a low voice with a sexy grin. "You'd enjoy being captured by me." My heart jumped in my throat, but I tried to remain cool.

"I'd like to see you try," I threw back at him. "But first you'll have to escape your own sandy death trap." I wiggled my feet out of the sand, stood up and washed my hands off in the water. He followed my every move with curious eyes.

"Sweet dreams, Anastasia." I wasn't sure if there was an underlying meaning to his words.

"Sweet dreams, Finn," I responded breathlessly.

Halfway back to the bonfire, I looked over my shoulder at him but he was gone. Seriously, how did he do that?

"Stasia! What happened to you? You're soaked!" Phoebe ran up to me in a panic.

"Just got a little too close to the water and a wave got me. I'm fine, I promise," I assured her. Carmen watched me with skeptical eyes and I got the feeling she'd seen what really happened to my jeans. When I got back to the fire, I rotated gradually; drying myself off.

"That wave sure was tall, dark and handsome." Carmen raised an eyebrow at me. "Who's the mystery boy?"

"It's nothing, really," I tried to convince her. Her face told me she wasn't buying it. "Okay, okay - his name's Finn. He's in my sixth period," I admitted. Her face paled.

"Finn? The Finn that's a Son of Daimon?"

"As far as I know. I mean I haven't asked him which Order he's in, but I saw four..." She grabbed my arm; interrupting me.

"Stay away from him, Stasia," she said with urgency. I heard an undercurrent of fear in her voice.

"What? Why?"

"He's cursed," she whispered. Cursed?

103

"Stasia! Carmen! Come on, we're leaving!" Willow ran over and took our hands, literally pulling us out of our conversation. Once we drug our tired feet back up to our suite I said goodnight, fell onto my bed and closed my eyes. I could still hear his voice and see his crooked smile in my mind. It should be illegal to be that hot. Carmen's warning disrupted my delirium. Cursed? People couldn't really be cursed, could they? What was he cursed with? Devastating good looks and a dark, sexy smile? She couldn't be serious. That just wasn't possible. Of course, two weeks ago I wouldn't have imagined any of this could be possible, yet there I was. Images from previous reveries flashed into my mind. His bloodied and beaten face, swinging an axe down on someone's neck, standing by as a woman was killed on the beach. With a sense of dread creeping down my spine, I had to admit it was very, very possible.

The world was blurry when I opened my eyes, but I could see movement coming towards me. I tried to roll over to get away but my body wouldn't listen. My stomach exploded and I instinctively curled into a fetal position. Something hard hit my shoulder. Footsteps walked away and people started yelling in the other room. Still curled into a ball, I took a moment to catch my breath. Oddly enough the pain had turned to hollow numbness. I guess when the pain becomes too much, your body mutes it for you. It was like a gift. Maybe that was what death felt like. Just never-ending numbness. The sound of glass breaking came from the next room, but as long as they were in there I knew I was okay. I knew once he came back he'd kill me. There was no way around it. At nine years old I was no match for him. But then again, the numbness wasn't so bad. It would be really easy to let it just take me. Then I wouldn't have to be scared anymore. I wouldn't have to feel pain anymore. Too bad I wasn't good at giving up.

Mustering as much energy as I could, I inched toward the living room closet on my stomach. Just a little bit farther... I reached up, turned the door knob and pulled. Pain from the movement erupted in every cell of my body and I fell back to the floor. I took a deep breath, pushed the door open farther and saw it on the third shelf up. I crawled on my hands and knees into the closet, when I heard them both come back into the living room. With adrenaline running through me, I stretched out my arm and pushed myself up. I heard a scream and a thump, but tried to block it out. He pulled the closet door completely open, right when I grabbed the handle. As I crumpled back onto the floor, he grabbed my left foot and pulled me from the closet. I rolled onto my back and saw a baseball bat in his hand, and through his legs I saw her unmoving body. It was heavy and I couldn't hold it up with my hurt arm, so I just angled it up towards him. He raised the bat above his head and I pulled the trigger.

I woke, drenched in sweat and sobbing in my bed. I pushed back the covers, pulled up my knees and tried to calm myself down. He can't hurt you now I told myself over and over. And it was true. When I'd shot him, I hit his right thigh. Enough to stop his attack, but not enough to kill him. He'd been in prison now for close to eight years. He killed his wife, my foster mother, when he hit her in the head with the bat, and was convicted based upon my testimony. I spent three weeks healing in a hospital and then the state found me a new home. But the memories never left me. Neither did the strength I gained from it.

I finally got my breathing under control and changed out of my sweaty clothes. I turned on my IPod, put in my ear buds and lulled myself to back sleep.

THIRTEEN

We received our first official assignment in History the next day. In groups of four, we had to research two specific Nereids; their strengths, weaknesses, what part they played in history, and write a ten page paper due in a month. Mrs. Leone rattled off the different groups while I crossed my fingers that Willow would be in my group.

"...Rhea, Willow, and Xavier. And the last group will be Lyric, Stasia, Maya, and Lexi. For the last ten minutes of class, you will meet with your group to discuss." So much for luck. I looked around and tried to figure out who Lyric, Maya or Lexi were when a girl waved at me. Thank goodness. She had an ethereal glow about her, and when she smiled the goodness radiating from her was enthralling. She had white-blonde hair with blunt cut bangs cascading down to her golden eyes. A wide silver cuff bracelet encrusted with sapphires clung to her wrist. A Siren.

"Hey Stasia, I'm Lyric," she greeted me and gestured to the girl sitting next to her. "And this is Lexi."

"Stasia? Isn't that short for Anastasia?" Lexi glared at me. She had strawberry blond, curly hair and big green eyes. A light dusting of freckles was sprinkled across her cheeks and nose. She reminded me of the Strawberry Shortcake doll I used to have, but without all the ruffles and overpowering strawberry smell.

"Uh, yeah." I couldn't figure out where her hostility came from. Lyric gave her a stern look and she sat back with a huff.

"I'm Maya," the third girl said, and smiled at me. I was instantly taken aback by her exotic looks. She had a Jamaican accent, rich brown skin and a mass of tiny braids making up her dark brown hair. Tiny turquoise beads were braided in at different places throughout. She had clear blue eyes that looked at me with warmth.

"I'm a Tyde, like you." She leaned forward like she was going to tell me a secret, pointed at the other two, and whispered loudly, "They're sea witches, A.K.A. Sirens."

"Abracadabra, bitches." Lexi wiggled her finger at us and Maya laughed. Lyric just sighed.

"If I was a witch, I'd turn you both into boogers and flick you across the room." That only made Maya laugh harder and Lexi almost choked on her Diet Coke.

"Ladies." We all jumped at Mrs. Leone's voice. "Your Nereids will be Kymo and Thetis. I hope you will take this assignment seriously, and I better not find any stickiness on your paper." She raised an eyebrow at us, but a corner of her mouth threatened to pull up into a smile. Maya put her hand over her mouth and tried to muffle her laughter. We nodded our heads and she walked over to the next group.

"Thetis? That'll take forever to write!" Lexi grumbled, and a pout formed on her face.

"It won't be that bad, and at least it won't be hard to research." Maya had finally composed herself.

"Who's Thetis?" I asked. Strawberry Shortcake gave me a weird look as if that was the dumbest question of all time. What was her deal?

"She used to be the leader of the Nereids, so we should be able to find all kinds of information about her," Lyric assured me. I wondered if I'd ever be able to keep the fifty Nereids straight. Why couldn't there just be ten?

Lightness filled my chest when I walked into sixth period and saw Finn sitting at our table. Unfortunately, the voice of reason in the back of my mind played Carmen's warning over and over again. But the second I made eye contact, all thoughts of a curse vanished. Plus, this was the first day I was going to actually do the 'experience' part of Oceanic Experience.

"Think you can do this?" Finn asked, once we were given the go ahead to start.

"If you can do it, I can do it," I countered.

"Then step aside, mademoiselle, and let me work my magic." He tried to step in front of the pool, but I made it there first.

"You don't think I'm going to let you have all the fun, do you?" I raised an eyebrow at him.

"By all means then, show me how it's done." He stepped back and grinned. "Just remember, you want to keep the water inside the pool." I just rolled my eyes at him. The chances of me being able to do anything at all were slim to none, so causing a splash wasn't really on my list of things to avoid.

Creating a whirlpool was just a warm-up to the rest of the class, but considering I'd just gotten to Lorelei and this was an advanced class, I was at a slight disadvantage. I had no idea if I was supposed to chant, sing, think happy thoughts or what. What if I couldn't do this? I stole a glance over at one of the other students doing it and tried to mimic her. I placed my left hand right above the water so that only my fingertips were touching. Tiny ripples immediately began spreading out from my fingertips. Maybe I could do this after all! Still touching the water, I pulled my fingertips inward so they were all touching, but also still in the water. Then I began to make small circles. At first nothing happened, but then the water started to churn ever so slightly.

Adrenaline shot through me. I was actually doing it! My excitement was a little premature, however. My hand seemed to have a mind of its own and I was having trouble controlling it. The whirlpool continued getting wider and faster with no end in sight. Finn was trying to tell me to calm down and focus, but I barely heard him. The only thing I could hear was the sound of waves crashing and a light melody. It was the same thing I had heard in the bathtub last week. Before I could figure out why I was hearing things, the smell of sea salt and coconut tickled my nose. Completely freaked out, I grabbed the side of the pool to make it stop. Instead, the water spread out towards all four sides of the glass; causing them to crack under the pressure. I squeezed my eyes shut and all at once the water exploded over the sides, soaking everything in a two foot radius. Including me and Finn.

There was a full moment of silence while everyone stared at us with their mouths gaping open. I glanced down at my drenched outfit and frowned. Finn, who was equally soaked, was now beaming at me with pride.

"So, what were you saying about keeping the water inside the pool?" I asked him sheepishly. Everyone moved at once; mopping up the floor, the desk, making sure the glass wasn't broken, and trying to dry us off. Fifteen minutes later our clothes were still damp, but the catastrophe had been cleaned up and we were back at it. Well, Finn was back at it. I was watching. Unfortunately for my wounded pride, he was extremely good at it.

Casually stepping in front of the pool, he barely had his hand above the water when it started swirling in a perfect whirlpool, then he made it swirl in the other direction just as easily.

"Show off." I crossed my arms and tried not to smile. That only resulted in more tricks. He put both hands above the water, which resulted in two whirlpools. Then a third one appeared, and then a fourth. They converged in the middle to become one.

"Just wait until I get good at this. My whirlpools will run laps around your whirlpools," I threatened him.

"I have no doubt about that," he said with a crooked grin.

"I am officially the worst Tyde of all time." I shook my head as we left the building. "I can't believe that just happened."

"I had the same problem when I first started," Finn reassured me.

"So you knew that would happen?"

He stopped in the middle of the sidewalk and faced me. "When your essence is that powerful, you have to learn how to harness your abilities and control them."

"My essence?" Wasn't that a brand of shampoo?

"The part of your soul that's tied to the sea. Think of it as a glass of water – most of the people here have glasses that are about twenty-five percent full. The more essence you have, the greater your abilities. We're born with our essence, but the Gods and Goddesses have the power to give us more. You could say their glasses are about two-hundred percent full. If they choose you, they give you a part of their own essence." He smiled at his own metaphor.

My mind went back to a conversation I'd had with my roommates. "What about direct descendants?" I squinted in the sunlight and remembered that my sunglasses were still in my bedroom.

"They're born with their glass around ninety percent full. The Gods and Goddesses don't have to give you more essence unless they've chosen you for something that requires one-hundred percent essence, which also makes you immortal." That caught my attention.

"Immortal? That can really happen?" No way.

"Well even if you're immortal, there are still things that can end your life. It's just harder to die." I caught the ghost of a smile on his lips.

"How can you tell how much essence I have?" I asked him; wondering if it showed somehow.

"I just know." His features hardened and he looked away. "There are a lot of things you don't know about me." I felt the hair on my arms lift as trepidation pushed its way into my mind.

"So tell me," I pleaded with him; wanting to comfort him and bring his smile back. One side of me was scared of what he might admit, but the other side longed to know who he was and what secrets he carried. The more time I spent with him, the more I wanted to know about him. It didn't matter to me what skeletons he had in the closet. Curse or no curse.

"That's not an option." His voice was low and rough all of a sudden. Anger flashed in his eyes and he met my gaze with conviction. "Meet me at the Cape this Friday night at eight-thirty. You need to practice."

He took my hand, threaded his fingers through mine like he did on the beach the night before and walked away; leaving me standing by myself, confused. When I got back to Maren Hall, Kira was sitting on the couch talking to Phoebe and Carmen. She jumped up when she saw me walk in.

"Hey Stasia!"

"How are you?" I asked her as she gave me a big hug.

"I'm good! I can't stay long, but I wanted to bring you something." She reached into her Roxy beach bag.

"This is for you." She handed me a wooden box with what looked like waves etched into its sides. Taking off the lid, my breath caught at what I found inside. It was a silver bracelet made up of beautiful blue stones. Turquoise. I looked up at Kira in surprise. Carmen and Phoebe ran over to get a closer look.

"Kira, this is amazing!" I felt my eyes getting moist as I took it out of the box.

"Oh my God, it's gorgeous!" Phoebe squealed.

"It was given to me by my mom when I started at Lorelei. I want you to have it." She smiled and put the bracelet on me. Not having a Tyde mother there with me, a big sister was the next best thing.

"I don't know what to say." I gave her another hug and admired it.

"Just seeing it on you is all the thanks I need," she gushed. "Turquoise is the stone that represents us. It protects the wearer from negative energy and brings good fortune. Ship captains used to wear it to ensure safe passage."

"If only it could help me pass biology safely," Carmen muttered. Phoebe poked her in the ribs.

"I've got to run, but you girls let me know if you need something." She locked eyes with on me and said, "We'll talk soon. Keep your phone on."

113

FOURTEEN

When Friday finally arrived, a flock of butterflies had taken up residence in my stomach. Finn wasn't in class again, so I was a little worried he wouldn't show. What would I do if he stood me up? I mean, it wasn't like it was a date. He wasn't obligated to me or anything. My palms started sweating and the butterflies doubled. It was just practice, so there was no reason to get all nervous. No different than in class. Except that it was completely different than in class. Alone in the dark, in the ocean, with only our bathing suits separating us? What was there to be nervous about? Unfortunately even this meager evening was more of a date than I'd ever had before. Boys tended to stay away from me in Atlanta, since 'charity case' didn't really make for an attractive quality. There were a couple boys I'd liked over the years, but they definitely didn't make me feel the way Finn did. The things he made me feel were frightening, thrilling and torturous all at the same time. The way he looked at me made every part of me come alive. I imagined what it would be like to touch his bare chest and have his arms around me. Just the thought made my body tingle.

My roommates had gone to the mainland to do some shopping and see a movie. I made up an excuse about my stomach hurting so I could stay back, but I still felt guilty. I wanted to tell them about Finn, but after Carmen's warning I was afraid of what they might say. Besides, it wasn't like there was anything to tell.

It was almost eight-thirty when I began walking toward the Cape. I watched the horizon catch fire as the sun set; leaving dramatic oranges and reds dancing across the darkening sky. The air was warm and the breeze wasn't chilly, even though I only wore a bathing suit. The Cape was completely abandoned except for a couple of seagulls and the charred remains of the bonfire. Several logs of driftwood still littered the sand, and I saw that someone had left a blue beach chair to fend for itself. I picked a spot farther up the beach to sit while I waited for Finn. The sand was warm and comforting beneath me and I dug my toes in. The moon had begun to rise over the ocean and night was threatening to take over completely. Seagulls skimmed the waves and hopped around on the sand, squawking at each other. One hopped over, eyeing me, then it gave me a squawk and came closer. As if hearing something, it turned its head to the water. I followed its eyes and a shock of electricity ran through me as a figure came out of the waves. Somewhere in the corner of my consciousness I sensed the bird fly away, but all of my concentration was on something else.

Wearing only dark blue swim trunks that hung low on his hips, he looked like something straight out of a Ralph Lauren commercial. My eyes ran down his body of their own accord. His broad shoulders were strong and defined, followed by a muscular chest and washboard stomach. Even in the low light I saw the water running down his sun-kissed skin and forced myself not to think about the parts of him I couldn't see. He walked toward me confidently and ran a hand through his wet hair to get it out of his eyes.

"Hey there." Finn grinned and sat down beside me. "Enjoying the view?"

I felt my face redden and was thankful for the fading light. I just hoped reading minds wasn't one of his abilities. I shrugged my shoulders. "Eh, it's alright. I've seen a million sunsets." My lousy lie won me a chuckle and a crooked grin.

"I didn't notice it. I was too busy watching something much more beautiful." He met my gaze with a confidence that left me breathless. His blue eyes seemed darker than normal and I allowed myself to drown in them while everything around us faded away. I knew I was dangerously close to falling for him, and once I fell, there would be no getting back up. Even knowing the risk I was taking, I kept walking toward the proverbial edge with reckless abandon. He caught a stray piece of blond hair blowing across my face and tucked it behind my ear. I froze when the tips of his fingers brushed my neck and shoulder. The heat they evoked lingered like glowing embers across my skin. His hand dropped and found mine, then he leaned closer and I saw something spark in his eyes as his lips curved upward. I held my breath.

"Time to see what you've got, Pasha." He stood up and brought me with him.

"What'd you call me?" I looked up at him with confusion.

"Pasha. It means 'beautiful star'," he translated for me as we walked hand in hand toward the ocean. He could call me anything and I'd probably answer to it. Well, almost anything.

The water resembled liquid silver as it lapped at the shore, and that familiar longing to swim under the waves hit me again as I fought the urge to run to them. I let go of Finn's hand when the water was up to my thighs and I felt the tingling sensation that always seemed to greet me. I stopped, closed my eyes and held my palms right above the foaming water. A million tiny bubbles broke against my palm and tickled my skin. The water felt alive. I smiled and opened my eyes, but Finn had disappeared. After scanning the waves, I saw him a couple yards out and swam out to him.

"What should I try first?" I asked once I got there.

"See if you can calm the waves," he suggested. Good one.

"No, seriously - what should I try first?"

"I am serious. Try it." He acted like I should be able to do it with both hands tied behind my back. Unfortunately I didn't have that same confidence in myself.

"But I don't know how." I frowned at him.

"Yes you do, just will it to be," he explained cryptically. This was ridiculous. He really expected me to stop the waves crashing onto the shore? Like I was any match for the tidal forces of the moon. At least he didn't have high expectations. A laugh tinged with hysteria bubbled up inside me and I faced the waves. Concentrating hard, I tried my best to picture them slowing down and becoming completely smooth. I pictured the water losing its foam as it flattened and stilled. Unfortunately, back in reality, the waves continued rolling toward the beach like normal. After staring at them for what seemed like an hour, I turned to Finn in frustration.

"This is pointless. I can't do it." Carmen's face popped in my mind. "Plus, don't you have to be descended from someone who has that ability?"

"Not always. Try again. This time face me." Like that would help my concentration. With zero faith in my abilities, I looked into Finn's eyes. They matched the darkness of the ocean and the rest of the world faded away. Remembering the feeling of the breaking bubbles, I reached my arms out and placed my palms on top of the water. Completely engulfed in Finn's eyes, I forgot all about what I was supposed to be doing. All I could think about was what it would feel like in his arms. Run my fingers through his hair. Then he smiled.

"Perfect," he said. That was an understatement. Wait...

"What's perfect?"

117

"What were you thinking about?" He cocked his head to the side and raised an eyebrow.

"Nothing," I spit out a little too quickly. At least he couldn't read minds. I filed that away in my 'good-to-know' folder.

"Obviously it's a little more than nothing - look what you're doing." He pointed behind me.

I turned to see the boiling ocean had turned into a tranquil lake. Completely still and utterly quiet, an eerie silence had fallen over the night. I glanced to my left where waves were crashing farther down the beach and saw the same to my right. The ocean-turned-lake was only in our immediate vicinity.

"Holy shit," was all I could manage. Finn laughed and it sounded louder amidst the calm of the ocean. "But this can't be me…I wasn't even trying yet!" I tried to argue, shocked by what I saw.

"It's all about harnessing the energy from your emotions, then transferring them to the water. You must have been thinking about something pretty powerful." His crooked grin was back, but my mind was on to a more frightening issue.

"How do I make it go back to normal?" It would be my dumb luck to break the ocean.

"Lift your hands," he instructed. My arms were still extended, so I took my palms off of the water. A concrete wall of sensations slammed into me. Adrenaline coursed through my veins and every emotion I'd ever felt assaulted me in an instant. Completely overwhelmed, my body went limp and I felt myself slip under the water. Finn's arms slid under my knees and back; lifting me up. I looked into his eyes, mere inches from my own.

"You okay?" He beamed at me.

"I think so," I replied, unsure of myself. "What the heck was that?"

118

"Your energy returning to you." I barely heard him as I became acutely aware of the amount of skin touching as he cradled me in his arms. Being held by him, I got the feeling nothing could ever hurt me.

"I knew you'd be amazing," he said with admiration, which quickly turned to sadness. He released my legs so I could stand on my own again, but I held onto his arms to test my strength. He steadied my waist and I felt the taut muscles in his arms as his skull and crossbones trace sparkled brightly just under the surface. My eyes moved over the rest of his torso as it glistened in the moonlight. I wanted to wrap up in him and never let go. I met his eyes. He watched me with something that resembled restraint. He cleared his throat, let go of my waist and ran his hands through his hair. With my heart beating out of my chest, I glanced back at the shore to see the waves had resumed crashing. It was as if time had stopped. The whole experience was exhilarating.

"I want to do it again!" I told him eagerly. But he shook his head.

"Let's stick to smaller things for now. You should pace yourself."

For the next hour we practiced making bubbles (which I did unknowingly when I had first gotten in the water), making little ripples, whirlpools like we did in class, and small waves. It was like I was meeting a part of myself for the first time, and it was as natural to me as breathing.

"So you've gotten the hang of some things above water," he paused and his face lit up, "but you haven't tried anything under the water. It's an entirely different experience."

"But it's dark - I won't be able to see anything," I countered.

"Afraid of the dark, Stasia?" With that, he disappeared beneath the surface. Left alone in the moonlight, I suddenly felt very alone. I thought I saw something move on shore, but then again it could have been just a trick of the moonlight. As a chilling feeling crept up my spine and settled in my chest, my heart rate quickened and I decided it was time to join Finn under the waves. With one last look toward the beach, I took a breath and dove under.

I was immediately shocked by how well I could see. It wasn't as bright as during the day, but everything had a glow; making it very easy to see. I spotted Finn a couple yards out emanating the same glow. Once he saw me, he continued swimming away from the beach. I followed him out as the ocean floor dropped farther and farther beneath us. He finally stopped and turned to face me, and I saw that his stormy blue eyes had taken on a completely new quality underwater. I saw flecks of teal and green amongst the darker blues. He grinned at me as his hair danced in the current, then he put both hands on my shoulders and ran them down the outside of my arms; stopping at the crook of my elbows. He pulled me closer and I noticed without our arms to tread water we began to sink quickly. A look of determination settled on his face and the grip on my arms tightened.

I stared back at him and tried to understand what he was doing. I tried to move my arms, but I'd have better luck getting out of a vice grip. Then I tried to push away by kicking my legs, but that turned out to be a futile effort as well. I looked up and realized just how far we had descended. Each inch we dropped was an inch between me and life sustaining oxygen. As my lungs burned for air, panic set in and I tried to think of a way to get away from him. Coming up with nothing, I continued to struggle, which only made the need for oxygen that much worse. Why was he doing this? Was he going to kill me? Why? His face remained so eerily still, while a terror I'd never felt before emerged from the depths of my soul.

Cursed. That's what Carmen had said. Thanks to my made-up excuse, no one even knew I was out there. He could anchor my body to the bottom of the sea and I would be eaten by sharks before they found me. I started to struggle again but my lungs were at their breaking point. Small black spots formed in my vision and Finn began to blur in front of me. I could only make out his lips moving.

'Just breathe' they said. What kind of sick joke was that? He was the one holding me captive underwater and he wanted me to just breathe? Now he was repeating it over and over. He was sick. Or crazy. Or both. My lungs were on fire and the urge to take a breath became intolerable. The small black spots turned to larger black splotches and I knew I'd lose consciousness soon. Suddenly, all on their own, my lips parted and my lungs inhaled.

FIFTEEN

Water immediately poured into my nose and throat and filled my lungs. I felt the pressure pushing against my chest. It was cold and foreign, and I waited for the pain to come, for the blackness to take over.

Then I exhaled. My eyes zeroed in on Finn, who was concentrating on me like a science experiment, and it frightened me all over again. Then I inhaled. And exhaled. No pain. No blackness strangling me into oblivion. Just me and Finn, suspended in the ocean. I started taking deeper breaths as my vision cleared and my energy returned. I watched him carefully and saw that he was breathing too. This couldn't be happening. People couldn't breathe underwater…it was impossible.

He smiled slowly at me and a red hot rage filled every fiber of my being. Having use of my arms again, I pushed away from him as hard as I could and kicked up to the surface. I broke through and immediately took a breath of fresh air. In the back of my mind I marveled at how easy it was to go from breathing water to breathing air again. Then I remembered why I was breathing water in the first place as Finn broke the surface beside me.

I swam towards shore. The waves greatly increased in size, and the thought crossed my mind that my anger had caused it. Good. Maybe they'd swallow him whole and keep him out there! I finally made it past them and onto the beach when I felt him right behind me. I whipped around and narrowed my eyes.

"Get away from me." I turned on my heel and kept walking.

"I wasn't trying to hurt you, Stasia."

I turned on him again as a fresh wave of anger engulfed me. "Drowning me is you NOT trying to hurt me? Is that supposed to make me feel better?!"

"I wouldn't have been able to convince you any other way."

"So that was your solution?!"

"I wouldn't have let anything happen to you." He tried to touch my arm, but I slid out of his reach and glared at him.

"How long were you deciding to hold me down there and watch me drown?! Did you ever consider the crazy possibility that I wouldn't be able to breathe underwater?"

"I can't explain how I know…you just have to trust me."

"Trust you? You want me to trust you after what just happened?" Tears poured down my face. He stepped closer.

"You're special, Stasia. You don't know the amazing things you're capable of. I want to show you who you really are." The tenderness in his eyes only upset me more.

"Don't say things like that! You don't even know me!" I put my hands on his chest and pushed him, but I could have been pushing against a cement wall for all the good it did. "You don't know the things I've been through! You don't know the things I've seen! Look at me, Finn. I'm not special! I'm broken!"

"Once you've been touched by evil, it never leaves you." I looked up at his words, laced with understanding. "But it doesn't define you. Evil didn't break you, Stasia, it built you up. Made you stronger." Looking up at him, I almost believed him. I narrowed my eyes.

123

"What do you know about evil? Do you know what it's like to be scared for your life every single day!? Do you?!" I pounded on his chest uselessly with my fists as emotions coursed through me. He just stood there silently and took all the abuse I could dish out. My anger eventually faded to humiliation, which turned to exhaustion. I collapsed against him with my hands and forehead pressed against his chest. I felt his fingers at the nape of my neck and his thumb lifted my chin.

"Anastasia…" he whispered. I heard the longing in his voice as he lightly ran his thumb over my lips. His eyes took me in and with no fight left, I gave in to them. The smell of the salt water that clung to his body filled my senses and I let the sound of the ocean caress my ears. He leaned closer and held my gaze. His closeness made my anger evaporate, replaced by a desire so strong it threatened to consume me. All I could think about were his lips, inches from my own.

"Kiss me…" I heard myself whisper. His other arm wrapped around my waist; pulling me to him abruptly. The next instant his mouth crushed against mine with such hunger, my own desire overpowered me and I lost myself to it. I wrapped my arms around his neck as the heat of his skin burned against mine. The coolness of his wet hair sizzled in my fingers as I clung to him.

His lips parted mine and I felt his tongue deepening the kiss. It did something to me I had no control over. I wanted more. I wanted all of him. Still kissing me, he easily lifted me up and I wrapped my legs around his waist. He carried me farther up toward the dunes and I felt the muscles in his shoulders as he lowered me down onto the cool sand. He gazed down at me with stormy, hooded eyes and I saw a trace of sadness in them again. He looked at war with himself, but finally pressed down on top of me; slipping one arm under the small of my back and pulling me against him again. My entire body responded to his touch. I ran my fingertips down his back and felt him shudder. Every kiss burned hotter than the one before. Every touch lit a new fire on my skin.

Too soon, he slowed our kisses until they were only light pecks. Ever so gently he kissed my cheeks, my nose and then my lips again. His mouth lingered and I fought the urge to pull him back down on top of me. Lying on his side, he delicately took my hand and threaded his fingers through mine in a gesture I was starting to love.

As much as he frightened me, he was unlocking an entirely new world for me. One with endless possibilities. The ability to breathe underwater? It was so unbelievable, I still wasn't sure I did it. I knew without a doubt there was no one else I'd rather have with me through this. I reached for him and he held me tight, lightly running his fingers through my hair. I felt a virtual safety net wrap around me as the security of his arms lifted some of the weight I'd always carried on my shoulders. The rest of the world felt miles away from us and I wanted to stay there forever.

"Promise me you'll give me a warning next time you want to convince me of something. I'll give you a red flag to wave or something." I smiled up at him lazily.

"I definitely will. I don't want to get beaten up again." He grinned back down at me.

"Since I can breathe underwater, should I expect my legs to morph into a fishtail?" I wiggled my feet in the air.

"I can assure you that won't happen." He rolled his eyes at me.

"Oh good, that would really hinder a lot things. Like walking. Or wearing pants." I frowned.

"Or playing kickball," Finn added, clearly amused by my logic.

"Or playing footsy." I tried to tickle his foot with my toes and noticed his leather anklet again.

"Black onyx?" I asked as I touched it with my foot.

"That's right – it's the stone of protection," he said. I tried to decide if I should ask him what he needed protection from, when I remembered my own new jewelry.

"Kira gave me a turquoise bracelet," I told him, and then sat up to show him.

"It fits you." He turned his attention to the ocean. "Although an aquamarine would be better."

I waited for more of an explanation. "Because it matches your eyes," he added, a little too rushed. I got the feeling that wasn't the reason he was really thinking of. I made a mental note to research aquamarine, since it must hold a special meaning for him. I remembered him saying it symbolized foresight and courage, but that was all I knew. If you needed protection, courage would have to be at the top of the important qualities list. Then something else hit me. Maybe he knew more about evil than I thought.

"Will the black onyx protect you from…a curse?"

His expression took on a surprised look. "A curse?"

"Well… I heard that you're, um…" A nervous knot tightened in my stomach and I looked down at the sand; running my fingers through it. There was no turning back now. "That you're cursed." I looked back up at him timidly. He laughed and shook his head.

"Is that what they're calling it these days?" He laughed darkly. His eyes locked onto mine; making it impossible for me to look away and all lightheartedness left his tone. "I'm not cursed, Stasia, it's something much worse than that." He leaned toward me. "I've been Chosen."

I felt my eyes widen. "You're….Chosen?" Well, that was certainly a new development. Suddenly I felt very small in comparison. "That's incredible! But I thought being Chosen was a great honor?"

His face turned menacing and he shifted away from me. "Not always. Sometimes being Chosen comes with a very high price."

126

He stood suddenly and walked to the water's edge. I followed farther behind, giving him room. He stopped at the water and ran his hand through his hair. Another habit of his I was beginning to fall in love with. In the moonlight his hair matched the black onyx stones glistening around his ankle. The pale light cast a sinister shadow on his face, making him appear dangerous. And beautiful. I reached for his hand.

"What price do you have to pay?" I asked quietly.

"Why do you want to know?" His jaw clenched and the unexpected ferocity in his eyes had me taking a step back. He reached for my hand and pulled me back to him. The anger was instantly replaced by complete surrender.

"I'm not the one who has to pay it," he whispered; running his finger across my lips again. He dropped his hand, turned and walked out into the ocean. I watched as he lightly skimmed his fingertips over the foaming water in a slow circular motion. The water around him began to dance. As I looked on, he seemed to become a part of the water; moving to the cadence of the waves. I found myself walking out to him without making a conscious decision to do so. He turned to face me as I approached, and I saw the teal and green hues in his eyes again. His hands eclipsed mine and slowly guided them across the top of the water in the same rhythm. As I looked in his eyes, I heard it.

Singing. The same melody I'd heard in the bathtub, in the ocean that first day, and in class. I closed my eyes and listened. What I thought was a woman's voice was actually just the soprano of a larger melody. Listening closer, I realized it resembled the sounds of a hundred violins. Flowing into my soul, it embraced me fully and I felt my body swaying to its tempo. Like a field of grain bending in unison to the wind, I let it take control of me. I opened my eyes to see that Finn was watching me. The sadness in his eyes had retreated and he eyed me with wonder.

"Can you hear it, Stasia?"

127

I nodded. "I think I feel it more than I hear it. It's amazing." I glanced down at the dancing water surrounding us. "What is it?"

"The ocean," his face brightened, "reaching out to you. Not everyone can hear it. It only embraces the pure of heart," he said; sounding wiser than his years. He lifted our hands and the sound began to fade as the water took on its silvery quality once again.

"I've heard it before, I just didn't know what it was."

"It was calling to you." He smiled knowingly.

On the way back up the beach, I began to feel slightly overwhelmed with all of the information I'd digested. "There's so much I still don't know. So much I have to learn."

"It comes with time." He looked at me with a sudden seriousness. "But right now we have a bigger issue."

"What's that?" I didn't know if I could handle any more earth shattering revelations tonight.

"Why you have sand all over you."

"I don't have…." Before I could finish, he swept my legs out from under me and caught me mid-fall. He lowered me onto my back on the sand. Not one to give up on a good fight, I caught him off balance and yanked him down beside me. Seeing my opportunity, I scrambled back to my feet and started up the beach to our sitting spot near the dunes. He easily caught up with me, then he picked me up and threw me over his shoulder.

"I win!" he declared as he lowered me down in front of the dunes.

"Well enjoy it now, because this'll be the last time I let that happen. I want a rematch."

His blue eyes lit up and a deliberate grin appeared. "Anytime you want to wrestle, I'm game."

I rolled my eyes at him and pushed his shoulder playfully. He smiled and wrapped me up in his arms. I smelled his woodsy scent mixed in with the sand and the sea as I breathed him in and closed my eyes. He smelled like a warm summer breeze.

"I've dreamt about you," I blurted out for no apparent reason. I felt the need to explain further. "I mean...I see you sometimes, in my dreams. Carmen told me they could be reveries."

"Is that how you do it?" he asked. I looked up in surprise at his words.

"You can...you actually do see me?" I whispered in disbelief.

"Your soul shouldn't be visible to anyone in reveries, not even me." His dark blue eyes brightened and he watched me closely. "But you've always just...appeared. Then poof, you're gone again."

As my real world and my dream world suddenly collided, I felt slightly off-kilter. And not in a good way.

"I thought you recognized me the first day I was here, but I wasn't sure. And you saved me...." I wasn't sure how to finish. He probably knew I could breathe under water then too. Why would he go to all that trouble if he knew I wouldn't die? "Why'd you save me if you knew I could breathe underwater?"

"You didn't know you could breathe underwater, plus I knew you were scared." He grinned at me, clearly amused by my question.

"I wasn't scared," I retorted.

"I must have imagined that look of sheer panic on your face then," he mocked, and I thought about how many looks of sheer panic he'd seen on my face in my reveries. No wonder he recognized it so quickly. How humiliating.

"The seaweed wrapped around my legs and wouldn't let go! Then all the fish..." I noticed how hard he was trying not to laugh. I sat up and put my hands on my hips. "I hope some seaweed attacks you someday so you know how it feels."

"I'll be sure to keep my seaweed machete on me at all times." He laughed.

"Not funny. You are officially banned from my reveries." I suppressed a giggle. I mean, who gets attacked by seaweed? Me - that's who.

He watched me for a moment, thoughtful. "Did you have one today?"

"No…" I recalled the entire day. No dreams. No blackouts. "Why?"

"Just wondering how frequent they are." But something told me that wasn't why he wanted to know. He looked at the ocean in deep thought.

"I don't understand how we could see each other in my reveries before we even met," I said; willing him to share his thoughts with me.

Instead he stood and pulled me up with him; tucking me in his arms. No matter how many times he touched me, it always felt like the first time. His skin sizzled against mine.

"The first time I saw you, I knew I would never be the same." He leaned down, lips inches from mine, and finished, "I didn't know if you were real. But then I touched you. Felt that you were really here and I knew you'd finally come back."

"Come back?" I whispered as he leaned down to kiss me. My question was lost as my entire body caught fire.

Sixteen

I listened to my phone beep for close to ten minutes, hoping I'd be able to tune it out and go back to sleep. I finally gave up and reached for it on my nightstand. Kira had texted me, wanting me to call her. I threw the covers back over my head and stretched my legs, still smiling from last night. I'd probably slept with a big goofy grin on my face too. Good thing I didn't share a room with anyone. Finn had walked me back to Maren Hall and then walked the short distance to Rostrum, right next door. Knowing he was so close brought another smile to my face. My heart pounded as I pictured him lying in bed sleeping; covers gathered around his waist, bare chest, messy hair...

A loud bang in the kitchen made me sit straight up in bed. I opened my door and saw Carmen bending over, cleaning the floor as curse words flew from her mouth.

"Shhh! You're going to wake up Stasia!" Phoebe shushed her from the living room.

"It's okay, Stasia's already awake." I smiled and sat down on the couch.

"How're you feeling? You missed an awesome movie last night!"

"Worst. Movie. Ever," Carmen muttered from the kitchen.

"Actually, I started feeling better after you guys left and I went down to the beach."

"By yourself?" Carmen looked up from her mess.

"Well..." I hesitated.

"You were with Finn, weren't you?" she accused me.

"Finn?" Phoebe squeaked, "As in Finn? Like, THE Finn?"

"Yes Phoebe, THE Finn. And he's not cursed, you guys, he's Chosen." I began to back pedal. I knew this wouldn't go well.

"Chosen or not Chosen, he's cursed. I heard that anyone who gets involved with him will lose their soul," Phoebe whispered, her eyes wide.

"They won't lose their soul, it's held captive in the Underworld," Carmen corrected her, "and their body will stay here, never to be reunited."

"Just an empty body, not really dead, but not really alive either," Phoebe added; grimacing.

"I seriously doubt that's true, you guys." I shook my head at them. They were starting to sound like a bad sci-fi movie.

Willow's bedroom door swung open and we all turned to say good morning, but stopped short when we saw the defeated look on her face. Her eyes were red and tears were streaming down her cheeks.

"Willow! What is it? What's wrong?" Phoebe ran over to her.

"She's gone." She stared at us blankly.

"Who's gone?" Carmen handed her a tissue.

"Nicolet. She's gone."

"What? How do you know? What happened!?" Phoebe cried.

"Who's Nicolet?" I asked. Willow's watery eyes shifted to me and her tears began to flow steadily.

"She's a graduate student here." Her face crumpled. "Was a graduate student here. I…I just met with her two days ago. I didn't hear from her yesterday, but I thought…I just thought…." Her sobs took over and Phoebe held her tightly; gesturing for Carmen to get more tissues.

My phone rang, so I ran back to my bedroom to grab it. It was Kira.

"Hey Stasia." I heard something heavy in her voice. "I'm sure you guys have already heard, but I wanted to call and talk to you." She sniffed and I knew she'd been crying. "One of the graduate students, my roommate.....she passed away. They found her. They think it was...a suicide." Her voice caught on the last part.

"Oh, Kira, I'm so sorry." I instantly felt horrible for not calling her back sooner.

"It doesn't seem real. I just don't understand." She was silent for a moment. "Is Willow alright? Nicolet was her mentor."

"She's really upset, but we're taking care of her. I hope you know I'm here for you too, Kira."

"Thanks Stasia, that means a lot to me." I could tell she was crying again. "I wanted to let you guys know there'll be a candlelight vigil for her on the beach at sunset."

"We'll be there."

That night we made our way down to the vigil. A dark shadow had descended upon the entire school, as word of Nicolet's suicide circulated. The rumor was that she had been missing since yesterday morning and a couple of Tritons found her body this morning near a boardwalk on the north side of campus. Her wrists had been slit.

A massive group of people converged on the beach for the candlelight vigil, each holding a small hurricane vase with a tea light candle inside. The whole beach flickered and came alive as the collective glow brightened with each new arrival. Lining the beach in both directions were much larger hurricane vases with candles running parallel to the ocean. They'd been secured in the sand just out of the reach of the waves. A beautifully ornate white table was placed in front of the row of candles, acting as a memorial. It was overflowing with beautiful exotic pink and orange hibiscus blooms and topped with several large picture frames. More colorful bouquets littered the sand below as people brought their own dedications.

As we descended the steps of the boardwalk, we were each handed our own candles smelling of white citrus. We followed Willow down to the table and saw that the flowers were much larger than they appeared from a distance. Intertwined with ivy and strips of lace, it was the most amazing arrangement I'd ever seen. Another hurricane vase sat in the center of the table with a single, large blue candle surrounded by pearls and turquoise stones. Willow pressed her hand to one of the frames, tears rolling down her cheeks. I gave her a light hug and faced the frame with her.

A beautiful young woman with bright red hair framing large green eyes smiled back at me. Images of a previous reverie exploded before my eyes. A flash of red catching my attention. A couple arguing on the beach. The woman lying on her side in the sand with blood pooling around her. I felt the blood drain from my face. It was Nicolet that I had watched die during my blackout. Last week.

I grabbed the edge of the table to keep from falling as a wave of nausea washed over me. I turned and ran back towards the boardwalk and slipped beneath it, surrounded by dunes and the sounds of people above. Clutching my stomach and trying to be quiet, I got sick. I started to shake uncontrollably and collapsed on the sand. I put my head in my hands, wrapped my arms around myself and rocked back and forth. The dream wasn't real. It couldn't be real.

"Stasia?"

I looked up to see my three roommates ducking under the boardwalk to join me.

"Oh, ew." Phoebe pinched her nose.

"Are you okay?" Willow rubbed my back while Carmen threw sand over the spot I had thrown up on. My skin tingled everywhere her hands touched me. I slowly stopped shaking and realized they were still waiting for an answer.

"I know it's her. I saw him. She died." I knew I wasn't making sense, but it was all I could make my mouth say.

"You knew Nicolet?" Carmen looked at me, perplexed.

"No. I...I saw her hair. I couldn't feel the wind."

"What do you mean?" I saw them looking at each other, probably wondering why they didn't bring some sort of tranquilizer for the crazy girl hiding under the boardwalk. I dropped my arms and shook my head; hoping to get rid of the hazy panic hugging my brain.

"I had a dream about her. Before I came here. I saw her die. She got stabbed."

"But she wasn't murdered, Stasia, and it just happened yesterday. It must have just been a dream. It's okay," Willow tried to comfort me.

"How could I dream about someone I don't know?"

"Maybe it was a reverie that morphed into a dream?" Phoebe guessed. Applause erupted from the beach, meaning the ceremony was starting. I had to get myself together. Willow was supposed to be the one who needed comforting, not me.

"It's okay, I'm okay. Let's go back out there, I think they're starting," I urged them.

"Are you sure? You still look a little pale..." Carmen helped me stand.

"Yeah, I'll be fine. Promise." I forced a smile as we made our way back out to the beach, but my legs were still shaking and I had an awful taste in my mouth.

As we walked to the front of the crowd, each person lowered their eyes at Willow and allowed us through.

"I still can't believe she would kill herself," Phoebe said softly; shaking her head. Suicide. They said she committed suicide, but I saw her being stabbed. I watched her blood disappear into the sand next to her lifeless body. She didn't commit suicide, she was murdered. At least she was according to my dream. Or reverie. How did I even know it was real? Maybe she really did commit suicide yesterday and the reverie was just a fluke. I groaned inwardly, since I had no way of knowing. If I could just remember what the man looked like. Dark hair? Or maybe brown? He was definitely big and very strong. She was no match for him. He was probably a Triton or Son of Daimon.

Son of Daimon. Finn. Why was Finn there? Was he keeping watch while the man killed her? Was he helping him? He obviously wasn't helping Nicolet. I couldn't shake away the thought that he had something to do with it. Why else would he have been there? And if it was real, how did she just die yesterday? I had to talk to Finn. He was the only person who could tell me what happened. I swept my eyes over the crowd looking for him, hoping he might be there. Was he a murderer? Is that what he'd been Chosen for? He said himself that he wasn't the one who had to pay the price of being Chosen. So it would make sense that the innocent people he killed would pay the price. My heart constricted with that chilling thought. My search halted as soon as my eyes fell upon Kira.

She stood to the right of the table in a simple black sundress. She looked like she'd been awake for days and had been crying for longer. My eyes began filling with tears at her obvious pain. Next to her were two other girls who appeared just as heartbroken. The pictures on the table kept distracting me, though. It felt as if Nicolet was staring right at me through the frame; accusing me. I couldn't help but wonder if she had seen Finn and I arguing as she was helplessly stabbed to death. I sent out a silent plea to her. I'm so sorry Nicolet. Please forgive me.

A tall blond woman stood in front of the table. Her long white dress billowed out around her in the ocean breeze. She bent over and lit the blue candle inside the large hurricane vase. There was a small wreath of white flowers set atop her head, resembling a crown. Bright blue sapphires dangled from her ears, neck and wrists. Her piercing blue eyes settled upon the crowd of grievers.

"That's Priscilla, she's our Maven," Carmen whispered in my ear. I stared back at her blankly, hoping for more of an explanation. "You know, the head mistress, leader, priestess, whatever you wanna call it."

When Priscilla started to speak, my chin hit the ground and a shadow of dread fell over me. I'd heard that voice before. "We've come too far to have this orphan girl ruin everything." I studied her long blond hair and the glow she emanated. It was definitely her. I could still visualize her in my dream, gliding down the hallway with Isadora as I tried to blend in with the wall.

"Ladies and Gentlemen, tonight we mourn the loss of a great student, friend and Tyde, Nicolet Stephens," she announced. The light breeze carried her voice over the crowd. "She will be greatly missed."

She went on to speak of Nicolet's many accomplishments and what she had meant to the House of Lorelei. I heard an agonizing sob as Kira held onto the other two girls. I glanced over at Willow. Her usually flowing blond hair had been pulled up into a messy bun and her blue eyes were splotchy and red. Her shorts and tank top were wrinkled and disheveled. Her bottom lip quivered slightly as she held back her tears. I squeezed her hand.

Priscilla picked up the hurricane vase delicately; her bracelets clinking against each other. Several more women in similar flowing white dresses joined her at the table. They stood perfectly still and held hands. They were each extremely beautiful, but that wasn't what made them so captivating. It was as if the sun shone from within them, broadcasting beauty and allure to the world. If it was possible to gather every new spring blossom, every savory smell of a summer garden, and every sparkle of morning dew and then combine them into one creature, the result would be standing before us. It was difficult to look directly at them without becoming completely overcome by their brilliance.

As they all closed their eyes, a beautiful sound like none other began to flow from them. The song of a Siren. It was a haunting cry that filled the night air and wrapped around every living creature. I felt it enter my conscious, resonate throughout my senses and settle into my soul. It trumped my thoughts and numbed my feelings. Becoming uncomfortable with the intrusion, I pushed the sensation back out, away from my ears and back into the breeze. Although it resisted, I was finally able to think again and felt my own emotions returning to me. Everyone around me appeared to be in some kind of trance. I looked up at Priscilla and inhaled sharply. Her emotionless eyes were boring into mine with a burning fury I could almost feel. The song ended abruptly and Priscilla immediately reverted back to her role as caring Maven. Everyone around me began moving and whispering again, but her chilling gaze stayed with me.

At the water's edge, she scooped up a sample of the ocean in a small glass and brought it back to the table. She raised her arms, looked up at the sky and regally proclaimed, "It shall come to pass." Then she poured the sea water over the burning candle on the table. The second it touched the flame the water snuffed it out. Simultaneously, every other candle on the beach and in our hands did the same. We were instantly drenched in darkness and a suffocating silence. I looked around anxiously as uneasiness wrapped around me, but no one else seemed to be worried about this sudden turn of events, so I tried to remain calm. Just as quickly as they had gone out, the candles danced back to life and the night filled with a warm glow once more. Priscilla bowed her head, walked around the table and gave Kira a small box. They turned to leave and everyone else began to make their way back to the boardwalk.

As the beach cleared, Priscilla walked towards us. Her cold blue eyes locked on mine and she gave me a practiced smile that didn't reach her eyes. She stopped in front of us; dissecting us one by one before speaking.

"Willow, it is customary that you receive a personal item of your mentor's upon graduation." Even at a close distance her voice held a certain amount of esteem and conviction. "Since these are extenuating circumstances, I believe you should receive that gift tonight."

She held out a purple velvet pouch with ribbon drawstrings. Willow wiped away a few tears that escaped her eyes and anxiously untied the drawstrings; pouring the contents into her palm. A breathtaking silver ring set with a turquoise stone sat in her hand. She slipped it onto her ring finger and held it against her chest.

"This means so much to me, thank you." Willow's eyes were bright with tears again.

"It once belonged to Nicolet's great grandmother. I know you will take great care of it, Willow. I know how much Nicolet meant to you." Priscilla bowed her head towards Willow and slipped past us.

"Willow?" Kira came up behind us and I gave her the biggest hug I could manage. She held onto me tightly and I felt tears dampen my shoulder. She straightened and wiped her eyes.

"I have something for you." She turned to Willow and handed her a piece of paper rolled up, secured with a lace ribbon. "I found this among Nicolet's things. I think you should have it." As Willow took the paper, Kira grasped both of her hands and her eyes widened with urgency.

"The contents are very old. Make sure it stays protected."

Willow nodded and embraced Kira in a hug, "Thank you. I'll keep it safe, but…what is it?"

"An old poem-" Kira stopped as someone called to her from the boardwalk, then focused back on us, looking defeated. "I have to go." She gave me another quick hug and started to walk away. Hesitating, she placed her hands on top of Willow's slender shoulders. "Nicolet loved you so much. Don't ever forget that."

"Thank you Kira." Willow glanced down at the paper as she walked away.

"Open it, open it!" Phoebe insisted; peeking over Willow's shoulder.

Willow slid the lace ribbon off the paper and unrolled it carefully. The piece of paper was browning around the edges and looked like it belonged to a different century. I worried it would crumble any moment and be carried off by the wind. The words scrawled down the paper looked like a work of art; looping and swirling into elaborate designs. Unfortunately the work of art wasn't written in English.

"What language is that?" Carmen wondered aloud.

"I don't know." Willow turned the paper sideways, trying to make sense of it. "I've never seen it before. I'll have to look through my books."

"Let's Google it!" Phoebe exclaimed, attempting excitement for Willow's sake. "I love a good treasure hunt!"

"I'm pretty sure treasure hunts never include googling things." She gave Phoebe an 'are-you-serious look. "But if you want to put some money on it, I'm down."

"Ten bucks," Phoebe suggested.

"Twenty," Carmen countered. She twirled a finger around her dark hair and lifted an eyebrow; daring Phoebe to up the price again.

"Thirty."

"Forty."

"Okay, okay," I put my hands up. "You'll be selling me and Willow off by the time you settle on a price. How about whoever figures out what the paper says gets a free meal at any restaurant, paid for by the other roommates?"

"Only if that includes dessert," Phoebe upped the ante.

"Deal," I said.

"Deal," Willow and Carmen agreed.

"Speaking of dessert, who wants brownies?" Willow smiled for the first time that day. Baking was her form of therapy. We took the boardwalk that led back to Maren. I saw a flash of movement out of the corner of my eye beneath us in the dunes, but when I looked closer only saw darkness and the swaying of grass.

SEVENTEEN

"You're telling me you were in his bed and nothing happened. I don't buy it." Phoebe shook her head at Carmen. A plate full of brownies sat on the coffee table as we lounged around talking in the living room that night.

"It's true! Logan was a total gentleman." Carmen winked at me.

"I saw that! You liar! You better tell me what happened or I'll throw your precious bag off the balcony!" She lunged for Carmen's Louis Vuitton bag.

"Okay, okay!" Carmen laughed at her. "Seriously, we lit some candles, got naked….and played poker." She shrieked as Phoebe started throwing pillows at her.

"I hate you. I've only had one boyfriend, and on one of our dates, his mom drove us to the movie and gave us the sex talk! In the car! I wanted to throw myself into oncoming traffic."

"Speak of the devil…" Carmen said under her breath, reaching for her phone, as it alerted her of a text with Caribbean steel drums.

"Whatever, Phoebs. Ian's been chasing you for months and you won't even look at him," Willow challenged her as she set her sights on a brownie.

"Who's Ian?" I asked curiously.

"It's not that I don't like him, I just don't know…"

"Excuses, excuses, Phoebs. He wants you, he's hot. What's so hard about that?" Carmen insisted.

"Who's Ian?" I asked again, louder this time.

"He's hot, I know, I know..." Phoebe sighed, "but he's a Son of Daimon. They kind of creep me out."

"If somebody doesn't tell me who Ian is, I'll just go ask Olivia!" That finally got their attention.

"I'm surprised you haven't met him yet...he's one of your boyfriend's friends." Carmen made kissing noises at me.

"Nobody said Finn's my boyfriend!" I put my hands on my hips.

"I knew it! You slept with him, didn't you?" Carmen started bouncing in her seat beside me.

"NO! He is NOT my boyfriend and I did NOT sleep with him!"

"But she really likes him...uh oh, her face is getting red. Yep, she likes him, alright." Willow grinned at me and Phoebe chewed on her fingernails in deep thought.

I threw my hands up. "Fine, I like him. Happy?"

"Very. Just watch out for your soul." Carmen continued eating her brownie with a smug look on her face. "I'm just saying."

"You don't think he's creepy?" Phoebe scrunched her nose like we were talking about zombies.

"He's definitely dark, but nowhere close to creepy." I chuckled at her.

"It's not like he's a pedophile." Carmen frowned at her, exasperated. "He's a Son of Daimon. They're mysterious, hot and sexy. What could go wrong? Plus, I heard he's going to ask you to the Cimmerian Shade Ball."

"Really?" Phoebe's eyes got wide. She turned to me. "Are you going with Finn?"

"You guys, we aren't together! I've never even heard of the Cimmerian Shade Ball." My heart squeezed. Would he ask me to go? What if he didn't?

"Mmmhmm...you sooo slept with him," Carmen mumbled as she furiously typed away on her phone.

"It's the annual dance the Sons have on the night of some important meteor shower. I can't remember what's so significant about that shower, but I think it has to do with Aquarius," Willow explained while licking brownie crumbs off her fingers. "I've never been, but I hear it's a big deal. Real formal. Like, prom dresses and tuxes formal. But of course it's invite only."

"Although….as far as I know, your precious Finnegan has never attended," Carmen said dramatically.

"Why not?" I asked. She looked at me like I was missing something obvious.

"Can you say 'cursed'? No girl in their right mind would go out with him." She looked at me and waited for me to realize she was referring to me. I changed the subject.

"He did show me some cool stuff though." I scooted to the edge of the cushion and leaned forward. "He showed me that I can manipulate waves." I heard them gasp. "I actually made them stop! It was wild!"

"Maybe you can help Carmen figure it out." Phoebe teased from the kitchen as she poured an entire bottle of Hershey's syrup into her milk glass. Apparently she liked a little milk with her chocolate.

"I don't need help!" Although Carmen was grinning, I caught a hint of jealousy in her eyes. "I've been doing it for years, so I'll be the one teaching her." She flipped her dark hair back over her shoulder.

"That's not the best part, though." I paused dramatically. "I can breathe…underwater!"

My announcement was met with silence. Then they all started talking at once.

"What?!"

"That's amazing!"

"You're so lucky!"

"No way! How's it work?"

"I don't know, I just…started breathing water." I shrugged and purposely left out the whole Finn-tried-to-drown-me part. "It was pretty crazy."

Willow's eyes widened. "That means you must have an affinity for a sea animal!"

"It does?"

"The sea turtles!" Phoebe jumped up and almost spilled her milky chocolate. "They must have recognized you! That's why they were around you!" I realized it made perfect sense. It would also explain the images I saw when I touched the turtle. Wow. Controlling water, breathing underwater and an affinity to sea turtles. This was seriously blowing my mind.

"So what does that mean? To have an affinity?" I questioned her. "Are they going to follow me around every time I go in the ocean?" I didn't remember any sea turtles the night Finn and I were swimming. And drowning. And then breathing. And…

"It means you have a special connection with them, so you can communicate with them somehow. It's different for each person," Willow explained; reaching for another brownie.

Phoebe sat back down beside me. "I've only known one person who had that kind of affinity, and it was this guy who could communicate with sting rays. Talk about weird. I don't think I'd want to be BFF's with one of those." She made a disgusted face. "But sea turtles are awesome! They get huge and live for like, eighty years. And the baby turtles are adorable!"

"Have you ever watched them hatch?" Willow asked me.

"I've seen it on the National Geographic channel, does that count?" I tried to remember what the documentary showed. I'm pretty sure that halfway through Laura Beth came in and changed the channel to something much more thought provoking, like Jersey Shore.

Carmen looked up from her text messages with Logan to add to the conversation. "It's really cool to see - the female turtles lay their eggs on the beach, then leave. After they hatch, the babies find their way to the ocean by following the moonlight shining off the water."

"We'll have to take you to see it!" Phoebe declared. "They're an endangered species but we can still get really close. They usually hatch right around this time. They stay in the nest for a couple nights after they hatch, then when they're strong enough they run to the ocean. If the moon isn't shining, we get flashlights to help them go the right way." She rubbed her chin and raised an eyebrow at me. "You know, we could just throw you in the ocean...I bet they'd follow you anywhere." She laughed, but I had a feeling she was probably right.

When Sunday rolled around, I lazily shuffled into the living room to find Phoebe and Willow watching the Weather Channel and painting their toenails. Phoebe was balancing a bottle of neon green on her knees, and Willow was in the process of filling up the room with used cotton balls.

"Dang, Willow. How many toenails do you have?" I ruffled her already messy hair and made myself comfortable on the couch.

"Note to self." She paused to toss another used cotton ball in the pile. "Any nail polish with glitter in it requires turpentine for removal."

"I might have an electric sander in my room if you think that'll help?" I snickered. She tried to throw a Q-tip at me but it fell short; landing on the floor three feet in front of me.

"Oh!" Phoebe pointed at the TV, grinning from ear to ear. "Hurricane Faye's coming to visit!" By her level of excitement, you'd think she'd just announced Prince William was coming instead.

"Hurricane Faye? Isn't that a bad thing?" I'd never been through a hurricane before, but I couldn't imagine that staying on a tiny piece of land surrounded by water was ideal.

She just giggled like I was being ridiculous. "Of course not! We break out the popcorn and enjoy the show!"

"But it's a hurricane," I emphasized. "It could wipe out this entire island and all of us with it." Did the word 'hurricane' mean something different around here?

"We never leave for hurricanes. I've been through three since I've been here." Willow looked up from her toes. "It's pretty amazing to witness."

Amazing sure, but from a front row seat right on the beach? Not so much. Something surfaced in my memory. "You know...I saw a documentary once about a hurricane that hit Galveston, Texas at the turn of the last century. There was a school on the beach just like us. But no one was able to warn them about the hurricane, so they didn't know to leave. When the water started rising, the nuns tied themselves to the little girls to keep everyone together."

"What happened?" Phoebe's face turned white.

"When the hurricane hit, as each girl drowned, she weighed down the others and the nuns couldn't keep everyone above water. When they dug through the ruins of the school looking for survivors, they found all the girls and nuns still tied to each other. All of them had died."

"That's awful...." Willow looked up from her toes, her face grave.

"I know. I can't even imagine how scary that would be, which leads me to my next question. Why are we not running for the nearest mountain town?" I scratched my head.

Carmen came out of her bedroom. "Duh, our ancestors came from the sea." She tossed some silver nail polish to Willow and picked up a magazine; flipping through it absentmindedly. "So don't get your panties in a wad. They placed a protective shield around the campus. We're golden. Plus, we used all the extra death-by-drowning rope tying Phoebe to the balcony last year. Now that was fun to watch." She blew a kiss to Phoebe who caught it and pretended to shove it in her mouth, chew it up and finally spit it out on the floor.

"Don't ask." Phoebe squelched the question already on the tip of my tongue, so I decided on another one.

"So why can't we make the hurricanes veer off course and stay out to sea or make them fall apart before they reach land?" I thought of all the lives that could be saved and the millions of dollars in damages that could be prevented.

"Messing with the balance of nature is a risky business. Especially something as powerful as hurricanes." Willow blew on her shiny metallic silver toenails to dry them. "It's forbidden by the Sanctions."

"What are the 'Sanctions'?" I needed a dictionary for all these new words.

"Basically they're the rules we have to follow. There aren't many, but they definitely enforce them," Willow explained.

"Most of us aren't powerful enough to do much harm anyway." Phoebe shrugged. "I mean, what kind of damage could my little sand tornado cause?"

"It could devastate an ant farm," I said in all seriousness. "Mass chaos would erupt and the death toll could rise to as much as twenty. I wouldn't want that on my conscience if I were you." Carmen laughed in her orange juice.

"The complete and total annihilation of an entire sand castle, that's what," Willow added.

"I foresee some serious chafing if it got in your bathing suit." Carmen looked up from her magazine, and continued. "And you thought razor burn was painful…"

"And don't get me started on how it feels in your eyes. We could all go blind in a matter of minutes," Willow threw out. We all erupted into a fit of giggles, except for Phoebe.

"Laugh it up now, but a gigantic sandstorm is next on my list and you three," she narrowed her eyes at each of us, "will be my next victims, so you better sleep with one eye open."

Carmen stood up suddenly. "Logan and his friends are going down to the beach in a little while. The hurricane's already kicking up some huge waves so they're going surfing. Which means you guys are coming out there with me." She looked at us expectantly. "So get your bathing suits on." She didn't wait for an answer, instead she disappeared into her bedroom.

"Anybody want to go to the beach? I heard Carmen's going…" Phoebe yelled sarcastically at Carmen's closed door. We stifled our laughter.

"I heard that!" Carmen said through her closed door. "I want bathing suits on A.S.A.P.! I'd hate to drag ya'll down there butt naked!"

A couple minutes later I had my bikini on and my thoughts inevitably drifted back to Finn. Would he be down there today? Did I want him to be there? Yes. Definitely, yes. I took out my phone and started to write him a text. Then deleted it. What was I supposed to say? 'Hey, was hoping to talk to you and find out if you're a murderer. Meet me at the beach in ten.' Yeah right. I'm sure he'd run down right away and welcome me with open arms. Right before he strangled me to death for being a complete moron.

EIGHTEEN

By the time we got down to the beach it was already teeming with activity. The sun was shining and the temperature was over ninety degrees. The smell of suntan lotion and salt mixed with sea grass greeted us. The breeze off the ocean made the heat bearable, but I could tell it was stronger than usual as my hair whipped around my head. I pulled out a ponytail holder and threw it up out of the way as my eyes scanned the ocean. Carmen was right; the waves had doubled in size overnight. They formed farther out and gathered speed and height as they raced towards shore. Long barrels, ideal for surfing, rolled continuously over the length of the beach; crashing and then regrouping as they ate away at the sand. The rhythmic pulse became hypnotic and I stared at them with a sense of wonder and…something else. Pride. A part of me belonged to that vast expanse of blue water circling the horizon as far as the eye could see. An entire world hidden beneath the surface, it harbored undiscovered secrets and its power could ravage entire continents. Its immense strength commanded respect and humbled the strongest of creatures.

"So, you gonna stand there all day like a statue or join the rest of us soaking up the sunshine?" I looked down at my roommates, who were all laying on the blanket squinting up at me. I laughed and found a spot on the blanket to stretch out on. I scanned the water for any surfers resembling Finn but they were all too far away to tell.

"Phoebe, isn't that Ian?" Carmen lowered her sunglasses and pointed.

"Well, don't point at him!" Phoebe smacked her hand down, but kept her eyes down the beach on the dark haired guy walking toward us. As he got closer I noticed just how good-looking he was. His dark hair was cut short, he had a diamond stud in each ear and wore a necklace of black onyx around his neck. He walked with a slight lean, making him look a little ghetto, but in a badass sort of way. I looked over at Phoebe and noticed she was fidgeting with her hair and watching him nervously as he approached. A slow, crooked smile spread across his face, and for an instant he reminded me of Finn.

"Girls." He nodded at the rest of us smoothly and extended a hand to Phoebe. "Want to walk?" Obviously not a man of many words. She glanced at us anxiously and I saw the unease in her eyes. I smiled encouragingly at her as she took his hand. They would make a cute couple; Phoebe with her pink and gray camouflage bikini, and Ian in his black trunks and laid-back style. As they walked away, Carmen put her sunglasses back on, laid back down and sighed. "Ah, young love. Makes me want to hurl."

"Do you think he'll ask her to the Ball?" I silently hoped he would. It would be great to have Phoebe there with me in the event I got asked. If I got asked. And if I said yes. Who was I kidding? When I said yes. Not that I'd even seen him since Friday night. And what if I found out he was a murderer? Why couldn't I have normal boy issues? Preferably the kind that didn't involve drowning in the ocean or murder.

"He definitely will." Carmen sat up and mimicked Ian's head nod and smooth voice, "Me. You. Ball. Saturday." I died laughing at her bad imitation. I closed my eyes to ward off the blinding sun. I'd taken off my sunglasses so I wouldn't have raccoon eyes, but it made it hard to see anything.

"Anybody up for some beach volleyball?" I looked up at Logan and Noah, resembling Greek gods, standing in front of us. Bronzed and muscular, they were the picture of perfection. Almost too perfect. The kind of perfect that made you question if you were seeing who they really were. And what they were trying to hide. Or maybe I was just paranoid. "You girls look like you could use some exercise..." Logan pulled down his Ray Ban sunglasses and looked at us; raising a light brown eyebrow.

"You can't handle this," Carmen told him as she rubbed more lotion on her legs, un-phased by his fighting words. Unlike Phoebe, she had the ability to hide all nervousness and insecurities. She had an air of confidence that made guys fall all over themselves. I probably should have taken some notes.

"Prove it," Noah answered Carmen and reached out his hand to me. Instead of taking it, I stood on my own. He looked momentarily hurt, but then smiled down at Willow. "You in?"

Willow sat up on her elbows and shook her head. "I'm allergic to exercise. Ya'll have fun."

"Your loss," Logan called back to her as we walked towards a makeshift volleyball court. It was basically a net with the surrounding court drawn in the sand. I'd played volleyball once and it definitely wasn't a pretty sight. I was hoping my skills had improved since then, but I wasn't too optimistic. With me and Noah playing against Carmen and Logan, I had a feeling Noah was on the losing end of that bargain. He palmed the ball, threw it in the air and gracefully served it over the net toward Carmen. She jumped and spiked it over the net before I even realized what was happening.

"Come on, Stasia, the ball's not going to defend itself!" Noah called out playfully, but I just rolled my eyes. The more we played, the more I realized volleyball wasn't my sport. After a horrific showing on my part, Logan and Carmen high-fived as the winning shot arced over the net and through my un-talented arms. Noah came over and gave me a high-five anyway.

"Good game, partner." He tried to give me a hug before I moved out of his reach. "Ya'll should come up to Rostrum and party with us." He looked around tentatively and in a hushed voice asked, "Do you get high?"

"I don't smoke," I retorted, unimpressed.

"That's not what I asked," he sneered at me, and took a step closer. I took a step back.

"I don't get high, either." I stood my ground this time and looked him in the eye with conviction.

"You don't know what you're missing." He shook his head at me. His tone turned slightly condescending. "You don't have to be scared. There's nothing wrong with it. Just like smoking cigarettes, really. Just better. And Logan's mentor just made a run to Wilmington to get a bag of some really good stuff." I got the distinct impression he assumed I was innocent and gullible, just waiting for someone like him to come along and corrupt me. Unfortunately for him, I wasn't innocent or gullible. I didn't need lessons from him or anyone else, for that matter. What he didn't know was that I'd been around drugs since I was about eight years old. When your foster parents choose partying for three days straight over feeding you, it tended to stick with you.

"I'm not smoking grass with you, Noah."

"Well, well…" He smirked at me, not expecting me to know another word for weed. "Maybe she's not so goody-goody after all." He stepped closer to me again and tried to put his arm around my waist, but I twisted out of his grip and stared daggers at him.

"Do not make the mistake of thinking you know me," I said through gritted teeth. I tried my best to suppress the buried anger he'd unknowingly triggered. I glanced back at Carmen for backup, but she appeared to be in deep conversation with Logan.

153

"Come on, don't be like that. I thought you were gonna be cool." He tried again to put his arm around my shoulder, but a strong tan hand clamped down on his first.

"Touch her again and I'll kick your ass." I jumped back in surprise at Finn's voice. It was dripping with pure darkness, sexy and terrifying all at once. He was face to face with Noah, and even though he was only an inch or two taller, it might as well have been a foot. Fear crossed Noah's face, but disappeared just as quickly.

"What do you want, Morrison?" Noah growled, but the slight tremble in his voice gave him away. I could tell it wasn't lost to Finn's ears. He stepped even closer and grinned at him with malice.

"Finally met a girl who won't fall for your bullshit?" Finn's face turned sinister and his blue eyes flashed. "She deserves respect, and that's the one and only thing you're ever going to give her."

"Whatever, dude." Noah tried to blow off Finn's threat, but he wasn't fooling anybody.

Logan walked up and eyed Finn. "We got a problem, Noah?"

"Nah." Noah quickly looked me up and down and then smirked, "It's not worth it." Anger shot through me at his insult and I moved in between him and Finn.

"Screw you." I pushed him as hard as I could and surprisingly, he flew back and landed hard on the sand. Everyone turned to stare at me except Carmen, who was suddenly standing right beside me.

"Get your boy under control before I whip his ass too!" She stared angrily at Logan. "Nobody talks to my friends that way!" I looked down at Noah, who was rubbing his chest, and saw two hand-sized bruises beginning to show. Did I really do that?

"She deserves it if she's hanging out with 'death boy'!" Logan helped Noah up off the sand, but when he turned back around, Finn tackled him; holding him down in the sand by his throat.

"Finn!" I called out to him. People were beginning to gather around us. "Come on...let him go, let's just leave."

"Stay away from her," he growled at Logan before looking up at Noah, whose face was drained of color. "Or you'll regret it."

He gave Logan a smile dripping with evil and released him abruptly; pushing his head back in the sand. Logan rubbed his neck where Finn's grip had left a red mark. Every muscle in Finn's body was tense, and I had a feeling he wanted nothing more than to kill them both. He radiated malevolence and my stomach turned to ice as I remembered his hands around another guy's neck right before he pulled out an axe.

"Asshole," Carmen muttered towards Logan before walking away. Willow ran over to us.

"Are ya'll okay? What happened?"

Finn looked back at the two retreating guys and narrowed his eyes. "We handled it."

"And I'm never talking to Logan again," Carmen added.

"I'm sorry, Carmen. I didn't mean for-" I began, before she interrupted me.

"It's not your fault he's a loser. I'm just glad I was there to watch you shove Noah in the sand! Those bruises will be a nice reminder to him not to mess with you. Let me see those muscles!" She squeezed my biceps and Willow's eyes got big.

"You did what?"

"Finn!" Two dark haired guys holding surfboards waved at him. "You comin', man?" Finn took my hand and pulled me away from Willow and Carmen.

He searched my face urgently. "I have to go," he said, his tone solemn. "Be careful who you hang out with, Stasia." Before I had a chance to argue, he walked away. I watched as he took his surfboard from one of the guys, jumped in the waves and easily started paddling out.

When I got back to our blanket, Carmen was telling Willow what happened and I felt my defenses go up at Finn's warning. I didn't need a babysitter. I could take care of myself. And besides, Noah wasn't the one who had stood on the same beach while Nicolet was killed. I watched as he dropped into a wave, whipped his surfboard around the top of it and rode it out like he'd done it a million times before. He dove into the water, retrieved his board and started paddling back out to do it all over again. Everything he did was so controlled and poised. And incredibly sexy.

When there was a lull in the waves, the three boys sat and talked on their boards. It made me wonder what the Sons of Daimon did in their spare time. I saw them in class and surfing, but besides that they were a complete mystery. Each one had an air of darkness, but Finn outweighed them all in that department. I could see why Noah was frightened of him...I got the feeling he'd never lost a fight. It was the darkness he exuded that made him so volatile and intimidating. Something inside me told me he would stop at nothing to protect someone he loved, and would definitely fight for what he believed in. It was a level of intensity that would tear a normal person apart, but Finn carried it with confidence and grace.

The sight of Kira walking along the beach pulled me from my thoughts. We hadn't talked since the candlelight vigil. Instead of a bathing suit, she was barefoot and wore a yellow strapless sundress. A long necklace of freshwater pearls hung from her neck and her blond hair was swept up on top of her head. I jogged down the beach to greet her and her face lit up when she saw me coming.

"Look at you!" She glanced down at my bathing suit and beamed with pride. "We'll make a beach bum out of you yet!" I embraced her in a hug and was hit with the scent of coconut and something fruity. I noticed the cup she held, filled to the brim with a slushy yellow concoction and a bright pink straw poking out. She winked at me.

"Come on, let's take a walk and catch up." We walked down by the water and she handed me the drink. It was definitely alcoholic and probably the best thing I'd ever tasted.

"Mmm...what is it?" I asked her as I stole another sip. It tasted like a Caribbean vacation in a glass.

"Malibu coconut rum and pineapple juice. My favorite. I was hanging out at Banana Cabana with everybody and just needed to get away, so I decided to take a walk on the beach. It always helps clear my head."

"How're you holding up?" I asked cautiously.

"The best I can, I guess." She took a long sip. "They came and took all of Nicolet's stuff. That was really hard. But I hid a bunch of it so I could keep a part of her. I know somebody else will have to move in, but I'm hoping they'll wait a couple days. I don't know if I can handle that yet. Her absence is unbearable, but having someone else in her room, her bathroom...." She looked so devastated, I wished there was something I could do to make her feel better.

"If you ever want to stay with us, just let me know. You're always welcome."

"I might take you up on that. It's just so quiet at home since...." She sighed. "I just don't understand how this could have happened. She wouldn't have killed herself. I know she wouldn't have." The sadness in her face gave me new motivation to figure it out. If for no other reason than to give Kira closure. Nicolet didn't kill herself. She was murdered. And I was going to prove it.

"What if she didn't?" She looked up at me, startled by my question. "Is there anyone you can think of that would want to hurt her for any reason?"

She shook her head fiercely. "Definitely not. Everybody liked Nicolet. She didn't have any enemies."

"Was she acting weird or anything?" I tried to dig a little deeper.

"Not really….she was always going on and on about some sort of conspiracy theory stuff, but I was used to that with her being a history major and all."

"What kind of conspiracy?"

"I'm not really sure, to be honest, and she never really explained it. But I'd see her reading books and writing things down in that notebook of hers. I tried to find it yesterday to see if there may be something in there to tell me why she did what she did, but they took it with the rest of her stuff."

I remembered the piece of paper she gave Willow and wondered if there was more meaning behind the mystery words than we thought. If she was into conspiracy theories, maybe she was killed because she got too close to the truth. I needed to get my hands on that notebook.

"Do you know what they would have done with her stuff? Maybe we can find the notebook?"

"I'm not sure, but if I had to guess I'd say they sent it back to her family in Savannah." She glanced at me, worried. "You don't need to worry yourself about this, Stasia. You've got enough on your plate as it is. You need to concentrate on your classes and making a home here at Lorelei. If there was some sort of foul play, I'm sure the authorities will pick up on it and investigate." She quickly changed the subject back to me. "So tell me how things are going with you! How do you like your roommates?"

"Oh, they're wonderful, Kira. You couldn't have put me with three better girls."

"I had a feeling you'd like them. Any guys caught your attention, yet? I bet they're knocking your door down…" She grinned at me.

"I've seen a couple cute ones, but…" I decided to keep Finn a secret and went with the old cliché, "I'm keeping my options open."

"Uh huh, I know how it is. You don't have to explain it to me." She nudged my arm.

"No really! I haven't met anybody yet!"

She just smirked at me. "So what about abilities? Do you have any questions, yet? I feel so bad that we haven't gotten to sit down and talk yet. When things calm down we will." I knew she was eager to help me, but Isadora and Priscilla's conversation about questioning her kept repeating in my mind. I didn't want Kira getting hurt. Or worse, killed.

"Nothing specific, no." Her face showed her disappointment, so I asked one question that seemed safe enough. "I'd really like to know what my trace means so I can figure out who I'm descended from."

"Well I've been doing some research on that because it's obviously rare and I knew you would eventually begin to wonder. But I couldn't find a trace like yours documented anywhere. The only thing that I may have figured out is that the trace's swirls are made up of seaweed." My mind automatically went to the sea weed reaching for me and surrounding me. I looked down at my trace and ran my finger along the three swirls in the shape of an upside down triangle. It would make sense if I had a connection to it. "But that doesn't tell us anything, except that the Nereid you're descended from has a connection with seaweed. However, that's pretty common among the Nereids. What's interesting about yours is the fact that the seaweed isn't the whole trace; it simply makes up the design of your trace. It's only a part of it. I'm not really sure what that means, but I promise I'll keep trying to find something." She gave me a supportive smile.

"Do you think it's because I was gone for so long? Maybe it just morphed into something new since I was never around any other Tydes?"

"No, that wouldn't happen. The design of your trace can't change once it's there," Kira said and shook her head.

"Do they just magically show up, or are we born with them?"

"It's beneath the skin at birth, but barely visible until that part of your body is exposed to the particular item you're connected to. Once that happens, it's sort of...triggered, and it shows on top of your skin. Usually a child's parents will expose them and bring their trace out at a young age. So I'm assuming your parents did just that while you were still a baby." My parents. That was a foreign concept.

"Are we born with our abilities? Willow told me they reach maturity at eighteen, but do we always have them?"

"Yes, but they don't start to come out until about age fourteen or fifteen. Sometimes it can be younger though, or older. Have any of your abilities started coming out yet?" she asked. Getting the feeling she knew more than I thought she did about my abilities, I decided to give her a little bit of information, hoping that would satisfy her for a while.

"I was able to manipulate water a little bit in my Oceanic Experience class, but that's about it." I tried to make it sound like it wasn't a big deal.

"Well I have a feeling your abilities will start to show themselves very soon, so whenever you want to talk or practice, you know how to find me." She gave me another supportive smile but remained thoughtful. I felt bad for not confiding in her, but I didn't feel like I had a choice. If Isadora was grilling her for information, the best thing I could do was not give her any...for her protection and mine. I only hoped I was doing the right thing.

Nineteen

Later that night, we gathered around the TV and watched the Weather Channel while Hurricane Faye churned closer and closer out in the Atlantic. Classes were cancelled for Monday since the eye was supposed to make landfall mid-morning, and the weather was forecasted to go downhill swiftly overnight as Faye approached. According to Carmen the shield around campus kept the storm surge out, but the full force of the wind and rain would still hit us. The Weather Channel had meteorologists stationed up and down the coast, but not on Bald Head. We'd have a front row seat anyway, so we didn't need to watch a meteorologist getting blown around on television to know what was going on outside. I had to admit I was a little bit giddy, having never been through a hurricane before. Dee had called an hour ago worried out of her mind. I couldn't explain the shield around campus, but I told her there was nothing to worry about, that the school had been there for centuries and we'd be fine. I thought I calmed her down, but I was still expecting several more hysterical calls tomorrow.

"What about this one?" Phoebe skipped out of her room. She'd been trying on dresses all night, parading around the living room for our opinions. Ian had, in fact, asked her to the Ball and after spending the entire day with him, she announced she was no longer creeped out by him. Finn still hadn't asked me, and I wasn't real optimistic that he planned to. Especially since he'd never even been to one. But maybe that was because he'd never had someone he wanted to ask. Who was I kidding? There was no way he'd gone through school without a girlfriend. Instead of picturing Finn with another girl, which inadvertently made my blood pressure rise, I tried to concentrate on Phoebe's newest dress. It wasn't my style, but somehow it worked for her. It was bright pink, strapless and very short. From the waistline it puffed out in several layers, giving it a very eighties look.

"Maybe if you were Cindy Lauper." Carmen wrinkled her nose at it and Willow smacked her arm and gave her the look. Carmen shrugged her shoulders innocently. "What? She said to be honest."

"She's right, it's a little much. Maybe something longer would be better..." Phoebe thought out loud and disappeared back into her bedroom.

"Did you guys hear that Keto was planning to visit Lorelei, but had to wait because of the hurricane?" Willow asked.

"Keto is who the Sirens are descended from, right?" I said, proud of myself for remembering something.

"Yep, and she's the leader of the Nereids now. And therefore the leader of both the Tydes and Sirens. So she's kind of a big deal," Carmen told me.

"We're doing a paper on Thetis and Kymo in History and one of the girls said that Thetis used to be the leader. What happened to her?"

"Willow, you want to take that one?" Carmen deflected. Willow looked up from her laptop.

"Well, Thetis could never get the Sirens and Tydes to stop warring with each other and it finally got to be too much for her, among other things. So she actually ended her own life. Keto took over after that because she was the second strongest Nereid, and Thetis's only child had been Achilles, who was killed forever ago in the Trojan War."

I read about Achilles in ninth grade, but the only thing I remembered was that his mother dipped him in the River Styx in order to make him immortal, by holding onto his heel. Therefore, his heel was the only part of him left unprotected. That very heel was how he was killed, which is where the term 'Achilles heel' came from. I definitely hadn't thought there was any truth behind it. Boy was I wrong.

"If Achilles's mom was Thetis, why wasn't he automatically immortal?" I asked Willow.

"His father was human. I can't remember his name, though."

"So how did Thetis kill herself if she was immortal?"

"There are ways," she answered cryptically.

"I heard that when Keto visited the House of Eudora in England, she was magnificent. She held a huge party and even talked to the students. That's almost unheard of," Phoebe said from her bedroom. "I can't wait to meet her."

"Isn't she known for being deceitful, though?" I asked. "That's what Kira said."

"That was just her reputation because of things that happened a long time ago. I think she's a great leader," Phoebe gushed, as she gave up trying on dresses and joined us.

"I don't like it. The Goddess of sea monsters (a.k.a. Sirens) should never be the leader of the Tydes. It's just not right, if you ask me." Carmen crossed her arms and glowered at Phoebe. "Our new Maven's a Siren, too. I don't trust her one bit."

"Priscilla?" I asked.

"Yep. She became Maven a year ago when Vanora left. She was transferred to another school. In Australia maybe? Something like that." Carmen shrugged.

"Was Vanora a Siren too?

"She was a Tyde. I don't know why they transferred her. Everyone loved her here because she actually cared about us. She was very involved with everything. Unlike Priscilla. She's always M.I.A.," Willow explained to me.

"Milking Innocent Animals?" Carmen sneered. Phoebe snorted and I almost spit out my Mountain Dew.

"No! Missing In Action!" Willow coughed; choking on her own laughter. We laughed so hard we started crying, and then spent the next hour coming up with everything else M.I.A. could possibly stand for.

After the giggles subsided, I followed Willow into the kitchen to make cookies. I grabbed a bowl from the cabinet and noticed my trace was shimmering and changing colors more than usual. That was the last thing I remembered before it happened. The world tilted and everything went black.

I stood on a long boardwalk facing the ocean. The first thing I noticed was the all-consuming darkness. The second thing I noticed was lightning flashing. From its brief sparks of light, I could see the turbulent waves mere feet from the boardwalk. A sign in the sand nearby was already halfway underwater. The blades of grass on the dunes were completely bent over in the wind and I could tell it was raining sideways, but I didn't feel either of them. A piece of bright orange tape caught my eye, so I kneeled down to get a closer look. There were four stakes connected by the orange tape; creating a square. I could see writing on the tape and tried to make out what it said. It read 'Bald Head Island Conservancy'. Something was being protected. I pushed the sand aside within the square and found small oval eggs. I picked one up and held it in my hand. Sea turtles. These were their nests. The water was getting higher by the minute and would inevitably swallow up the eggs; crushing them in the surf. There were more nests to my right. More eggs. I squinted down the beach, hoping to see some sign of civilization or help, but the only lights were far down the beach. I didn't have time to get help. I had to move them. Jumping down off the boardwalk, I found a spot between two large dunes and dug a wide hole big enough for all of the eggs. I pulled myself back up onto the boardwalk, just in time to see a colossal wave engulf the entire boardwalk, taking the eggs and orange tape below with it.

"NO!" I yelled and jumped into the water. I tried to grab the eggs I saw before they were stolen by the sea, but they were so slippery I couldn't hold onto them. One by one they were battered and smashed, then drug out into the ocean.

"NO!" I yelled. "Don't take them!" My heart broke over and over as if my own children were being carried out into the darkness, never to be seen again. All those turtles. All those babies...

"Stasia! Stasia, wake up!" My eyes flew open and I pushed whoever was hovering over me out of the way; clumsily getting to my feet. I ran into my room, found my flip flops and bolted out the door. I had to save them. I couldn't let all those babies die!

"Stasia! Where are you going? Wait!" I vaguely heard them calling after me as I took the stairs two at a time and made my way out the back door of Maren Hall. Flying down the boardwalk, I jumped onto the sand and sprinted up the beach as fast as I could. There were people behind me yelling something, but I wasn't listening. All I could think about were those eggs. The baby turtles. I couldn't let them die. After running for what felt like hours, I finally spotted it. Orange tape. I flopped down beside the first square and started digging. About ten whole eggs were cradled in the cool sand.

"Stasia! Please stop and tell us what's going on!" Willow tugged on my arm, but I shook her off and moved on to the next nest. One by one, I made sure the eggs were safe. At the last nest, my legs gave out from under me and I fell on the soft sand.

"Thank God they're safe!" I sighed with relief.

"You better have a damn good reason why we're running for our lives on the beach in the middle of the night!" Carmen sat down beside me, breathing hard.

"Stop being so dramatic, Carmen," Phoebe said. "Tell us what happened, Stasia." She rubbed my arm supportively.

"I saw them die. They washed away. All of them." Hot tears burned my eyes and I was helpless to stop them from spilling over. If these eggs were safe, what nests did I see get destroyed? According to the tape, I was on Bald Head. The boardwalk I had stood on was right above us. It had to be these eggs. I watched the waves rolling in to the shore and noticed how much bigger they had gotten since this afternoon. It hit me like a ton of bricks. The hurricane. I remembered the wind. The blinding rain. The rising water. I wasn't having a reverie or even a dream. I was seeing something that hadn't happened yet. I was seeing into the future. A new panic took over. "We have to move them! Before the hurricane comes!"

"But they're protected by the shield! They'll be fine." Carmen dismissed my worries.

"It doesn't extend this far. They'll wash away. I saw it happen."

"What do you mean, you saw it happen?" Phoebe's forehead scrunched in confusion.

Suddenly exhausted, I tried to explain. "When I blacked out….I had a vision. I saw it happen."

"Are you talking about foresight?" Carmen shook her head, unbelieving. "You have reveries, Stasia, not foresight. No descendant has ever had foresight."

"It couldn't have been a reverie, the hurricane isn't here yet!" I threw up my arms in frustration. "In my vision, the hurricane was here and it washed all of the eggs out to sea. We have to hurry!"

"Are you sure?" Carmen asked at me, still skeptical.

"I'm sure, Carmen." I closed my eyes, hoping to stop the tears, but that just made them come faster.

"We could move them closer to our beach where they'll be protected by the shield?" suggested Phoebe.

"You know it's illegal to touch the eggs," Willow countered. "We should call someone from the island to come and get them."

"There's no time. We have to move them now. It could be too late by the time we went and got someone. We don't have much time."

"She's right," Phoebe agreed with me. "We can't just leave them."

After several more convincing arguments, Willow gave in. We decided the best thing to do was go back to Maren and get our clothes baskets, pad them with towels and then transport the eggs to our protected beach. We took off running. I just hoped we made it back before it was too late.

Twenty minutes later, clothes baskets and blankets in hand, we split up and each made our way toward a different nest. The weather was quickly going downhill. The rain came down in sheets and persistent wind howled around us. Phoebe jogged down to the last nest. It was closest to the water, therefore more susceptible to the increasing waves. Carmen and Willow ran past me to the other nests.

I knelt down and gently removed each egg from the first nest and placed them into the clothes basket. I secured them with the blanket; preparing them for the walk back. I moved onto the next nest and did the same. The water had risen to my calves and the rain was blowing sideways. I could barely see Phoebe down the beach as she struggled in the much larger waves.

Carmen made her way over to me and set her basket down. "I got them all except for one, it slipped out of my hand!" she yelled over the wind. Her dark hair was plastered against her head and mascara ran down her cheeks.

"I just hope we can get them back without breaking any!" I called up to her. Willow joined us, having retrieved as many eggs as she could.

"Where's Phoebe?" she yelled.

"She was right over there!" Carmen leaned into the wind and pointed up the beach. The nest Phoebe had been emptying was now under at least three feet of water and her basket was floating away, held captive by the waves. I looked around frantically but didn't see her.

"Take the baskets!" I yelled to Carmen and Willow. "I'm going to find her!"

As I maneuvered my way down the beach, the water rose up to my thighs. I was having difficulty keeping my balance in the strong current, and the waves crashing into me were relentless. I could hardly see my hand in front of my face. This wasn't going to work! There was only one thing to do. I dove into the water.

Beneath the water, my vision magically cleared. Not sure how to find her, I tried to swim in a zigzag pattern; hoping she hadn't been swept out too far. The current was still strong, but I was able to counteract it pretty well and stay on course. I spotted something bright green blowing in the current just a couple of yards away and instinctively swam toward it. Phoebe's shirt. She was sinking. I wrapped my arms around her and kicked toward the surface.

"Phoebe!" I called out to her, but there was no response. "Phoebe!" Her lips were blue and her eyes had rolled back in her head. I struggled to keep her head above water and swim at the same time. I'd never had any lifeguard training and had no idea what I was doing. I kicked as hard as I could with my legs, but I knew I wasn't getting anywhere. The rain assaulted my face, making it hard to see where we were in relation to the beach. I could be swimming out to sea for all I knew. Wave after wave crashed over us, trying to pull her from my arms. I latched onto her as tightly as I could and shut my eyes. I'd controlled the waves once before, I could do it again. I concentrated on breathing and tried to slow my heart rate. Be calm. Be calm. Be calm. I tried to project my feelings into the water. Another wave crashed over us and we tumbled helplessly below the water. Somehow I held onto her shirt and was able to pull her back up to me as I kicked to the surface again. It wasn't working! She was going to drown out here in this God forsaken hurricane. Another wave hit us from the side; instantly ripping Phoebe away from me.

"Phoebe!!" I screamed, knowing she couldn't hear me. My eyes stayed locked on her green shirt as she was tossed around like a rag doll.

I lost sight of her as a wave crashed directly on top of me; pulling me under and slamming me against the ocean floor. The back of my head hit something solid, a sharp pain shot down my neck, and I decided I'd had enough. An inferno sparked deep within my soul and grew into an all-consuming, emblazoned fury. My vision sharpened immediately and a powerful sensation shot through my limbs; filling me with added strength and resolve. I pushed off the bottom with my feet and propelled myself back up to the surface easily. glared at the boiling ocean with hatred, like I was staring down an old opponent in the ring before a fight. It would NOT break my will and it would NOT take my friend. I unleashed what sounded like a roar filled with pain and anguish, and then brought both of my hands down on top of the water with such force it stung. Words flowed from my mouth with a ferocity I hadn't known I possessed.

"You will not take any lives tonight!! Give her back to me!! Now!!" I yelled at the top of my lungs and squeezed my eyes shut.

I hit bottom with a thud, which momentarily knocked the breath out of me. I looked down at the ocean floor. The ocean floor? I tried to get my bearings and realized the ocean had receded in about a five yard radius all around me, as if I was standing in an oversized bubble. The waves sloshed up against the sides, unable to reach me. Miraculously Phoebe was laying a couple of feet away from me, still unconscious and ashen. She had long gashes along her arms and legs. I lifted her up and tried to remember how long a person could go without oxygen before brain damage set in. I felt like we'd been in the water for hours. Surprisingly, as I walked towards shore, the protective bubble followed; allowing me to walk all the way up to the beach untouched by the waves. Finally on the sand, Carmen and Willow took Phoebe from me and silently stared at me wide-eyed. I hoped Carmen wouldn't ask me to show her how to do what I'd just done, because I had absolutely no idea.

Carmen gently rolled Phoebe onto her back and began trying to resuscitate her. Every ounce of energy left me and I collapsed on the sand. The stinging rain battered my body. I made an effort to catch my breath, but the wind just kept blowing sand in my face; clogging my nose and mouth. I shakily lifted myself up and crawled on all fours to where Phoebe lay on the sand. I tried to wipe off my face, but the sand had mixed with my tears and I only succeeded in scratching my skin. I gave up and fell down beside her. Willow cradled her head while Carmen performed CPR. I just looked on helplessly.

Time slowed as I silently watched the frenzy around Phoebe. Willow and Carmen were saying something to me, but all I heard was the howling of the wind. Something caught my eye through the rain a couple of yards away. Movement. I saw a figure retreating into the night, but I was too exhausted to worry about it. Instead I tried to concentrate on Phoebe's cold, limp hand in mine. I tried squeezing it and started talking to her.

170

"Phoebe, you gotta wake up," I whispered, as tears streamed down my sandy face. "Please wake up."

Carmen continued to administer CPR; rhythmically breathing into her mouth and pushing on her chest. Over and over and over. Suddenly, Willow opened her eyes and released Phoebe's head. Phoebe began coughing violently as water spewed from her mouth. My heart swelled, and Carmen turned her onto her side. She continued to cough for several more minutes as all the water was expelled from her lungs. Willow moved behind her and placed her palms on the cuts and bruises decorating her arms. She slowly opened her bloodshot eyes and focused on me. Her lips were returning to a normal color, but her face was still deathly pale. Her hair was twisted around her head and matted from the sand.

"Why are you all wet?" she asked weakly, and attempted a smile.

"You decided to go for a swim," I told her, and Carmen smothered her in a hug.

"Don't you ever do that to me again!" Tears of relief rolled down her cheeks.

Phoebe just smiled up at her. "And you said you weren't going to do mouth-to-mouth when you saved my life."

TWENTY

The next day I awakened to driving rain and screeching wind. What sleep I had gotten was restless. There were too many thoughts floating around in my head. After almost losing Phoebe none of us wanted her out of our sight, so we all piled into the living room. Phoebe was still asleep on the couch, Carmen was on the floor and Willow had curled up in the arm chair. How she slept like that was beyond me. I tiptoed to the balcony doors and peeked out through the blinds. The only thing visible was the rain blowing completely sideways. I looked down at the beach I couldn't see and hoped the turtle eggs were still safe. The four foot wide hole we had dug among the dunes put them within the safety of the shield, but I had no idea when they would hatch. I planned to check on them several times a day until then. I couldn't let them down. If it was the last thing I'd do, I was going to make sure they made it into the ocean unscathed.

The one tiny detail I'd spent all night coming to grips with was that I saw into the future. Not just saw, but actually experienced it. I was there. Between reveries and visions of the future, my true reality was becoming more and more complicated. During a reverie, I seemed cognizant of what was happening; I knew I was sleeping and where my body was. But in a vision, I had no idea that I'd randomly blacked out and subsequently travelled days or weeks in time. I only realized it after I woke up, which was slightly unsettling. What if I blacked out in the shower? Or swimming? And what if I did something stupid during one because I didn't know I was in a vision? What if I saw myself? Would I disrupt the space-time continuum, ending all life as we knew it? I had no idea how these things worked.

The other small technicality weighing on my mind was that if this last blackout had been a vision of the future, then the first one would have been too. That explained how I saw Nicolet's death a week before it actually happened. It also explained why Finn asked me if I had a reverie Friday. He had seen me earlier that day. It was just the 'me' from a week ago. So what I saw during my blackout at the party in Atlanta had been real. It just hadn't happened yet. Which meant Nicolet didn't kill herself. Which meant she really was murdered. And the only people that were there were Nicolet, the man who killed her, me and Finn.

A buzzing sound from my bedroom made me jump. A new text. From Finn. My heart jumped into my throat.

Finn: Meet me on the beach

Me: In a hurricane? I texted back. He was out of his mind.

Finn: Trust me

Me: You're crazy

Finn: About you

"Stasia?"

"Morning Sunshine!" I walked back into the living room. Phoebe propped herself up on the couch and stretched. She immediately clutched her throat in agony.

"Ow. I feel like somebody strangled me. It hurts to swallow." She leaned back and closed her eyes. My phone beeped from my bedroom.

"You need to rest, Phoebs, you went through a lot last night." I pulled the blanket back over her and smoothed her hair back. We had all painstakingly taken showers when we got back to our suite, but it was a little easier for Phoebe since she could command the sand to jump off of her body at will. Pretty cool if you ask me, considering I would never need an exfoliation ever again. I lost about ten layers of skin in the process of scrubbing it off. "Okay...but will you tell Carmen..." She was asleep again before she could finish. Willow shifted in her chair and mumbled something about bacon cupcakes. I chuckled and darted back into my bedroom.

He couldn't be serious.

Finn: See you in 5 min

That was three minutes ago. So he just assumed I was going to go along with his brilliant idea? He was probably out there, standing in the rain, soaking wet, waiting for me. I mean, I couldn't just leave him out there to catch pneumonia, right? Or what if he got hit by a piece of flying debris? It could happen. Damn. He was definitely going to pay for this one.

I searched my wardrobe for anything remotely waterproof, or at least water-resistant. I finally found a pair of black wind pants, a red ski jacket (maybe if I got washed away, the Coast Guard would be able to spot me), and pulled my hair up into my Georgia Bulldogs hat. It might be more fitting to wear Phoebe's wet suit and goggles, but this would have to do for now. I couldn't believe I was doing this. There weren't many people I'd venture out in a hurricane for. Against my better judgment, Finn was apparently becoming one of them. I tried to sneak through the living room, but my wind pants were anything but quiet. Just as I turned the doorknob, Willow turned in her chair again and I froze mid-step. Holding my breath, I clicked the door shut, turned around and walked right into Olivia and Cassie.

"Going for an early morning jog on the beach?" Olivia smirked, and they both laughed hysterically. Why couldn't they just say 'hey' and keep walking? "You might want an umbrella though, I heard it's supposed to rain."

"Oh my God, Olivia. Is that a zit on your chin? It must really hurt, it's huge!" I leaned in and stared at her face with mock horror.

"What?" Olivia looked accusingly at Cassie. "Why didn't you tell me I had Mt. Everest on my face before we went downstairs!" She pushed past her into their suite.

"Olivia, wait!" Cassie called after her. I hopped onto the elevator before the doors closed and smiled despite myself.

Down in the lobby, a group of girls were gathered around one of the large big screens watching a movie since the satellites were out. I felt their stares and heard the whispers in my direction as I walked by as nonchalantly as possible. Oh yeah, Finn was definitely going to pay for this.

I hesitated at the double doors. How was I supposed to find him in a hurricane? What if I got blown away? And worse, what if everyone saw me get blown away? It would be all over YouTube within minutes. I looked back at the lobby to see how many witnesses there were. Only twenty or so. Excellent. I turned back toward the door and almost had a heart attack. Finn stood on the other side snickering at me. I was glad he thought this was funny. Using all of my strength, I wrenched open the door. With the wind counteracting my movements, I had to slide out quickly before getting crushed.

"What part of 'go out into a hurricane' did you think was a good idea?" I glared up at Finn, but he had vanished. Something touched my hand and he reappeared right in front of me.

"How'd you do that?" I yelled, realizing a second too late it wasn't necessary. It was like we were back inside, except...we weren't. The rain had stopped and the deafening sound of the wind had disappeared as well. I was also sparkling.

"I've cloaked us." Finn grinned, proud of himself. "It's one of my abilities."

"You what?" He was sparkling as well. Instead of answering, his grin widened and he released my hand. He disappeared and I was back out in the hurricane. Rain battered my face and the sound of the wind screamed in my ears. Thankfully he grabbed my hand again.

"Don't do that!" I scolded him, as he tried not to laugh. "You think you're real funny, don't you? Just because you borrowed an invisibility cloak from Harry Potter doesn't mean you can just-" He let go of my hand again. I reached out through the blinding rain, hoping to grab him but my hands couldn't find anything solid. Knowing he was watching me, I put my hands on my hips and yelled over the wind. "If you don't cloak me right now, I'm going back inside and never speaking to you ever again!" I felt his hand in mine again and he reappeared, along with the protection of his cloak. Unfortunately I was already dripping wet.

"I just wanted to see if you'd melt," he explained with feigned innocence.

"I'm not that sweet," I retorted, and wiped the water off my face with my free hand. I tried my best to be mad at him. It was difficult, considering he was the embodiment of temptation and continually wreaked havoc on my emotions.

"Neither am I," he answered, a conspiring gleam in his eye. He pulled me down the steps and onto the beach. I noticed we weren't technically the ones sparkling, the cloak attached to us was. It was draped around us like a blanket, sticking to our bodies and keeping the rest of the world out. I glanced sideways at him, wondering how many times he'd cloaked himself around me without my knowledge. I thought about all those times I felt like I was being watched. I probably was.

Unlike me, his faded jeans and blue t-shirt were completely dry; his hair lay perfectly across his brow, also untouched by the hurricane. I felt like a wet dog in comparison. The sand beneath our bare feet was wet, but I was glad for that one connection to the beach. I couldn't feel the air or smell the water. Otherwise, I couldn't be sure we were really outside. The rain and wind whirled around the cloak, creating a misting effect that made it impossible to see. I felt like we were walking through a storm cloud.

"Where are we going?" I asked.

"Almost there." We could walk right off of a cliff and I'd never know the difference. Suddenly the sand beneath our feet turned to wooden planks. He turned to face me and the cloak blasted outward, encompassing a large gazebo. It hung down the sides of the roof and glittered all around us. It was awe-inspiring.

"Wow." I spun in a circle, taking it all in. "How do you do that?"

"I just will it to be." He shrugged his shoulders like it was no big deal. "As long as we're under the cloak, no one else can hear or see us." I didn't miss the ghost of a smile that crossed his lips. Unfortunately a twinge of fear overshadowed my sense of adventure. I'd been cloaked by a possible murderer. In the middle of a hurricane. The possible 'accidents' that could happen to cause my death were endless. I pushed down my worries and put on a face of confidence.

"So now that you've got me here, what do you intend to do with me?" I looked around, curiously. "And where have you taken me?"

"To a gazebo," he responded slyly; watching me carefully. He picked up a small wooden box similar to Kira's, but this one looked much older. The wood was weathered and smooth, with dark engravings covering its top and sides.

"I have something for you." From the box, he pulled out a small blue velvet pouch and handed it to me. Surprised, I held it gingerly and looked at him for the meaning behind it. He gazed back at me with amusement.

"It's inside the bag." He grinned at me. With shaking fingers, I untied the ribbon and pulled the top of the bag open. I reached inside and pulled out the most beautiful necklace I'd ever seen. The delicate chain was black in color; a dark metal I didn't recognize. From the chain hung a large oval pendant of the same metal, made up of swirls and loops that encased an oval blue-green colored gemstone.

"It's an aquamarine," he told me in almost a whisper. The beauty of it illuminated the gazebo with a brilliance I felt deep down in my heart. As I placed it in my hand to get a better look, my skin tingled under its weight. It had a very gothic quality to it, and I could tell it was as old as the box it came in.

"Finn." Completely at a loss for words, all I could do was stare at it. "This is....I can't take this."

"Of course you can. It belongs to you now." He peered at me with curiosity. "Plus, it matches your dress."

"My dress?" Last time I checked I didn't have on a dress.

"The one you're going to wear to the Ball." I smiled as I realized what he was saying.

"Are you asking me to the Cimmerian Shade Ball, Finn?"

He took a step toward me, eyes never leaving mine. "Are you saying you'll go with me, Stasia?"

"I heard you don't go to those kinds of things," I challenged him.

"I don't." He moved even closer to me, gently taking the necklace and placing it back in the velvet bag. Pulling the ribbon closed, he dropped it into the pocket of my wind pants. His hand grazed my leg; sending sparks all the way down to my feet. Holding my gaze, he pulled the hat off my head and brushed my wet hair back from my shoulders. I waited for his fingers to get caught in the mass of tangles I knew had been created by the wind, but thankfully that didn't happen. The thought brought on a nervous smile and he grinned back at me. His eyes dropped to my lips, and when they met mine again they were stormy and filled with white hot desire. He took my hand.

"Will you go to the Cimmerian Shade Ball with me, Anastasia?" he asked in a low voice.

"Yes," I breathed, lost completely in his closeness. A voice in the back of my head reassured me that if he was asking me to the Ball, he didn't plan on ending my life...which was a plus. He smiled, picked me up and spun me around. I placed my hands on either side of his cheeks and slowly leaned down to give him a kiss. It was just a light peck, but his soft lips ignited a fire inside me. Still holding me, he sat down on the wooden bench of the gazebo. I straddled him as he leaned back against the railing and pulled me close. He lightly kissed the tender skin below my ear, which sent a frenzy of sensations through my body. He made his way up my chin and toward my mouth. I closed my eyes, anticipating a kiss that didn't come.

I opened my eyes to see that his were filled with a painful conflict I didn't understand. I touched his cheek and watched as the pain slowly receded. The raw vulnerability I saw in his eyes would haunt me forever. It was a look I knew well, because it was one I'd seen many times in my own reflection. When all of your defenses were stripped away, the only thing left was surrender. Only then could you see the true size of the burden a person carried. Only then could you see the toll it had taken on their soul. His silent pleas broke my heart.

"You don't have to be strong all the time, Finn." I don't know why, but I felt it was what he needed to hear. His eyes searched mine and he smiled, and I felt the special bond we already shared growing stronger with each passing moment. With a slowness that threatened to make the fire inside me explode, he kissed me. What started out as slow and gentle quickly turned into something more urgent and powerful. A low moan sounded from deep within him and he unzipped my jacket; pushing it down and off my arms. I felt his hand at the small of my back; the tips of his fingers dangerously low as his other hand pulled the strap of my tank top off my shoulder. With a hunger that was almost tangible, he ran his lips along my collarbone and shoulder; licking the same spot and sending waves of pleasure through me.

Bringing his mouth to mine, I gently kissed first his bottom lip, then the top. He bit my lip lightly and gave it a tug, then began kissing me in earnest again. A longing so strong took hold of me and all I could do was feel. I ran my fingers through his soft hair and clutched a handful, eagerly holding his lips to mine. He ran his hands up my thighs, gripped my waist, and slid my body closer; pressing me against him. I felt his body tense and he broke our kiss and leaned his forehead against mine; leaving both of us breathing hard. He slowly opened his eyes.

"You have no idea what you do to me," he said as he looked up at me with restraint. He stood and lowered me to my feet in front of him. He straightened, took both my hands with a slight smirk, and suddenly looked very regal. He extended his arms and stepped back as if dancing; bringing me back towards him and lifting one hand above my head to spin me around. He caught my waist awkwardly and dipped me dramatically. The blood rushed to my head and a giggle escaped my lips.

"If we have to actually dance at the Ball, you're in big trouble." I laughed at him.

He stood me upright, bowed, and with a horrible French/English accent grinned up at me. "Right you are, mademoiselle."

Twenty-one

"Yep, just as I suspected." Carmen placed her palm on my forehead. "Two degrees above crazy."

Although Finn cloaked me all the way back to the dorm, the damage to my clothes and hair had been done. I heard a fork drop and several gasps when I walked back into our suite. Their breakfast plates were immediately abandoned as Carmen started in on a game of twenty questions and Willow practically threw me in the shower, mumbling something about me getting sick. Once in dry clothes, I found a blanket and made myself a nice cozy spot on the couch beside Phoebe.

"I hope he had a good reason for dragging you out in the middle of a hurricane!" Willow scowled at me. "He needs a lesson in common sense."

"Well, if you call asking me to the Ball and giving me a necklace a good reason, than I guess he did." I grinned and heard Phoebe squeal beside me. She jumped across the couch and wrapped her arms around me.

"We get to go together! We have to find dresses! Oh my God, this is going to be so much fun! We can go shopping tomorrow if the hurricane's gone, and I need to find some jewelry too-"

"Calm down, Cinderella. You don't even know if she said yes..." Carmen interrupted her. They looked at me in anticipation.

"Well, duh." I rolled my eyes and Phoebe squealed again. "But look what he gave me. Isn't it the most gorgeous thing you've ever seen?" I pulled the necklace out of its velvet bag.

"Does he have any cute brothers?" Carmen's face lit up.

"Stasia, that is so romantic," Phoebe gushed. "I mean, he gave you a necklace and asked you out in the middle of a hurricane!"

"I'm seriously beginning to worry about you guys." Willow sighed from the armchair and looked up from her laptop with discord. "Being asked out in the middle of a hurricane is not romantic. It's totally reckless and irresponsible."

"And totally hot," added Carmen. "Let me see that necklace"

She turned it over in her hand a couple times. "It looks old. Does it belong to somebody in his family?" she asked.

"I don't know. All he said is that it belongs to me now." I contemplated her question. It seemed ludicrous to think he'd given me something of that much value. I'd been seeing him for three years in my dreams, but we just officially met less than two weeks ago.

"I got it!" Willow bounced in her chair and pointed at her laptop screen. Before we could ask her what she was talking about, she bolted into her bedroom. She came back with a notebook and the piece of paper that belonged to Nicolet; rolling it out flat on the coffee table.

"It's written in an early form of the Greek language," she explained to us, "so all I have to do is find a website to tell me exactly how early...." She began writing furiously, looking from the screen to her notebook and back again.

"Oh, good. One less thing for me to figure out." Carmen pointed at all of us. "Start saving up your money, 'cause you'll be paying for my meal at the nicest restaurant on the east coast." She grinned and turned her attention back to the necklace. "What kind of stone is this?"

"It's an aquamarine. He told me before that it stands for courage and...." My breath caught and I looked up. "...foresight."

"Do you think he knows you might have....?" Phoebe blinked at me.

"I never told him. I mean, I just figured it out last night. How could he possibly know?"

"Maybe it's just a coincidence?" Carmen suggested. "I mean, we don't know for sure you actually have foresight." She shrugged her shoulders.

"That's a really big coincidence, if you ask me," Phoebe commented as she peeked over Willow's shoulder. I leaned back on the couch; my mind reeling. Even if no one else believed me, I knew it was true. I knew I had seen into the future. Twice. Was it possible that Finn knew it too? He knew I could breathe underwater, so it wouldn't be a long shot. How could he know so much about me? Who was he?

The next day as storm clouds gave way to partly cloudy skies, we decided it would be the perfect day for dress shopping since classes were cancelled again. Although the storm surge was prevented, the wind still caused damage to trees and anything else not bolted down. While the maintenance crews cleaned up the campus, we took the ferry to the mainland. We piled into Carmen's black Audi and headed to some boutiques Carmen knew of in Wilmington. I honestly didn't know what I was looking for since I'd never been to a Ball. I'd never been to the prom either, but I had a feeling the Cimmerian Shade Ball would be absolutely nothing like the dances back home. Considering that back in Atlanta, kids only stayed at the dances as long as their buzz lasted, which ended up being about thirty minutes. Then everyone left to go to the after party, which was the real event of the evening. The actual dance was more of pit stop and an excuse to get dressed up before the real fun began. Thanks to Laura Beth I wasn't usually invited to the after parties, so more often than not I didn't bother going to the dance either. Why get all dressed up for nothing?

But this was completely different. This wasn't some high school dance with punch and streamers. It was a Ball. This was an exclusive event that had been held for countless generations. I wanted to look beautiful. Most importantly, I wanted to feel beautiful. I wasn't just a normal human girl anymore; I was a descendant of the Nereids. A Tyde. I was part of a legacy that was established centuries ago, and I was finished hiding in the shadows, simply surviving. I was ready to live the life I deserved to live. After everything I'd been through, I was ready to be happy.

We had gone to several boutiques before we realized that unless we wanted a wedding dress or a bridesmaid dress, we'd have to look elsewhere. After we stopped at Panera Bread for lunch, we decided to go to a shop Carmen heard about that offered a more eclectic selection of gowns. After driving to an outlying swampy area, we sat in Carmen's car and stared up at a daunting Victorian manor. It was surrounded by live oak trees with Spanish moss draped on their branches and two sprawling cemeteries flanking the house. The house itself had been neglected over the years and showed signs of wear. The paint was peeling off of the exterior, and several black shutters hung from their hinges. The wraparound porch had warped in several places; giving it a wavy appearance.

"Are you sure about this, Carmen?" Willow hesitated. Carmen shrugged her shoulders and looked out at the tombstones warily.

"I heard she's off her rocker, but she makes rockin' dresses." She laughed at her own joke.

"I have a bad feeling some of her customers ended up with a permanent address in her cemeteries." Phoebe scrunched up her nose.

"You guys are so dramatic." I sighed and opened the car door. "We've got her outnumbered four to one." My stomach was a little queasy with nerves, but I tried hard not to let on.

"All I'm saying is that if she comes at me with scissors or a butcher knife, I'm out." Phoebe put her hands up. As we walked down the winding sidewalk toward the house, I noticed a sign above the door that simply read "Seamstress." It reminded me of an old western town with signs above the doors that just read 'Blacksmith' or 'General Store'. The old weathered tombstones near the house added to the nostalgic feel. Before I could knock, the door swung open.

A demure woman in her early forties with long, straight black hair and large blue eyes stepped out of the door to greet us. She wore a dark red dress with a black lace overlay across the bodice, went lent her a slightly medieval look. It hung on her thin figure and pooled down at her feet. Twenty or thirty bracelets hung on both of her arms and a large red stone hung from a long necklace. She was strikingly beautiful.

"Hello." She gave us a warm smile. "May I help you girls with something today?"

"Um, we were hoping to look at some dresses?" Phoebe squeaked.

"Of course, of course." She stepped aside and gestured for us to come in. "My name is Natasha. The dresses are upstairs, so feel free to go on up and take a look.

185

I'll join you shortly." I followed her eyes to a wide antique staircase. Above it, a gothic-looking chandelier with candles hung precariously. The interior of the house had been given more attention than the exterior, but I could tell nothing had been changed from the original house. Expansive wool rugs covered the hardwood floors, and faded black and white photographs watched us from the walls as we passed by. If I didn't know any better, I'd say we had just arrived in a different era. We made our way up the creaking stairs as she disappeared into a room I assumed was the kitchen.

"Would you girls like some tea?" she called from below. I could tell Phoebe was trying to decide if she was going to poison us or chop us up for a stew.

"Sure, that'd be great!" Willow called back. She shrugged when Phoebe gave her a harsh look.

"If we all croak, it's your fault," she said in a hushed voice.

At the top of the stairs, a very shabby-chic dress shop stretched out before us. However, unlike the trendy décor crafted in mass warehouses, this was the real deal. An antique postmaster's desk greeted us at the entrance; holding a vintage cash register that probably still worked. Beside the cash register was a modern credit card machine. Which was a plus, since that's what I'd be using to pay for my dress. An old Singer sewing table covered in fabric, pins, measuring tape and spools of thread took up one corner. Lace curtains hung from each of the four square windows, and a romantic white chandelier hung from the ceiling with crystals raining down from the eight arms. Large, white ornate iron racks stood throughout the room holding an arrangement of different gowns. Each dress was a work of art in its own right; each one intricately sewn together shining with its own individual personality and character.

"Stasia!" Phoebe whispered at me.

"Why are we whispering?" I whispered back.

"I don't know!" she giggled. She held up a strapless gown made up of layer upon layer of silk cascading down to the floor. The bodice was cream colored with an empire waist, accentuated by a silver band. As the fabric floated to the floor, flames of teal, purple and orange danced up from the bottom. I pointed to a small door labeled 'Fitting Room' and she entered hesitantly. I turned and walked right into Natasha.

"Oh! I'm sorry!"

"Do not fret child, it's alright," she assured me, and then gazed at me almost lovingly. "What is your name, dear?"

"Stasia." She continued to stare at me and her blue eyes darkened; taking on an otherworldly quality.

"Dangerous waters await you, but destiny breathes within you. You shine with a pure beauty all your own."

"Um, thank you," I mumbled, unsure of how to respond to that.

She just smiled and placed the tray of glasses down on a small sitting table.

"Help yourselves to the tea, girls. It's a new herbal recipe I've created." I heard Phoebe mumble something about six feet under in the fitting room and hoped Natasha didn't hear it. If she did, she didn't show it. She glided over to the sewing table and began searching through a rack of dresses.

"Ta-da!" No longer whispering, Phoebe pranced out of the fitting room and twirled around. Accentuating her tiny waist, the different layers of fabric flowed out elegantly to the floor from the silver band. As the cream changed to teal, orange and purple, it reminded me of an exotic bird. She looked exquisite.

"It's beautiful!" Willow clasped her hands together.

"It looks like it was made for you, Phoebs!" I exclaimed, and Carmen shook her head in agreement.

187

"I am so getting this. It's perfect!" Phoebe twirled around again and grinned from ear to ear. "Did you find one yet?" She asked me.

"Not yet."

"I believe you'll find your taste matches this particular dress." I whirled around at the extreme closeness of her voice. Natasha stood mere inches from me, holding a bunch of fabric I assumed was a gown. Her eyes watched me knowingly and I began to get slightly uncomfortable as she continued to stare at me with a wide, almost proud smile on her face.

I took the dress and high-tailed it to the fitting room.

I carefully stepped into the dress and zipped the back up as far as I could. I twisted to see my reflection in the mirror. The woman looking back at me caught me off guard. She was...beautiful. The dress itself began over one shoulder and swooped down to cover my chest as it followed the curves of my body perfectly; down my waist and flaring out mid-thigh. Ironically the tag said this particular style was called 'mermaid'. The bright teal color matched my eyes perfectly, and gave the impression I was much tanner than I really was. It wasn't quite a teal though, more of a...

"Aquamarine," I whispered, as a shiver ran down my spine. An intricate swooping design embroidered in black started at the shoulder; snaking across the top of the dress and around to the back as it curved back in front, ending where the dress split mid-thigh. Black lace peeked out of the slit, which enhanced the gothic mood of the dress. It was as if it had been made to match the necklace Finn gave me. How could he have known? I heard Phoebe outside the door.

"You gonna hog it all for yourself or let the rest of us see it, too?" she teased me. I took one last look, unlatched the door and walked out. After a full minute of everyone gawking at me wide-eyed, Willow finally broke the silence.

"Wow. Stasia," she stared at me. "It's so...you."

"Damn. Finn isn't going to be able to keep his hands off you!" Carmen whistled and flashed a sinister grin. I looked down at the dress and smiled. It was perfect.

"I'll take it," I told Natasha.

"I had a feeling you might. It looks absolutely ravishing on you." She smiled approvingly and turned back to her sewing table.

After some tea (void of poison), we paid for our dresses and headed for the door where Natasha shook each of our hands. I noticed she held onto mine a second too long, and studied my trace. I wondered if she knew what she was looking at.

"If you girls need anything at all, let me know. And come back any time. I don't get many visitors, so it's always a treat." We made our way down the front steps.

"Oh, and girls?" Phoebe and I turned. "Enjoy the meteor shower. I hear it's quite lovely." She smiled with a gleam in her eye. Goose bumps popped up on my arms. Not once had we mentioned the Ball.

With that harrowing conversation, Phoebe practically slid over the hood of Carmen's car to get to the passenger door and away from Natasha.

"Well that wasn't creepy at all..." Carmen said sarcastically as she put the car in reverse. Natasha remained on the porch as we pulled out of the driveway. I turned to look at her one last time, but she had vanished.

Twenty Two

"This might be difficult," Phoebe said as she chewed on her fingernails, deep in thought. The sand before us was flat and unassuming. Unfortunately we hadn't marked the new nest, so it was going to be a challenge to find them without digging up the entire beach. Then again, perhaps the eggs could find me instead. I dropped to my knees and skimmed my hand atop the sand to see if I could somehow sense the hatchlings. I inched forward carefully and continued to sweep my hand back and forth. When something close to static electricity shocked my pinky finger, I stopped and started moving my hand back over that same place. More tiny electrical currents shot into my fingers and I beamed up at Phoebe with excitement.

"I think I found them!" I started digging carefully through the sand to uncover them.

"Wait, I have a better way." Phoebe dropped to her knees, too. She expertly held her hands above the nest and the sand retreated; gently uncovering the eggs. We leaned over to get a better look and saw that they appeared perfectly intact, except for several small cracks. There was no movement or signs of life, but they weren't broken. That was all we could hope for at this point.

Phoebe placed a hand on my shoulder. "I think they're gonna be just fine."

"I wish we could tell if they're still alive." I looked on as Phoebe held her palms above the nest and commanded the sand to fill it back in. We inspected Phoebe's work and decided you'd never know we had been there. And you definitely couldn't tell there was a nest of sea turtle eggs beneath the sand. We brushed our legs off and returned to Maren.

A sliver of moonlight streaming in the window spotlighted my new dress; giving it a stage to shine. Lying in bed, I turned onto my side to admire it. The material shimmered as it swayed from the blowing vent on the floor, and it seemed to have a life all its own. The black lace added an element of mystery to the otherwise vibrant dress, and the embroidered design drew your attention down the length of it. I couldn't believe I'd be wearing it to an official Ball in a couple of days.

A slight chill swirled around me. I reached down to pull up the comforter, but my hands didn't find it. The other issue was that my bed had disappeared. I was standing back on the wide platform surrounded by water. I felt the breeze at my back and looked over my shoulder. My heels were only an inch from the edge of the platform. Water churned at least ten stories below me; sloshing up against one of the large pylons. I forced my feet forward and tried to put as much distance between myself and certain death as quickly as possible. I'd have to work on where I appeared in these reveries. A ten story fall was not tempting whatsoever. The platform looked exactly as it had the last time I was there, with the exception of blood splatters everywhere. There was a large circle drawn in the middle as if it was a landing pad. Why would there be a landing pad out in the middle of the ocean?

A two story tower stood at one corner with a rotating light at the top that resembled a small lighthouse. With no artificial light for miles, I was surprised at how many stars I could see. I didn't know that many stars even existed. I took a seat and leaned back on my elbows. The chill of the platform brought out goose bumps on my legs. I was dressed in what I wore to bed, which happened to be thin shorts and an even thinner tank top. No wonder I was freezing! I'd have to start wearing warmer clothes to bed. I shrugged and turned my attention back to the sky. I easily located the constellations I was used to seeing, like the big dipper or Orion's belt, but the impressive amount of additional stars distracted me from their shapes. I raised my hand to the sky, closed one eye and connected the dots of Orion with my finger. I could actually make out his entire body and bow. I imagined what it would have been like long ago when people believed the Gods were depicted in the stars. From my spot on the platform, I could see why they were so preoccupied with the heavens.

A cough from the other side of the platform had me jumping to my feet. With my eyes adjusted to the darkness, I could see someone sitting against the wall of the tower, arms resting on their knees, head down. I crept forward. As I got closer I saw something wrapped around his hands with several strips of fabric hanging from them. Gloves.

"Finn?" I whispered. The person's head snapped up at my voice. He stood and walked towards me slowly, as if every movement brought excruciating pain. He wore yellow basketball shorts and no shirt. The light from the stars reflected on his strong torso and I forced myself not to drool.

"Why are you here?" he asked harshly. I closed the distance between us and touched his shoulder, but he jerked away; not facing me.

"I...I think I'm having a reverie. I don't know how I got here," I stumbled over my words.

"You should leave." The ice in his voice cut deep and I instantly got defensive.

"It's not like I can control these things, Finn! I can't help when and where I show up." When he reluctantly turned towards me, his eyes fell to his feet and an exhausted-sounding sigh left his body. I was shocked by what I saw. His left cheek was bloody, a deep gash ran from his ear to his collarbone, and his left shoulder was bruised with another large cut in his bicep. Although the trace on his forearm had dulled slightly, it remained untouched. I reached out to him but he shrank away.

"What happened to you?" I asked gingerly.

"Nothing." He tried to turn away from me again, but I grabbed both of his hands and held him firmly in front of me. The roughness of the leather wrapped around them rubbed against my palms and reminded me of how very male he was. He gave off a distinct aura of conviction and strength that made my knees weak.

"This doesn't look like nothing. Who did this to you?"

"This time it was Cage and Ricker." He shook his head and looked down. Then more so to himself than me, he muttered, "I've got to figure this out. I'm running out of time."

"This time? Who are Cage and Ricker?"

"They're Sons too," he replied, "and my roommates."

"What? Why would they do this to you?" I could feel my anger rising.

"They're helping me," he dropped his head and sighed.

"I don't get it, Finn. How is fighting with you helping you?"

"This doesn't concern you, Stasia," he growled at me, clearly frustrated. "It's not something you need to know about yet."

"Doesn't concern me? It's way too late for that." I took a step toward him. "I don't like seeing you like this."

"Which is why you should leave." I heard the anguish in his voice.

"No. I care about you, Finn. I can handle whatever this is." He looked back at me with stubbornness, then finally resignation. His shoulders sagged.

"You don't know that. You can't know that. It's not up to you-" As if he'd said too much, he clamped his mouth shut and closed his eyes. I wrapped my arms around him and laid my head against his firm chest. The tension in his muscles made it feel like I was hugging a brick wall. After a moment of hesitation, his body relaxed and his breathing slowed. My gaze drifted to his hurt shoulder and I noticed the bruises had already receded. Pulling out of his arms, I inspected the gashes that were on his arm and neck. The gaping holes had closed and were beginning to turn a dark pink as his skin healed and renewed itself. I looked to his face next. His cheek was no longer swollen and the blood I saw was completely gone. I searched his eyes and he attempted a grin.

"Another ability," he replied simply.

"The other time I saw you here...that's why you were completely healed the next day. No wonder..." I remembered the double axe. The question spilled from my lips before I could stop it. "Did you kill him?" This brought on a full smile and he laughed.

"What do you think?" he raised an eyebrow. I stared at him in disbelief, but he just grinned.

"Fortunately for Ian, I let him live," he replied smugly.

"Ian? That's who you were fighting?"

"Not fighting. Preparing," he corrected me.

"Did you help kill Nicolet?" Might as well throw out all the questions on my mind.

"No."

"But you were there. Why haven't you told anyone what we saw? That she was murdered?"

"Why haven't you?"

"'Cause no one would believe me."

"Exactly."

We walked around the periphery of the platform. "But I don't want to talk about who I've killed and who I haven't killed." I looked up at him and tried to figure out if he was kidding as chills ran down my spine, but his face told me nothing. Our conversation only confused me more. We reached the edge and I hesitantly peered down at the water below. Finn sat down with ease and let his feet dangle. He held out his hand for me to sit next to him. My heart was beating out of my chest and I was having trouble breathing, but I wasn't going to let him see my fear. I painstakingly lowered myself down and dangled my legs over the side, too. My breath came out ragged and I tried to calm my nerves. I rubbed my arms as a sudden blast of cold air hit me. My barely-there tank top didn't do much to keep me warm. Finn moved closer to me and put his arm around me.

"The clothes I sleep in aren't really made for midnight trips out at sea," I muttered.

His eyes moved over my body, then back up to meet mine as he grinned at me playfully. "I gotta tell you, I've always liked your choice of clothing during your nighttime reveries."

"You mean the lack of clothing?" I raised an eyebrow at him.

"Maybe." He dropped his head and looked up at me pretending to be bashful; his wicked smile telling me what he was really thinking.

"From now on, I'm wearing a muu muu to bed." I crossed my arms.

"You're going to wear a cow to bed?" Finn scrunched his nose at me; making me giggle.

"No! You've never heard of a muu muu?" He shook his head. "It's one of those long night gowns that grandmas like to wear."

"I don't care if you wear a muu muu or a tutu, you'll still be beautiful."

"That's the sweetest thing anyone's ever said to me," I joked with him. "And you get extra points for making it rhyme."

"I write love poems when I'm not rapping. It comes naturally." He winked at me.

"If you start rapping, I promise you I'll throw myself off this platform."

"Well we can't have that. I'd have to jump in after you, and these aren't my swim trunks. Lucky for us, I don't rap on days that end in Y." Finn laughed, and then asked, "So, do you know where we are?"

I looked from side to side. "In the middle of the ocean?"

"Almost." In a tour guide voice, he announced, "You are sitting on the official Frying Pan Shoals Light Station."

"Frying Pan?" I looked up at him skeptically.

"Hey, I wasn't the one who came up with it. Don't ask me why they named it after something you cook eggs in. All I know is that it's a type of lighthouse to warn ships about the Frying Pan Shoals sticking out from the Cape." I looked out at the water, trying to see any sign of light in the distance.

"So, this is off the coast of Bald Head?" I continued squinting but didn't see anything.

"That's right. The shoals are really just mounds of sand that got built up by the currents of the Atlantic running into the current of the Cape Fear River as it emptied into it. They extend at least twenty miles out into the ocean. Hundreds of ships have run aground and sunk, so the Coast Guard built the station and they let us use it as long as we maintain the tower and the inside."

"The inside?"

"We're actually on top of the light station. The light tower is over there, of course," he pointed to the tower on the opposite corner, "but the actual station is more like a really big square house. We're just sitting on the roof. To get back down into the station you go through the tower."

"Really? I just thought this was a landing pad or a platform."

"The Sons stay here a lot. Right below us are several living rooms, kitchens, and rooms to sleep in. This is also where the Ball will be held this weekend."

"Wow." I gazed up at the stars above. "I love it. It's so peaceful out here."

"That's why I come here so much. Being surrounded by only water, I feel more like myself than anywhere else. But I could always tell something was still missing for me." He looked at me with a steadiness that increased my heart beat. "Now I know that something," he leaned closer to me, "was you."

My entire body warmed at his words. "I change my mind. That was the sweetest thing anyone's ever said to me." He caught a stray hair and tucked it behind my ear. In the distance I heard a low melody. It was different from the melody we had heard in the ocean, but similar at the same time.

"Do you hear that?" I asked him.

He tilted his head, listening too, but shook his head. "Nope, I don't hear anything."

"It's a song…" I looked up at him, but instantly became disoriented as the platform below me changed to sheets and a wall stood where Finn had sat two seconds before. My bedroom.

"No!" I put my head in my hands. "You have got to be kidding me. Ugh!" I fell back; hitting my pillow in a cloud of disappointment. I'd be perfectly happy staying with Finn at the light station until dawn, but obviously my body had other plans. I had to figure out how to control these reveries. I closed my eyes and opened them just as quickly when I realized I still heard the melody, only it was much louder. I felt an odd pull to go to the beach. Fine time for the sea to be calling to me. Two o'clock in the morning wasn't really conducive to playing in the waves. But something about this pull was different. I listened carefully to the melody again and concentrated on what the pull felt like. It hit me like a ton of bricks. I launched out of bed and threw on some yoga pants and a long sleeve t-shirt.

I made it to the beach in record time, somehow not waking anyone up along the way. The breeze off the ocean was still slightly chilly, but my additional clothing did wonders. The sand above the nest was as smooth and flat as earlier, so I got down on my hands and knees and found the nest quickly when I felt the spark of electricity. Right before I began to dig, I saw movement. A tiny section of sand shifted ever so slightly and then moved back the other way. A tiny head the size of my thumb peeked up out of the sand at me. The second it saw me it disappeared. I held my breath, and patiently awaited its reappearance. Then the sand began to move as multiple tiny heads popped out. One made a sound resembling a peep and their little flippers came to life as they pulled themselves on top of the sand. They were no bigger than my hand and already had beautifully intricate shells. In the shadow of the night they blended in well, only a couple of shades darker than the sand.

None of them sprinted to the ocean like I expected them to. They just shuffled around me, running into each other as well as my legs. Each time one touched me I felt the same small spark of electricity, only slightly stronger. It almost tickled. Several tried to pull themselves up onto my calves, with no luck. I held out my hand to one in particular and it pushed its way onto my palm. I gently rubbed its shell. It was rough to the touch, but still slightly malleable.

A small spark continued to pulse in my hand; raising the hair on my arms. A strong belonging overwhelmed me as I watched them scurrying in the sand. It was like seeing a beloved relative for the first time in years. I felt surrounded by acceptance and tears sprang to my eyes as I watched the hatchlings began to circle me almost as their elders had in the ocean last week. Wishing to be closer to them, I set down the one in my hand and slowly lowered down on my stomach, giving them time to move out of the way so I didn't crush any. I rested my chin on my hands and watched as they climbed over each other and tried to climb on me. I picked up another hatchling and put it in my palm. It looked at me briefly and clumsily made its way up my arm to my shoulder. I giggled as it padded up the back of my neck and attempted to hide in my hair. I carefully reached back and placed it back down on the sand. It immediately started crawling over one of its siblings for no apparent reason. Their energy was contagious and I lay like that for a long time just enjoying their company.

Eventually growing tired and remembering classes started back tomorrow, I lifted myself back up onto my knees. As if realizing my departure, the hatchlings began to dig back into their nest. One by one they disappeared, throwing sand over themselves with their flippers.

"Sweet dreams," I whispered. Somehow in the back of my mind I knew that when night fell again, they would be strong enough and feel safe enough to make their first monumental journey. And I was going to be there to watch over them as they did.

TWENTY-THREE

Puffy eyed and groggy, I threw on some khaki shorts and a light pink tank top the next morning. During the walk to our first class, Carmen and Willow chatted about the twenty drunken texts Carmen had received from Logan last night. Apparently, the first ten were consisted of begging and apologies, while the last ten were about how she was missing out on the best thing that could have happened to her. As you might expect, Carmen told him to go screw himself.

After bordering on comatose in my first two classes, I drank a Mountain Dew, hoping it would do the trick. After poking myself with a pencil for forty-five minutes to stay awake in third period, we met for the last fifteen minutes to discuss our history paper and I heard a couple more reasons to dislike Logan.

"Either you're in deep thought or you're about to pass out." Maya peered at me from across the table as she sipped her coffee. I looked up from my blank paper.

"I'm just really tired." I yawned and rubbed my eyes.

"Were you at that party at Rostrum?" Lyric asked. "I heard it was pretty crazy."

"I was." Lexi twirled a lock of her strawberry hair and eyed me suspiciously. "But I didn't see you there. Of course, I was too busy fighting Logan off. He was trying to hook up, but he was so drunk he couldn't even walk." She blew a bubble with the gum in her mouth and shrugged.

"I thought he was seeing somebody?" Lyric asked.

Lexi leaned forward dramatically. "I heard he broke it off with that girl Carmen because she's slept with half of the Tritons on campus."

"That's not true." I rubbed my forehead. My head hurt. And Lexi's gossip wasn't helping. "She broke it off with him because he's an asshole." Carmen could have slept with the whole school and I wouldn't have known, but that didn't matter. I wasn't going to let her talk crap about my friend.

"He's a player anyway. You shouldn't mess with that, girl." Maya shook her head at Lexi.

"Whatever," Lexi rolled her eyes. "Nobody said I want to marry the kid. What's wrong with having a little fun?" She licked her lips and I wanted to smack some sense into her, but I settled for tuning her out instead.

Willow and I met Carmen and Phoebe for lunch at the Hole, but all I could do was stare at the piece of pizza in front of me. The sun was beating down on me, draining what little energy I did have. I took a long drink of my water.

"You okay, Stasia?" Carmen asked me, squinting into the sun.

"Yeah, I'm good. Just tired."

"You haven't even touched your food." Willow held out her turkey sub. "You want some of my sub?"

"No that's okay; I just need a minute-" Willow started swirling in front of me, along with everything else.

Where were my sunglasses? The sun was burning the back of my eyelids, so I squeezed them shut a little tighter. The good news was that the sand beneath me was warm and cozy. Maybe I'd just lay there for a while. I'd get up in a minute. Something tickling my foot interrupted my sleepy thoughts. I cracked my eyes open and sat up. A tiny white crab was trying its best to torment my pinky toe. When I leaned forward to get a better look, it disappeared into a small hole where my foot had been. I suppose I'd attack the foot blocking my home too.

Looking around, I realized with consternation that I had no idea where I was. I'd never seen a place more breathtaking. I was perched on a thin beach surrounding a very extensive lagoon. The sand beneath me was stark white and the waves lapping at the shore were a bright, luminous aqua. Standing up, I brushed the fine, soft sand off my legs and took in the rest of the scenery. The colors were so vivid it almost hurt my eyes. Orange, yellow, and red fish darted back in forth in the perfectly clear water. Circling the beach in every direction was a lush, dense forest with towering palm trees, massive banana trees, and colorful hibiscus and plumeria trees. Something told me I was on an island, but with the exception of a small wooden kayak down the beach there were no other signs of life.

I meandered toward the water and stopped once I was knee deep. The water was surprisingly warm and a school of tiny silver fish tickled my ankles. I started to dive in when I realized I was wearing shorts and a tank top. Why hadn't I put on a bathing suit before I came out here? And most importantly, how did I get there in the first place? A scream broke my thoughts and I twisted around to find the source. I ran to the edge of the forest and stopped at the wall of trees, but could see nothing through the thick mass of green. I heard another muffled scream, so I pushed my way through as leaves and branches scraped against my arms and legs. It was immediately ten degrees cooler beneath the canopy and the fragrant smells of sage, oleander and sweet mint were intoxicating. Huge pink and orange exotic flowers added pops of color in every direction. Coconut palms, avocado pear trees, mimosa trees and orange trees were everywhere I looked. At least there was no danger of starving. I stumbled for a few more feet and found myself on a worn dirt path that continued in both directions. I stopped to listen and heard muffled voices to my left, so I took off in that direction.

The sound of bird calls above me in the trees followed me as I ran. It was actually closer to singing; a harmony of different sounds melting into one beautiful symphony. I caught sight of a couple toucans and parrots with blazing feathers of blue, yellow and red. They reminded me of Phoebe's dress. Where were my roommates? Were they here too? The path began to widen and a small house came into view. I stepped off the trail to blend back in with the forest; walking carefully so as not to make any noise. Peeking over the tall leaves of a banana tree, I was surprised at how small the house appeared. I didn't even know if I'd call it a house. There was only enough space for a door on the front and a skinny window on each side. Made up of a green stone, it was well camouflaged. Its roof was made up of rounded slats of wood.

Loud noises came from within the house and I hesitated, trying to decide what my next move should be. If I barged in ready to save the day, what would I do then? What if they had weapons? What if it was just kids playing around? I had no way of knowing from outside. Then I heard a woman yell and another loud thud. I inspected the ground around me for something that could double as a weapon. I heard a loud creak and looked over my shoulder as the door of the house opened. I crouched down and held my breath in anticipation. A woman stepped out and slammed the door behind her. She turned and pulled out a ring of keys; locking it. When I saw her face, my veins turned to ice. Her rich brown hair was pulled back and she had scratches down the length of her face, but there was no mistaking who it was. Isadora.

She touched her face and winced, mumbling something I couldn't hear. She passed my hiding place and disappeared into the forest. Still holding my breath, I listened for any other sounds coming from the house. Silence. The lack of noise was almost worse than the alternative. What if someone was dead in there? Did I really want to find a dead body? But if someone was hurt I had to help them. I checked to make sure Isadora wasn't coming back and scurried up to the front door. I tried the knob even though I saw her lock it, and not surprisingly it didn't budge. I moved around the side of the house and peered into one of the windows. What I saw inside had me stumbling backwards. Even though the exterior of the house couldn't be more than five feet wide, it was colossal inside. Was I hallucinating? I peered back in the window and blinked several times to make sure my eyes weren't playing tricks on me. I was looking into a sprawling living room that boasted a large stone fireplace with bookshelves on either side that extended floor to ceiling. A sitting area had been set up facing the fireplace with several plush couches and arm chairs. Behind that, a huge desk was flanked by even more shelves filled to the brim with books. A large painting of a woman hung on the side wall. My eyes traveled downward and I saw a figure slumped on the floor. I squinted and tried to make out more details, but the glare of the sun on the window made it impossible to see.

I tried to open the window but it was locked as well, so I stalked back into the forest and picked up a thick branch that was pointed on the end. Standing back from the window, I swung it into the glass with all of my strength. It created a large jagged hole just big enough for an arm. I gritted my teeth as the sharp edges caught and tore my skin open. I felt around for the latch and pushed it the other way, hoping to unlock the window. With blood dripping down my arm, I pulled on the window again and this time it gave easily. I lifted myself up and through the window. Jumping down onto a lavish rug, I ran to the opposite side of the room, hoping the person was still alive. Her long hair and slight build told me it was a woman. Her hands and feet were bound by a piece of rope. She looked unconscious, so I knelt down beside her and brushed her blond hair out of her face. I covered my mouth and tried not to scream. Kira. She had blood-matted hair and several large cuts and bruises on her face. I held my hand below her nose and felt a light stream of air that told me she was still breathing. A piece of tape covered her mouth.

"Kira!" I patted her face, gently trying to wake her "Kira, wake up!" She moaned but didn't open her eyes or move. I started to untie the rope around her feet when the world shifted. I fell sideways against the wall and everything went black.

"Give her room - she's not going to wake up if you're smothering her!"

"But shouldn't she be waking up by now?" I recognized Carmen and Phoebe arguing as I opened my eyes.

"Stasia!" Ignoring their cheers, I threw my legs over the side of my bed and pushed them out of the way. Immediately the room spun and I had to sit back down.

"Oh, no you don't. Not again." Carmen grabbed my shoulders and tried to lay me back down. I shoved her arms off.

"Kira's in trouble!" I frantically tried to stand back up, but my body had no energy to fight Carmen. I glanced down at my arms but didn't see any sign of scrapes or dripping blood.

"Stasia, calm down. Kira's fine. I just talked to her on the phone. She's fine." Willow told me in a soothing tone one would use to calm a confused child.

"No she's not, she's been kidnapped. She was tied up and unconscious!"

"She's okay, I promise. We just talked to her a couple minutes ago. She's on her way back from Wilmington. She's coming to see you tonight." Phoebe rubbed my arm. Pain swept over me like a dark wave and I closed my eyes. Was it a dream? But I wasn't sleeping; I was in The Hole-

My eyes flew open and I tried to sit up again. "It was a vision! I blacked out, didn't I?" I stared at them wildly as they shook their heads yes and watched me warily. "See, that's why she's fine now. Because it hasn't happened yet! I have to tell her-"

"Stasia, you have to calm down and rest. You hit your head and back really hard on the pavement when you blacked out. You need to lie down," Willow instructed; steadily holding my eyes. That would explain the incessant pounding in my head. I lay back on my pillow and closed my eyes again.

"Fine. But you'll see...you'll see." I couldn't make out what she said next because sleep pulled me under.

Twenty-four

The next time I woke up a single candle flickered on my dresser, but the rest of the room was dark. The deafening silence made me wonder how late it was, but the soothing dancing light of the candle across the wall had me hypnotized. The pounding in my head had died down some, but now it felt like it had been stuffed with cotton. I felt the back of my head and found a large knot that hurt to the touch. The slightest movement caused excruciating pain down my neck and the whole left side of my face. I must have fallen backwards from the bench we sat on. My back felt like it was one big bruise. The last thing I remembered was Willow's face spinning, and then I woke up on that beach.

I saw movement out of the corner of my eye and sat straight up in bed.

"Hello?" I whispered, my voice scratchy. A figure materialized near the window and my chest tightened in fear. He stepped into the light of the candle.

"Hi." Finn's grin was laced with mischief as he sat down on the side of the bed. "How're you feeling?" He shouldn't have been allowed to look that good. He was only wearing shorts and a t-shirt, but the way he moved and the confident vibe he carried with him made my heart race.

"I think I got run over by a truck." I attempted a smile and my cheek throbbed.

"So that's where the tire marks on your back came from…" He smirked at me. I started to laugh, but pain exploded in my head.

"Don't make me laugh." I closed my eyes and rubbed my temples, still smiling. "It hurts." He watched me for a moment and I was suddenly self-conscious of how appalling I must look. Had he been watching me the whole time I was asleep? What if I snored? Or drooled on my pillow?

"How long have you been here?" I asked him.

"Since about five o'clock this evening. No one knows I'm here though, and it's after hours. I've been cloaking myself when someone comes in." He winked at me and grinned at his own cleverness. By the lack of light outside, I'd have to say it was past nine o'clock p.m. The hottest guy on Earth had been in my bedroom all night, and I was lying in bed unconscious the whole time. There's nothing like a bruised body and a little concussion to impress a guy.

"How did you know where our suite was?"

"I saw Phoebe coming back this afternoon, so I cloaked myself and followed her up here. I slipped in through the door before she closed it."

"Had a lot of experience in the stalking department?" I teased him.

"I'm going to have to plead the fifth." He grinned at me.

I sat up on my elbows and eyed him curiously. "Have you followed me before?"

"Only a couple-"

"Finn!" I pushed him playfully. I immediately ran through everything I'd said and done in the last week and a half. What if he heard me talking about him? I was going to have to be more careful. Leave it to me to fall for the one guy who could make himself invisible.

"I just…wanted to see you." He looked down at my hand and rubbed his thumb across it, sending tingles up my arm. I waited for him to explain further, but he didn't.

"And….?" I prompted.

"Well, the first time I saw you from my balcony. You were going out in the ocean the weekend you got here. I was curious and a little worried, considering it was raining and I'd pulled you from the water the day before," he continued; rubbing my hand and watching me as he spoke. "I saw the turtles. I could tell they recognized you." At least I didn't do anything too embarrassing that day. Maybe since he seemed to know everything about me, he could clear something up for me.

"Phoebe thinks I have an affinity for sea turtles."

"She's right. The turtles sensed you were nearby, so they came to say hey."

"When I touched one of them I could see into his mind. It was wild."

"It's different for everyone, but my affinity is like that too. I can see into their mind and feel what they feel." I'd completely forgotten he would have an affinity too.

"Which animal do you have an affinity for?" Visions of dolphins or seals came to mind, but that didn't seem right.

"Are you sure you want to know the answer to that?" No.

"I wouldn't have asked if I didn't." I cracked a smile.

"They aren't as...likeable as sea turtles." Of course not.

"How bad could it be? There aren't that many scary things in the ocean. Except for electric eels. Or jelly fish. Or sharks – they can rip you apart just for fun." He smiled again and nodded his head. My eyes grew wide and my jaw dropped.

"Sharks?!" I gaped at him. "You have to be kidding me. Of all the creatures in the ocean, you have an affinity for sharks?" I shook my head, disbelieving. A mental picture of Finn swimming with a great white shark popped in my head.

"They aren't all bad, just misunderstood," he defended his affinity.

"You can't convince me they aren't scary as hell. I saw Jaws."

He laughed at me. "So does that mean you don't want to go swim with them?"

"Uh, I'd like to keep all my body parts. And my life. But thanks for the invite." Sharks? Unbelievable. But, I had to admit they were a perfect match; silent, sleek and deadly. He kicked off his shoes and turned to me.

"Move over," he instructed.

"Excuse me?"

"How can I lay down if you're taking up the whole bed?"

"Who says you're getting in my bed?"

"I'll be good, I promise." He grinned, but I wasn't sure if I believed him. "It'll make me feel better if I can be close to you and make sure you're alright." He batted his dark blue eyes at me. The thought of Finn in my bed made me all jittery. I just wished I wasn't black and blue with a headache the size of Alaska. He pulled off his shirt in one quick motion and I almost passed out at the sight of his bare chest in the candlelight. I picked my chin up off the floor and pulled back the covers. He slid underneath them and I snuggled up next to him; resting my head on his bare shoulder. I closed my eyes and breathed in his intoxicating scent. The heat coming off of his body wrapped around me and had me moving closer. His bronzed skin felt like silk, but the taut muscles beneath made me want to touch every part of him.

"Kira came by to see you earlier. She didn't wake you up, but she whispered to you how sorry she was for not being closer when it happened. She really cares about you." My vision came crashing back to me.

"I had a vision that Kira was kidnapped when I blacked out."

"I know."

"You do?" I looked up at him in surprise.

"I heard your roommates talking about it earlier."

"It's not the first one I've had," I told him, and hoped he believed me. I knew they weren't dreams or reveries. They were different. I just didn't know how to explain it.

"I know that too."

"So I do have foresight."

"Of course you do." It felt so good to have someone validate me, I wanted to hug him.

"Nobody else will believe me."

"It's just hard for them to accept. It's an extremely rare ability." He smiled down at me.

I propped myself up on my elbow. "Okay. How do you know so much about me? You knew I could breathe underwater, and I'm pretty sure you've known I had foresight for a while too."

"I can't tell you."

"Can't, or won't?"

"Can't." His eyes pleaded with me. "But you can trust me, Stasia. I promise." I was too tired to argue, so I just sighed and laid my head back down on his shoulder.

"Is there anything else you know about me that I should be aware of?" Maybe he could tell me if any other random abilities were going to show themselves soon.

"How beautiful you are?" He looked down at me adoringly. If he thought I was beautiful right then, he might need his eyes checked.

"That's old news." I snickered at him and pain shot through my head again. "Ow."

"That's what you get." He leaned down and kissed my forehead. My bedroom door opened.

"Stasia! You're awake!" I immediately glanced over at Finn, who had promptly disappeared. It was going to take a while to get used to that.

"Hey Willow!" I was happy to see her, but a little distracted knowing Finn was somewhere in there without her knowledge. I felt like I should let her know. She came and sat beside me on the bed.

"I'm about to go to bed, but I wanted to come in and do a little magic on you. I didn't want to do it until you were awake, so you wouldn't freak out when you woke up completely healed. I did that to someone else. It wasn't pretty." She wiggled her fingers. "Now lay back and enjoy."

"I have to admit that having a healer as one of my best friends is pretty awesome." I'd honestly never had a best friend before, but if I had to choose three to have in my life, it would be my roommates. They meant the world to me. I closed my eyes when I felt her hands cover my head. At the first touch the knot on my head screamed, but then all I felt was tingling. I could actually discern the pain being taken from my head and neck, replaced by a slight numbness. She lifted her hands.

"Better?"

"Much." I smiled up at her, suddenly lethargic. I felt like I'd just had a two hour massage in two minutes.

"Your body still needs to heal and regenerate its cells, so don't get any ideas about getting out of bed. Or going to classes tomorrow. Kira's already talked to your teachers."

"That all sounds good except for one thing. My stomach is eating my gall bladder as we speak."

She laughed at me. "I thought you might be hungry." She left and returned carrying a plate overflowing with pasta. "It's baked ziti and it's hot, so give it a little time to cool down."

"You rock." I closed my eyes; exhaustion washing over me.

"Sleep good and yell if you need something." She squeezed my hand and shut the door behind her. The baked ziti on my night stand was the best thing I'd seen all day (except for the definition of perfection lying beside me), and my stomach growled at the delicious aroma. Before I could even reach for the plate, the fork lifted on its own and dug into the cheesy pasta. Finn reappeared just as he took a big bite.

"Hey! That's mine!" I grabbed the fork from him. He licked his lips and made a big production of swallowing, then crawled back under the covers with me. I devoured the rest of it like I hadn't eaten in years. With my belly full and Finn's arms around me, I couldn't fight sleep off any longer.

"Sweet dreams, Finn," I whispered.

"Sweet dreams, Pasha."

Twenty-Five

A lullaby. It eased the drums pounding in my head. Not just one voice was singing to me though, it was more of a chorus made up of multiple voices. My eyes flew open. It was still dark. Maybe it wasn't too late.

"Finn! " I whispered loudly as I shook him. "Finn, wake up!"

"Mmm?"

"Come on, I have to check on the turtles." I shook him one more time and hopped out of bed. My body felt heavy and sluggish, but it was moving better than it had earlier tonight. My head still felt like it was stuffed with cotton and my tongue had turned to sandpaper, but I couldn't ignore the pull of the hatchlings. I could tell they were...waiting on me.

I pulled some sweatpants on over my boy shorts and a t-shirt over my tank top. The thought of Finn cloaked in my room while my roommates changed my clothes brought heat to my cheeks, but I tried to push the thought away.

"Please tell me the turtles are in the living room." Finn rubbed his eyes sleepily.

"They're on the beach and it's time for them to go to the ocean. I need to be there." I grabbed his hand and pulled him into the living room and out the door.

He reluctantly followed after me. "Damn. I was really hoping for the living room. Much closer."

I gave him a warning look and he grinned innocently at me. Down on the beach, I ran over to the nest and fell to my knees. My muscles were screaming and my head hurt, but that was the farthest thing from my mind. I placed my hands on the sand and felt the familiar electric spark in my fingers.

"They're still here! I didn't miss it!" Finn sat beside me as excitement pulsed through me.

"Is this where the nest is?" He peered at the undisturbed sand with doubt.

"Yep." I was thrilled be to sharing this with him. "Just wait." I scooted closer to him and rested up against him.

"The nests aren't usually this close to campus," he surmised.

"These weren't either, until a couple days ago. We moved them right before the hurricane hit so they'd be protected by the shield." I told him about my vision and how we had relocated the eggs. I started to tell him about Phoebe's almost-drowning fiasco but the look on his face stopped me. A mixture of overwhelming pride and astonishment sparkled in his eyes. Without a word he reached up and rubbed my cheek. I closed my eyes and leaned into his hand. The feel of his lips suddenly on mine created a domino effect of sensations that ran down my neck and cascaded over my body. I felt his arms wrap around me, but all I could think about was how soft his lips were and how they fit with mine so perfectly. I felt something nudge my leg and looked down. A smile spread across my face and an unexpected feeling of pure joy filled my heart.

"Hi there," I greeted the squirming hatchling. I picked it up and set it on Finn's palm. "This is Finn." The hatchling tried to scurry back to my hand. "He won't drop you. If he does, I'll kick his ass."

"You shouldn't use that kind of language around the baby," Finn retorted in a parenting voice as I swatted at him.

"You just concentrate on not dropping the baby." I patted the turtle on the head with my finger.

"They're so little," he said as he marveled at the miniature creature in his palm. Movement in the sand drew our attention back to the nest, and we watched as the rest of the hatchlings made their way out. Finn returned the hatchling to me and I kissed it gently on the head before placing him back on the sand with his siblings. They were frantically crawling over each other and bumping into me. I stood and gave them a straight path to the ocean. The moon above was almost full, and it shone down on the water; lighting the way. Their flippers working overtime, they scooted over the sand as fast as they could. Even large shells were obstacles for them. I watched for any hungry crabs or dive bombing birds looking for a snack. As the first turtle hit the surf, it was hit by a small wave and tumbled over and over. Pure instinct was the only thing pushing them to endure whatever it took to reach deeper water where they could swim. Watching their struggle, I felt tears spring to my eyes. Finn embraced me in a hug as they spilled over.

He rested his cheek on the top of my head and I felt him smile. "They'll be fine, Stasia. They know what to do." Several hatchlings were swimming on top of the waves before disappearing beneath the surface. I looked on like a proud mom as each and every one made it safely to the ocean and began their journey out to sea. I knew the statistics weren't in their favor, but I felt like I'd done a small part by making sure they found the water safely.

Finn looked down at me with concern. "It's time to get you back to bed."

I put my hands on my hips and gave him a cynical look. "Oh, really? And you're going to be the one to get me into bed?"

He turned toward me. "That's an honor I don't deserve." His eyes softened and he ran a finger over my lips. "But I'll spend every minute of the rest of my life trying to earn it." What was left of the walls around my heart melted away and collected in a puddle at my feet.

216

Once we were back inside Maren Hall, exhaustion made it hard to keep my eyes open. I leaned up against the sink in the bathroom and took inventory of my reflection. Surprisingly, I didn't look as bad as I felt. My hair was a complete disaster, but the rest of me had fared pretty well. I had a feeling Willow's magical hands had everything to do with that. I tried to stand upright but my legs gave out and I grabbed the counter for support. The bathroom door cracked open.

"You okay in there?"

"At the moment my bed seems really far away." I heard him chuckle as he came into the bathroom. He gently carried me back in the bedroom and laid me down on the bed.

"You're staying, aren't you?" I looked up at him through droopy eyelids.

"Of course." He smiled and kissed my forehead before sliding beneath the covers. In the safety of his arms, the entire world could blow up around me and I'd never know the difference.

"Good," I smiled; closing my eyes and immediately giving in to sleep.

The following morning I found a pink hibiscus flower in Finn's place. I plucked it from the sheet and smiled to myself. Finn had actually slept in my room last night. In my bed. I'd slept like a baby wrapped in the shelter of his arms. I rubbed my head and besides some tender skin, it was completely healed. Speaking of blacking out, I still hadn't had a chance to talk to Kira and warn her. I picked up my phone and hoped she was awake.

"Hello?"

"Hey Kira."

"Hey Stasia! How're you feeling?"

"Much better, thanks to Willow. I'm still a little sore, but for the most part I'm better."

"That's good to hear. You didn't look too good when I came by to see you last night."

"I heard you came by. Did my roommates tell you about my vision?" I had a feeling she wouldn't believe me either. I was right.

"They said you had a vision of me being kidnapped?" She sounded skeptical. "If that's true, that would mean you have foresight. No descendant I know of has ever been gifted with that ability."

"No descendant has ever had my trace either, but it's right here on my arm. I know I saw you get kidnapped. It was awful! Isadora dragged you into a house-"

"Isadora?" She sighed. "Stasia, why would she do something like that?"

"I don't know, but it's what I saw. I know it was real!" I said, exasperated.

"It was just a dream. I'm completely fine! Nothing's going to happen."

"You don't know that! I know what I saw, Kira."

"I'll be fine, I promise."

"But Kira-"

"I have to go, but I'll call you later to check on you, okay?"

"But-"

"Get some rest and promise you won't worry about me."

"Okay." I resigned myself to the fact she wasn't going to believe me.

"Promise me."

218

"Okay, I promise." Unfortunately I was getting pretty good at lying. I grabbed my IPod and put in my ear buds to drown out the world. How was I going to keep her safe if she didn't believe me? I knew what I saw, and Finn even confirmed they were visions. I was right about the hatchlings, and I knew I was right about Nicolet being murdered and Kira being kidnapped. I just didn't know how I was going to make anyone else see that.

"Time to wake up!" Carmen was suddenly on top of my bed. "Are you ready for Extreme Makeover: Stasia Edition?"

Saturday arrived quicker than I thought it would, and I couldn't believe I was going to an actual Ball that night. It seemed surreal. Thursday went by in a blur since I slept most of the day, and Friday was spent trying to catch up on what I'd missed during the last two days of classes. Of course, word had gotten around campus that I had blacked out, had a seizure and suffered from hallucinations. There was nothing like embellished rumors to boost your self-esteem. Whispers and wide-eyed looks followed me wherever I went. My plan to blend in was coming along nicely.

"I don't need an extreme makeover. I'm fine just the way I am," I grumbled at her. I started to pull the covers over my head but she seized them first.

"You promised," she pouted dramatically. "Are you going to deprive me of my dream?"

"If your dream is to give me a makeover, we need to find you a new one."

"You're just my first client. Soon people will be knocking down my door wanting my services."

"Right now I need your service in the kitchen." Willow peeked her head in the door and smiled at me. "Morning."

"A true artist's work is never done." Carmen sighed tragically and tossed my comforter completely off my bed. "Now get up before I send in reinforcements." She stopped at the door. "And by reinforcements, I mean Phoebe. She was so batty when she woke up, I had to sedate her. And the beast is beginning to stir." She flashed me a smile and disappeared.

With Carmen doing our hair and makeup, Willow demanded to oversee her work to make sure she didn't go too far. I was secretly glad. I still wanted to look like myself when she was done, just a prettier version. It was tradition for all of the girls to travel to the light station on the Son's yacht, where they were escorted into the Ball by their dates. I'd been contemplating how we would get from the boat to the top of the light station. I didn't get a good look, but I hadn't seen any elevators the last time I was there. If I was expected to climb ten flights of stairs, I wanted to know ahead of time so I could bring some tennis shoes and a tank of oxygen. The boat was leaving promptly at nine o'clock p.m., and rumor had it there was a meteor shower at midnight. It sounded like the stage was set for a magical night. My stomach squeezed with nervousness.

Twenty-six

"Comb."

"Hair spray."

"Bobby pin."

"Hair spray."

Carmen inspected her masterpiece (A.K.A. my hair), sprayed it one more time, and then scrunched her nose in concentration.

"Can I see it yet?" Carmen had my back to the bathroom mirror so I wouldn't see it until she was completely done.

"Almost ready." She smoothed down a couple more hairs and reached for the hair spray.

"If you put any more hairspray on it, it's going to look more like a helmet than a hairdo," Willow declared. "She's going to a Ball, not for a ride on a crotch rocket."

"She might be by the end of the night…" Her joke stopped short with Willow, but Phoebe snickered. " You don't know how hard the wind's going to be blowing. We can't afford to cut any corners." Carmen chewed on a bobby pin and circled me a couple more times.

"Done!" she announced loudly enough for the entire third floor to hear. She came around to face me, holding a small hand mirror.

"Now if you don't like it, lie and tell me you do." She grinned. She held the mirror low and raised it slowly for effect. "Wait for it…wait for it…"

"I've been waiting two hours." I groaned and tried to steal the mirror, but she pulled it out of my reach just in time.

"Patience, grasshopper. All good things come to those who- Hey!" Phoebe snatched the mirror from her and passed it to me; rolling her eyes. Carmen had done Phoebe's hair first and it looked absolutely amazing. Chunks of hair were pulled back into a messy bun at the crown of her head. The style accentuated each streak of blonde, red and brown perfectly. For an extra pop of color, Carmen tucked a feather matching the bottom of Phoebe's dress into the bun. I was reminded of the exotic birds I'd seen in my vision, but I figured this probably wasn't the best time to mention that.

Not having had my hair fixed that many times, I noticed how heavy all of the bobby pins were; not to mention the eight layers of hair spray that probably added a few pounds. I took a deep breath and looked in the mirror. A small section of hair had been French braided; starting from above my left eye and extending all the way down into the corner of a low side bun. It was elegant, classy and simple. I loved it.

"Oh, Carmen, it's beautiful." I moved my head from side to side to get a better look.

'You really like it?" Her face was beaming.

"I really do! You're amazing!" I jumped up and gave her a hug. She held me at a distance, but patted my back.

"Easy, trigger. No sudden movements. Don't go messing up my hard work. You can come home a hot mess, but when you step off that boat in..." she checked her watch, "two hours, I want every head to turn." I jumped down from the stool, gave her a kiss on the cheek and ran into the kitchen to eat a snack before the make-up portion of the extreme makeover started.

An hour and a half later, Phoebe and I stood on the boardwalk of the marina along with about a hundred other girls dressed in exquisite gowns, also waiting to board the yacht. I looked down at my own dress nervously for the twentieth time. Despite my anxiety, I swore it was created just for me. I ran my hands down it and smoothed the posh fabric. I touched the aquamarine necklace Finn had given me. The skin beneath it tingled each time it moved, but oddly enough it calmed my nerves. I looked up as the large white yacht I'd seen my first day on the island slowly pulled in to dock. It bore a resemblance to an oversized Ferrari on water with its sleek exterior and dark windows. I couldn't even imagine what the inside would look like. I'd never been on a boat, much less a million dollar yacht.

"Please tell me that's not Olivia." I followed Phoebe's eyes and spotted the girl she was glaring at. She was in a skin-tight blood red gown that followed every curve of her body down to her glittering silver heels. It was definitely Olivia. She was talking animatedly to two other girls I'd seen around Maren. "Maybe she'll fall overboard before we get there."

"She can't be that bad. Girls like her are all talk," I said. If there was one thing I'd learned in life, it was that everyone had a story – good or bad. I wondered what Olivia's story was. Right then her piercing eyes locked in on us. She gave us her best condescending smile and swiftly turned her back on us. I hoped she didn't have a super hearing ability.

"Well, her 'all talk' really works my nerves," Phoebe huffed; still glaring at her.

The crowd of girls began to move and I craned my neck to see if we were boarding. A single file line was beginning to form, as each girl walked up a ramp and disappeared onto the yacht's deck. Several guys in black suits, who I assumed were Sons, stood on both sides; extending their hands to help each girl aboard. Finally it was my turn. I held up the bottom of my gown and delicately stepped onto the ramp. For some odd reason I was reminded of the movie Titanic and the scene where Rose stepped off solid ground in her dress for the last time. All I was missing was a wide brimmed hat and a prescription grade case of resentment.

The ramp itself was a little unsteady and had too many places for the heel of a shoe to get caught. I held onto the two guys' hands and stepped onto the immaculate wooden floor of the deck. Phoebe joined me a second later. We were shuffled through a small opening that led to a sizeable room oozing with opulence. Clusters of candles adorned small tables throughout the room, and soft music played from hidden speakers; adding to the ambiance. A plush white carpet spread across the floor, meeting walls painted a warm golden color. They were trimmed with elaborate white molding that punctuated the lavish surroundings. Phoebe and I chose a loveseat that was a shade darker than the walls. Extravagant frames covered the walls containing pictures of guys, all with dark hair. According to the plates below, group pictures had been taken of each graduating class.

The boat started to move and my pulse quickened, knowing I was getting closer and closer to seeing Finn. Most importantly, I knew I'd have to walk back down that plank without falling and breaking an ankle, or worse, falling into the water. My hair definitely wouldn't survive that. Carmen would be pissed.

I thought about Kira as waiters in white uniforms handed out glasses filled with ice water. I planned on texting Kira later since I hadn't talked to her today. The memory of her blond hair hanging limply over her bruised face flashed in my mind, and a wave of nausea passed over me. I set down my glass and squeezed my eyes shut. I quickly realized it wasn't the disturbing image, but the boat's motion that was causing it. I hadn't even thought about sea sickness! Falling in the water might not be so bad after I puked all over my dress. For the next thirty minutes I concentrated solely on keeping my dinner down and calming my nerves. Phoebe had been talking non-stop about nothing in particular, which told me she was nervous too.

The yacht inched to a stop, and the other girls began to stand up. I couldn't see anything out of the dark windows lining the room, but I knew what loomed above us. And who. My palms started to sweat.

"Showtime." Phoebe's eyes glittered with anticipation. When we stood up, the sea sickness in my stomach morphed into a million butterflies. Why was I so nervous? It was just Finn. Who was I kidding? That was exactly why I was so nervous. He would never be 'just Finn'. We followed the line of girls and gave our clutches to a Son who was creating an organized pile. I guess they assumed it was easier to leave our belongings on the boat. That phone call to Kira would have to wait.

When we stepped out onto the deck, we caught a glimpse of the rustic-looking contraption that would lift us up to the light station ten stories above.

"Oh, hell no." Phoebe shook her head vehemently. "I am not getting on that thing." It greatly resembled a hot air balloon basket, except there was just a single metal bar going across one side that swung out; acting as the entrance as well as the exit. Four steel ropes connected to the corners were all linked to a winch high above, and I could just imagine the Sons assembling this out of spare materials they found lying around. I wasn't sure I was ready to trust their handy work with my life. I watched as a girl in a flowing lavender gown began to step in, but the Son manning the basket shook his head and said something that made her get back in line.

"Anastasia Whitman?" The same Son was now calling out my name. Phoebe looked at me with alarm and my heart seized up. Were they doing this by reverse alphabetical order? That seemed odd.

"Yes?" I stepped out of line and raised my hand. He gestured for me to come to the front. I gave Phoebe one last confused look and walked past fifty or so girls to the front of the line, while each one glared at me jealously as I walked by.

"Is there a reason I'm going first?" I whispered to the Son who was now holding out his hand to help me in to the basket.

"It's tradition," he said simply. I stepped in, completely confused.

"What do you mean?" I asked, but before he could answer the winch above me came to life and the basket started to rise. Holding on tightly, I looked out over the water shining in the moonlight and a blanket of silence fell over the night. The view was beautiful, but I made sure not to look down. Why did I have to go first? Was it because of Finn? Did he arrange this? I looked up to see where I was going and saw a catwalk extending out from the main building, which I would have to walk down. My heart was threatening to jump out of my chest and I felt my hands shaking. The winch came to a stop as I reached my destination. A crowd of dark haired guys stood about five yards away on the other end of the catwalk, and for one horrible second, I imagined Finn standing me up; leaving me humiliated in front of everyone. I'd have to be lowered all the way back down in a cloud of shame, to be taken back to the island.

Then a figure stepped out from the crowd. My heart stopped and my mouth went dry. Wearing a black suit over a dark gray shirt, he confidently sauntered down the catwalk towards me. His dark hair was perfectly swept across his forehead, and his dark blue eyes were slightly shadowed. He stopped a foot in front of me and the corners of his mouth lifted in a crooked grin.

"Welcome to the Cimmerian Shade Ball, Anastasia," he said formally with a gleam in his eye, then in a hushed voice added, "You look absolutely stunning." With a wink, he extended his hand and I tried to remember how to put one foot in front of the other. We walked across the catwalk towards the crowd of guys awaiting their own dates' arrival in the basket of death. The crowd split down the middle to allow us passage. Each guy respectfully nodded their head at Finn as we walked by. Before I could figure out the reason for all the pomp and circumstance centered around him, we took a sharp left turn down a dimly lit hallway and climbed several stairs that led to an unassuming door. It opened from the other side, and when we stepped out into the crisp night air, I was entirely unprepared for the scene I saw before me.

The Light Station had been transformed into a page straight out of a black and white fairy tale. Rows and rows of lights were strung along the entire length of the platform; resembling a thousand tiny fireflies hovering above our heads. Black carpet concealed the concrete beneath, with a dusting of glitter that gave it the appearance of diamonds. As we walked the glitter lifted and swirled around our feet. Thirty or forty formal tables were set up around the perimeter with stark white covers hanging over the chairs, each secured with a wide piece of black lace. Elaborate centerpieces overflowing with large white flowers and even larger black feathers sat on black and white damask tablecloths. Placed in the middle of the floor were at least fifty trees in white planters hanging with dark red fruit. At around six to seven feet tall, they encircled a shiny black dance floor. The glow of enchantment was awe-inspiring, and the Ball exuded prestige and tradition. In the middle of the ocean, the darkness of night pulsed with its grandeur.

"Wow. This is incredible." I smiled up at Finn and realized he'd been watching me.

"Thirsty?" he offered.

"Definitely." With his hand at the small of my back, he guided me back towards the tower. We walked through a side door and I carefully made my way down yet another flight of stairs. Whoever built this station obviously hadn't taken high heels into consideration. This time the stairs ended in a spacious room full of comfortable couches and chairs. Floor to ceiling windows lined two opposite walls, and a lengthy bar recessed into another wall. I looked at Finn.

"It's a mocktail bar." He smiled down at me.

"A what?"

"A mocktail bar. It has all of the normal drinks and cocktails, just without the alcohol," he explained. I'd never heard of a mocktail bar, but it sounded pretty good. I tried to remember names of popular cocktails.

"How about a pina colada?" I didn't know exactly what it would be called without the alcohol.

"One fake pina colada coming up." I giggled at him as he headed to the bar, and then decided to inspect the many culinary options around me. There were several tables set up around the room brimming with food.

One table was set up fondue style, hosting large bowls filled to the brim with melted chocolate, caramel, and cream cheese icing. Chunks of pineapple, bananas, strawberries and other fruits were stacked on platters available for dipping. Another table overflowed with an array of pastries and cakes.

My mouth began to water when Finn appeared holding a tall hurricane glass filled with yellow deliciousness. A large wedge of pineapple hugged the rim and a cherry garnished the coconut cream on top. I took a sip and my taste buds were assaulted by the savoriness of a tropical island. It also reminded me of Kira's drink. I took another sip and Finn eyed me with amusement.

"Hey dude!" A large hand attached to a tall, curly-haired guy clamped down on Finn's shoulder. "I was wondering if you'd ever make it to one of these." His dark brown eyes were warm and his smile was genuine.

Finn punched him in the side playfully and nodded towards him. "This is Dominic," he introduced me.

I shook Dominic's hand and smiled politely. "I'm Stasia."

"I know." His grin contradicted his ominous tone.

A cute girl with long auburn hair, wearing a silk green gown walked up to stand beside him. She had wide green eyes that matched her dress and a tiny button nose.

"Claudia wanted me to introduce her to the Scion," he told Finn. Finn glanced my way anxiously while I racked my brain for what the word 'Scion' meant.

"I'm Finn," he affirmed and shook her hand.

"It's such an honor to meet you," Claudia gushed. "So when's your birthday?" Finn flinched.

"Claudia," warned Dominic, as if her question might be too personal. "Come on, let's go dance. See ya'll later," he called to us as he grabbed her elbow and practically dragged her away.

I turned to Finn with suspicion. "Is there something you're not telling me?" His face gave nothing away.

"There's a lot of things I'm not telling you." Well at least he was honest.

"I was waiting for her to ask you to autograph her forehead."

He wrapped his arm around my shoulder smugly. "It's hard work being this good looking."

I just rolled my eyes. "Why did Dominic call you the Scion?"

"Just a nickname." He shrugged his shoulders.

"And why did I have to be lifted up first? I thought I was going to get mobbed by the other girls." I lifted my eyebrows at him, wanting an answer.

"The most beautiful girl always goes first." He surreptitiously changed the subject. "How 'bout we go back up?" I narrowed my eyes at him, letting him know this wasn't over, and allowed him to guide me back outside. I looked around for Phoebe. If she had a breakdown while being lifted in the basket, I'd never forgive myself. I spotted her with Ian on the other side of the dance floor and waved at her. She waved back and smiled. It appeared she'd made it up unscathed.

Twenty-Seven

We spent the next hour or so mingling with other couples. Faces and names started blending together, but one thing stuck out in my mind. All of the Sons treated Finn with a higher level of respect than anyone else. Some of the guys even seemed nervous around him.

Something else that stuck out in my mind was Olivia's hateful gaze following my every move. Maybe she really was as bad as Phoebe and Carmen said.

We passed by several of the potted trees on the way back to the bar, so I took the opportunity to take a closer look at their ripe fruit. They were close to the size and shape of a lemon.

"Pomegranate," Finn said carefully, as if speaking the word aloud was taboo.

"Is that what this is?" I cradled one in my hand and leaned in to smell it, when Finn stopped me.

"It's also called the fruit of the dead." His foreboding tone had me releasing the fruit and taking a step back. His features hardened and the muscle in his jaw flexed with anger. He looked away and took my hand; pulling me away from the trees. His entire body tensed and I followed his eyes toward the tower. An older man in a black suit with striking silver hair observed us emotionlessly.

"I'll be right back," he said, without breaking eye contact with the somber man. The stormy expression on his face didn't look like he wanted to discuss the weather. He was the first person I'd seen that exuded more darkness than Finn. His body seemed to blur and shift within the shadows of the tower. It was very unsettling and I forced myself to look away.

"Anastasia?" I looked up into the small, cold eyes of a petite girl with light brown hair, wearing a blue dress. She held a champagne flute with her pinky finger extended high in the air and instantly reminded me of Laura Beth, which was not necessarily a good thing.

"Yes?"

"So it's true?" she asked with a hostile undertone.

"Is what true?"

She stared at me. "Don't you think it's a little ironic that you're here with the Scion?" She twirled a ring on her finger that had a bright blue stone. A sapphire, maybe? If she was a Siren that could explain her hostility toward me, being a Tyde.

"I have no idea what you're talking about." I turned to face her, not concealing my frustration.

"Stasia!" Phoebe ran up to the table and threw her arms around me. Thankful for the interruption, I turned my back to the Siren and patted the chair beside me.

"Hey Phoebs! Have a seat." She sat down beside me and I could tell pinky girl was put out by her sudden appearance. She turned on her heel and stomped away without another word.

"Who was that?" Phoebe asked as she took a sip of something pink. Her face was flushed and her eyes were shining with excitement.

"Your guess is as good as mine. So, are you having fun? Ian looks pretty good tonight – he cleans up nice."

A Texas-sized grin spread across her face. "This is the best dance I've ever been to! I found some of these little guys…" She held up an airplane bottle of vodka with one hand and lifted her glass carelessly with the other. The pink concoction inside sloshed out and onto the table. "Whoops!" She giggled and continued, "And…I have the hottest date here. Besides Finn, of course," She winked at me and I couldn't help but laugh. Somebody was going to have one hell of a hangover in the morning.

"Speak of the devil!" She bolted out of her chair and threw her arms up with excitement. "Hey Finn!" She hugged him and stumbled away to find Ian. Finn chuckled and handed me another pina colada. I immediately took a sip. I could drink these all night.

"You are truly a gentleman," I told Finn in a horrible British accent. "These mocktails are bloody delicious."

"This gentleman would like to ask his lady to dance," he answered in an equally terrible accent. He stood and extended his hand formally. I took it and raised my eyebrows in feigned surprise.

"His lady?"

He raised my hand to his mouth; holding my gaze the entire time and gently pressing his lips to it. "His lady," he confirmed with obvious devotion, and pulled me out to the dance floor as a slow song began. I watched the lights above play across his handsome face and wished I could hear his thoughts.

"Who was that man you were talking to earlier?"

"A friend," he answered vaguely, and then searching my eyes, he whispered, "I need to ask you a question."

"Okay, shoot." I smiled up at him.

"Do you trust me?"

I took a moment to think about his question. On one hand, he wouldn't tell me certain things about himself, he only gave me cryptic answers and seemed to know way too much about me. On the other hand, I felt completely safe with him, even though I had every reason to believe he was capable of murder. I knew he wouldn't intentionally do anything to hurt me, and my intuition told me he was actually guarding me from something. Keeping me safe. I just didn't know what that 'something' was yet. I wasn't sure I wanted to know.

"Yes," I answered with certainty.

"Good." His features relaxed and he let out a breath. "I need you to trust me, Stasia. No matter what."

"I'm much stronger than you give me credit for. I want you to know you can tell me anything. I can handle it."

"Be careful what you ask for," he warned, more to himself than me. Desperation flashed in his eyes as he looked over my shoulder at the ocean. Eventually, he met my gaze again. His was so unguarded and pure, it left me breathless. I looked down at my feet, momentarily overwhelmed by my own emotions. Every time he looked at me, my resolve wavered and I knew it was only a matter of time before I fell hard for him. Which terrified me.

"Do I still make you nervous?" He cocked his head to the side with a devilish grin.

"Nope. Not at all," I tried to lie convincingly.

"You're not a good liar, Stasia." He hid a smirk as he repeated a similar conversation of ours. Suddenly he cloaked us and we were covered with sparkles from head to toe. Finn stopped dancing abruptly and pulled me close; the intention clear in his hooded eyes. An emotional frenzy sparked inside me and my breath came faster as he leaned in ever so slowly. His mouth brushed mine lightly, enticing me. I grinned and took the bait; kissing his bottom lip and biting it gently before pulling back. Taking my challenge, he delicately kissed the skin beneath my ear down to my collarbone. Goose bumps raised on my skin as every sensation became heightened. Couples danced around us, completely oblivious that we were making out right in front of them. The thought sent a thrill through me. He touched my necklace and looked at me with warmth.

"It looks magnificent on you," he said in a low voice, and a thought occurred to me.

"How did you know it would match my dress?" A forced whisper was all I could manage.

He paused, and his eyes were filled with desire. "You aren't the only one with foresight, Pasha." My eyes widened, but before I could respond, he kissed me with a searing urgency that made my entire body ache with longing. He broke our kiss, grabbed my hand and led me towards the same door we entered through earlier. He pulled me down a different hallway and we fell against a wall. I was trapped against it from the pressure of his body on mine. The flame burning inside me threatened to explode into a raging inferno as his hands seemed to be everywhere at once. He moved backwards, taking me with him and we crashed through a door; landing clumsily onto a well-placed chaise lounge chair.

I fell on top of him, but he flipped us over effortlessly so that I was lying on my back instead. His lips grazed mine, sending tingles down to my toes, then moved downward as he kissed my neck. I tilted my head back to give him full access. His cool lips offset the heat of his tongue and waves of passion took hold of my body. He continued kissing the other side of my neck as his right hand gripped my waist with hunger and pulled me against him. I tucked my hands inside his jacket and ran them along his strong shoulders, urging him to continue.

His lips met mine again and suddenly there were way too many layers of clothing between us. I wanted to touch him and feel the heat coming off of his skin as it caressed mine. His strong hold on my waist released and his hand moved up my rib cage, inching ever higher. My chest suddenly felt fuller, anticipating his touch. His hand lingered just below, as if he was trying to decide if he should continue. His palm moved to my side so that only his thumb grazed the bodice of my dress, causing the skin beneath to tingle and ache. Suddenly, he grasped my waist again with what seemed like a lot of effort.

"Don't stop..." I whispered and put my hand over his, trying to guide it higher again. He easily threaded his fingers through mine, preventing it. He leaned back to look at me.

"I have to stop myself before I lose all control and rip that beautiful dress to shreds." The fate of my dress was the last thing on my mind, but he grinned and crouched on his knees in front of me; pulling me into a sitting position. He smoothed down a couple of hairs that had broken free of the iron clad hair spray and watched me with pure adoration. Feeling slightly ashamed at my own lack of inhibitions, I felt myself blush as he took my hands in his. Then the lights went out.

I instantly latched onto him and heard him snicker. "It's just midnight, love. It's time for the meteor shower." I could actually hear him smirking at me.

"I knew that…" I stood quickly, feeling foolish. He took my hand again and led me back outside. Everyone else had gathered on the dance floor with their faces lifted to the sky. All artificial light had been shut off so we could see the true beauty of the moon and stars. They were exquisite. No longer cloaked, I felt oddly exposed. Finn wrapped his arm around me and my heart swelled. I held onto him, reveling in our most recent cloaked make-out session. I glanced down at my dress to make sure it didn't look too rumpled, then I remembered the last thing Finn said before sweeping me off my feet.

He had foresight, too! A refreshing wave of relief washed over me, knowing I wasn't alone in my random blackouts and visions. Is that how he knew I had the same ability? Suddenly I had a million questions. Did he have blackouts too? What else had he seen? How long had he been having visions?

Unfortunately my questions would have to wait. Oohs and aahs came from the crowd once the meteor shower began. Out here surrounded by only darkness and water, each burning meteor took your breath away. It was truly beautiful to behold.

"Do you see those two bright stars?" Finn asked me, and I followed his finger. "They're part of the constellation

Aquarius. He's the water-bearer of the sky. Right below him is the constellation Pisces. He's pouring water down to Pisces, which we all know is a fish. The reason this meteor shower is important to us is because it originates out of Aquarius. It comes once a year and symbolizes the water bearer showering the world with new life and spiritual awakening. It represents the washing away of the past, leaving room for a fresh start." He peered down at me, somehow understanding the magnitude of his explanation to me.

Since arriving at Lorelei, I'd felt the past washing away to be replaced by a new freedom to reinvent not only myself, but my future. A fresh start was exactly what I had been wanting, and I felt like Aquarius had been showering me lately with new life and spiritual awakening. I smiled up at the water-bearer and silently thanked him as he spun above us in the night sky.

Thirty minutes and two cramps in my neck later, the lights came back on. Beach music blasted from the speakers and Finn turned to me, eyes sparkling.

"It's time for that dance," he said as he extended his hand. I looked at the dance floor and noticed no one else had taken the opportunity to embarrass themselves, so why should we?

"There's no one else dancing yet."

"That's because they're waiting for us."

He was right; all the other couples were watching us curiously. The guys seemed to know what was going on, but the girls all looked confused. My eyes met Olivia's and she gave me a look that could wither every flower in a twenty mile radius.

"And exactly why are all of these people waiting on us?" I felt a massive attack of stage fright coming on.

"Tradition."

"Is there a book somewhere that says no other Sons can dance until Finn Morrison does? ' Cause if there is, I'd like to find it and burn it." He just laughed at me and pulled me out onto the dance floor with our audience looking on.

"Just follow my lead," he whispered to me. This couldn't go well. I expected some sort of cha-cha or rumba or something else equally mortifying, but instead he took my hand and began moving his feet. I immediately understood which dance we were doing. Shagging was actually something I'd done before, but that didn't calm my stage fright by any means. I started to relax a little bit and got in step with Finn. Under the firefly lights with an empty dance floor, my adrenaline started pumping and I couldn't believe how much fun I was having. Finally, after ten anxiety filled minutes, other couples came out to the dance floor.

To our left, Ian was trying to teach Phoebe the steps as she continually ran into him, due to watching her feet the whole time. To our right, I saw something I never thought I would witness: Olivia smiling and laughing. She was dancing with a tall good-looking guy who gazed at her like the sun rose and set in her eyes. Smiling at my own dance partner, I couldn't remember the last time I was this happy.

Twenty-eight

Too soon, the lights flickered to announce the end of the Ball. I found my shoes, which I had kicked off at some point between The Temptations and The Embers, and started to follow the other couples as they filed back downstairs to the catwalk, but Finn held back. He took my hand and guided me to the now empty dance floor.

"For my lady." He bowed before me and presented me with a single rose he seemingly manifested out of thin air. Instead of the customary red or yellow, this particular rose was dark as midnight; a rich, soft ebony that reminded me of a raven's feather. The embodiment of darkness was captured beautifully in its black petals, but the symbolism of the rose itself lit a startling contradiction between life and death; both intertwined within one fragile flower. A flower I currently held gently in my hand. Its sweet aroma drifted up to my nose.

"It's beautiful, Finn," I breathed, unable to take my eyes off it.

"Just like its new owner." He flashed a dazzling smile down at me and took my hand.

He escorted me back downstairs through the small hallway, and when we rounded the corner it took me a second to realize what I was seeing. The other girls had already been lowered via the basket of death to the yacht below, and the catwalk stretched out before me with eleven Sons lining the left side. Each held a single black rose just like Finn's. One by one, they offered me their flower and nodded their head respectfully. I wasn't sure if they were nodding at me or Finn, but it didn't really matter. I'd never had anyone show me that kind of recognition. I was used to hiding in the shadows. By the time we arrived at the basket, I cradled a dozen black roses in my arms. I knew my face had to be a bright shade of red from the heat I felt coming off of it, but I didn't care. At that moment, I felt like royalty; a princess swept off her feet by a dark, sexy angel of mystery. Finn produced a strip of black lace and wrapped it around the flowers; securing them together.

"You are too much." I smiled widely at him. He narrowed his eyes and stepped closer.

"And I've only just begun seducing you with my unwavering charm, mademoiselle," he purred in his horrible British/French accent; his mouth lifting up in a crooked grin I couldn't resist. Standing on my tip-toes, I gave him a light kiss. His arm went around my waist while his other cradled the back of my head, and he pulled me to him for a much deeper kiss. The eleven Sons watching on the catwalk and the hundreds of girls waiting below faded from my consciousness as I willingly drowned in him. The dark magical quality of the roses in my arms and the night surrounding us folded around me; embracing and warming my heart. His kisses stopped abruptly as he cupped my chin; forcing me to gaze into his stormy eyes. My legs suddenly trembled.

"I will stop at nothing to protect you, Anastasia. I want you to remember that." The desperation in his eyes and the urgency of his voice tightened my chest with trepidation. I nodded in agreement, not knowing how to respond to his sudden pledge of protection. What did he think I needed safeguarding from? Fear quivered in the pit of my stomach, but I tried to push it down. His shoulders relaxed and his crooked grin returned.

"Sweet dreams, Stasia." Finn kissed my hand and looked up at me through his long lashes.

"Sweet dreams, Finn." I didn't want to leave his side. I knew I would feel his absence like a cold wind blowing around my heart. I reluctantly stepped into the basket, steadied myself and met his smiling eyes again. The winch came to life and I was being lowered. He became smaller and smaller until I could no longer see him.

"Stasia!" Phoebe broke my trance. She ran to the basket, but was held back by the Son opening the bar for me. The deck was pitching back and forth violently, making it difficult to find my balance. I carefully took several steps before she had her arms around me. She handed me my clutch and looked down at my roses with awe.

"Ohhh, how beauth-iful! I've nefer then black roth-es before!" She bent down to smell them and I felt a buzzing in my clutch. She looked at me with a lopsided smile and poked my shoulder with her finger. On the sobriety scale, Phoebe would be at the too-drunk-to-be-in-public level. "Youuu are one luckyyy girl, Stasthia. You bether hold on to him," she slurred at me and I laughed; taking her arm and leading her inside. My phone buzzed again.

"Come on, let's sit down and have some water." I cocked an eyebrow at her. I could tell she was seeing at least four 'Stathias' at the moment. I motioned for a waiter and asked for a very big glass of water and something to eat. I checked my phone and saw I had a voicemail.

At first I only heard rapid breathing, so I pressed the phone to my ear. "Stasia!" More panting, followed by a soft whimper. "You were…right…You were right. I don't know what she'll do… " My blood turned to ice as I heard a rustling sound and a hushed whisper. "The….Fortunate Isle…hurry…ple-." A loud smack sounded and she whimpered again before the line went dead.

I stared at my phone for a moment in shock. It was coming true. My vision. It was actually happening. I yanked Phoebe to her feet and dragged her back outside.

"Hey, wherrrre we goin' Stasthia?" She looked at me in confusion. I held both her cheeks and tried to force her to focus.

"Phoebe, listen. My vision's coming true. We have to help Kira." As my words sunk in, her eyes widened and her mouth dropped open. She seemed to sober up with lightning speed.

"Call Willow." She was right. I found Willow's number and pressed 'Call'. I prayed she would answer. It was a little after two in the morning.

"Stasia?" I could tell by her hoarse voice that I'd woken her up.

"Willow!"

"Hey-"

"My vision's coming true." There was no time for small talk. "Kira's been taken. We have to do something!" I could hear her sitting up in bed.

"Wait - calm down, calm down. Tell me what happened." I told her about Kira's message. She was silent for a moment, which made me highly aware of the unending terror beginning to strangle me.

"Are you sure she said The Fortunate Isle?" she asked.

"Yes. That's exactly what she said," I confirmed quickly. "Do you know where that is?"

"No, but Nicolet's poem might."

"What do you mean?" Phoebe was trying to talk into the phone at the same time, so I put Willow on speaker so she'd stop climbing on me.

"I figured it out…what it says. Hold on." I could hear her moving papers around. "Okay, listen to this:

most fortunate of Isles

belongs to the blessed and true

which of itself and without favour,

slumbers beneath the blue.

242

anchor off her shore
whilst shifting currents slew
cease the tidal surge
and arrive her sprites to woo
hidden amongst the mangroves
beyond the blue lagoon
stands the house of thetis
seen only by those deemed true
she whispers to the creatures
and answers to the blue
the heart of the Isle rejoices
its soul to be renewed.

"Oh my God." I stared out at the water, almost incoherent. "That's where we have to go." Panic broke my trance and I shook my head to clear it. "We have to go find her! I don't know how, but-"

"Hold on, there's numbers written on the back," she stopped me. I could almost hear the wheels turning in her head. "I didn't understand what they could mean, because they looked so recent. But now it makes sense."

"What are they?"

"Coordinates. Longitude and latitude."

"Thath's perfect! We just neeth to find a way to geth there!" Phoebe clutched my arm, her eyes wide with fear. I squeezed her hand and handed her the water to drink.

"Okay, I just looked the coordinates up and it's basically in the middle of the ocean," Willow said. I glanced at Phoebe.

"We neeth a boat," she whispered, and I nodded. We were on a boat, but the chances of me stealing this yacht were pretty slim. Especially with a hundred girls on it and the fact that I had no idea how to drive a yacht. Phoebe looked around and raised an eyebrow, obviously thinking what I was thinking.

"No. There's no way we'd able to take this one." I shook my head at her. "We'd have to find another one somehow."

"Or you could just use mine." We whirled around at her silky voice. Olivia leaned up against the railing with crossed arms. Phoebe immediately took off in her direction.

"You were listening to us!? Go back inside you evil bit-" I clamped my hand over her mouth and stared at Olivia.

"You have a boat?" I asked her. She nodded her head slowly and peered down at Phoebe with a smirk. "And you would let us use it?" I laughed; sarcasm evident in my voice. She sauntered over to us.

"You won't be using it. I will take you in my boat." She made sure the distinction was clear. Phoebe squirmed, and muffled curse words came through my hand as she glared at Olivia.

"Why would you help us?" I found it very hard to believe that Olivia would help us sail out in the ocean out of the goodness of her heart. I wasn't even positive she had a heart.

"I have my reasons." She looked down at her cuticles as if our conversation was boring her.

"Stasia, I'll get Carmen and we'll meet you guys at the marina, okay?" I had forgotten about Willow on the phone.

"Hurry, Willow! And don't forget the poem!" I called out to her before she hung up. I released Phoebe and focused intently on Olivia.

"Kira's life could depend on us. If you have any doubts about helping us, then tell me right now and we'll find another way."

"It's not Kira I'm worried about." She stared daggers at me. "But yeah, I'm sure. And if Phoebe and that girl Curly or Cartman-"

"Carmen," I corrected her.

"Whatever. If they cause any trouble, you're on your own. Got it?" I didn't like this one bit. But from what I could see, this mean self-centered devil girl was the only way I was getting to the Fortunate Isle.

Twenty-Nine

Twenty minutes later, the three of us stood on the empty boardwalk at the marina waiting for Carmen and Willow. In front of us was yet another yacht, only smaller. I didn't know how long it would take to get to the Isle, but I was suddenly thankful we'd be taking the journey in style. I needed rest, and Phoebe needed to sleep off her drunken stupor so she didn't lash out at Olivia and get herself thrown overboard.

"There they are!" Phoebe waved frantically at them as they made their way toward us. They eyed Olivia warily but stayed quiet. It looked like Willow had packed for a month-long journey at sea, until I figured out what exactly she was carrying. She had gathered up some clothes for us, along with a ton of snack food. I could have kissed her right then and there. My body had been in that dress long enough, and I was starving. We all followed Olivia towards the back of the yacht. We all stepped down onto the deck except for Phoebe, who was already looking a little green. I held my arms out to her as she clumsily stepped over the rail and onto the deck.

"This is my parents' yacht and I'm not supposed to have anybody on it without asking them, so don't mess anything up unless you want to pay for it." She turned on her heel and we all looked at each other in disgust.

She walked us through the first level of the boat, which housed three bedrooms and two bathrooms. Phoebe and I claimed one room, while Carmen and Willow claimed the other. I changed into the jeans and t-shirt Willow brought for me and collapsed onto the soft queen-sized bed. The rooms were cozy, with a small chest of drawers and an arm chair. The walls were a pale yellow color that reminded me of a sunrise. There was one small window looking out on the water. I glanced over at my twelve black roses sitting on the dresser. There was already a vase in the room with fake flowers in it, so I replaced them with mine instead. They made me think of Finn and the amazing night we had, and my entire body went numb with delirium. The last thing I heard before I went to sleep was Phoebe throwing up in the bathroom. Something about Phoebe puking on Olivia's personal property made me smile.

When I woke up sunlight was streaming in through the window above my head, and it took me a couple of minutes to remember where I was. My scalp was in pain from the fifty bobby pins in my hair. I reached up and tried to fish some of them out, with no luck. Phoebe's side of the bed was empty and I had no idea what time it was, so I got up and searched the other two bedrooms. Both empty. I climbed a carpeted spiral staircase at the end of the hall to the second level of the yacht. An immaculate living room opened up before me, surrounded by windows looking out over the ocean. Carmen and Phoebe had made themselves at home on two enormous half-moon shaped leather couches facing each other in the middle of the room. Their attention was on a sixty-inch flat screen TV that retracted down from the ceiling. They wore matching fluffy white terrycloth robes with fuzzy slippers. A tray of doughnuts, cinnamon rolls, strawberries and scones sat on the coffee table, along with a pitcher of orange juice.

Carmen grinned up at me. "It's about time you woke up."

"What time is it?" I asked groggily; still trying to find those elusive bobby pins poking into my skull.

"Just ten-thirty."

"Ten-thirty? Where are we? Where are Willow and Olivia?"

"Yes, don't know, and upstairs," she rattled off the answers in order. I observed Phoebe, who was not looking very good this morning. The hair that had been so elegantly styled last night was now in one big knot on her head, and her face was drained of color. The bags under her eyes were apparent even from far away.

"How're you feeling, Phoebs?"

"I'm never drinking ever again." She craned her neck to see me from the couch; squinting from the light coming through the windows. I bent down and gave her a quick hug.

"You want to take advantage of the witch's money with us?" Carmen asked with unrestrained satisfaction and snickered.

"That's okay, ya'll seem to be doing a fine job of that already." I leaned down closer and raised an eyebrow. "Ya'll better behave or she's not going to help us. At the moment she's all we've got."

"We'll try our best, but if I see a shark swim by, there's a good possibility she'll accidentally fall in the water and get eaten." They collapsed into a fit of giggles. I shook my head at them and walked up the staircase to the third and top level of the yacht. Speaking of sharks, I wanted to call Finn, but I definitely didn't have any cell phone service out here. I would feel much better if he were there with me. I had no idea what I was doing or what I was going to do once we arrived. What if we couldn't find the Isle? What if we got hurt? What if Kira got killed? I tried to force all of those morbid thoughts out of my mind as I stepped into what looked like the yacht's control room. There were two large plush chairs facing a litany of keyboards, buttons and levers that I hoped Olivia knew how to operate. There was a small leather couch at the back of the room where Willow and Olivia were engrossed in a laptop. I spotted Nicolet's poem on the small table in front of them.

"Hey Stasia!" Only Willow looked up at my entrance. She patted the cushion beside her for me to sit. "How are you feeling?"

"I'm okay, but I'll feel better when we find the Isle. Have you guys had any luck?" I peeked at the laptop screen.

"Well we're already locked in on the coordinates and heading straight towards them." She shared a stressed look with Olivia. "Our problem isn't finding the Fortunate Isle, though. It's the whole getting on the Fortunate Isle part that we're worried about." I could tell they'd been at this for hours. Olivia took a swig of Diet Coke, stood up and stretched.

"You thirsty? Hungry?" She was looking at me, but I had trouble reconciling her nice tone with the person saying them. No sarcasm at all.

"Um, sure. That would be awesome." As she walked away I raised both eyebrows at Willow and she shrugged her shoulders. She eyed my hair and already started taking out the bobby pins I couldn't find on my own. She gave me a grave look while she worked.

"Like I was saying, we think we'll be able to find the Isle just fine. We should be there by tomorrow. But making it onto the island is a whole different issue."

"Are there walls or something? High cliffs? A crocodile-infested moat?"

"No, worse - a protective shield. Just like the one around Lorelei, except this one keeps everything and everyone out. You have to be approved to go onto the island." Well this was definitely a major roadblock.

"Approved?" I asked, slightly frustrated. Was there a secret knock we needed to know or something?

"Not everyone is allowed admittance. And we have no idea what those specific qualifications are. We've been studying the poem and we think we've figured out a couple of things, but executing them might be a challenge."

"Why is the island so protected? What's so special about it?"

"The Fortunate Isle is an island the Nereids have lived on for centuries," Olivia explained as she came up the stairs with a glass of orange juice and jelly toast. "Mostly it's used by the more…important ones." She set the food down in front of me and I dug in immediately. Willow nodded.

"By 'important', she means the strongest, or the leaders. Thetis and Keto have always lived there. Several have left since Keto took over, though." As I gobbled down every last bit of the toast and orange juice, I thought about the island. It sounded like a sanctuary untouched by the outside world. If my vision was true, the place I had been would match that description. It surpassed anything I'd ever seen. I guessed getting there in a vision was slightly different than in real life, though.

"So if the Isle is so sacred, how do you think Isadora was allowed entrance?" I asked them.

"The only thing we can come up with is that Keto changed some of the long standing rules around admittance and who's deemed worthy." Willow put hand quotes around the word worthy. Suddenly feeling disheartened, I put my head in my hands. Willow wrapped her arm around my shoulder and sent healing tingles across my back. They wound down into all of my muscles; releasing the tension and helping me breathe easier.

"Thank you." I smiled at her, then picked the poem up from the table and read the first stanza out loud.

> most fortunate of Isles
> belongs to the blessed and true
> which of itself and without favour,
> slumbers beneath the blue.

"What do you think it means by 'slumber'? Is the island...asleep?" I asked Willow apprehensively.

"I'm not sure. Olivia thinks it means someone has actually put it to sleep. Or turned it 'off' in a sense."

"It's the most likely possibility if Sirens like Isadora are being allowed in," Olivia added; looking up from the laptop.

"How can we be sure the poem has anything to do with our current situation?" I tried unsuccessfully to put the puzzle pieces together.

"Unfortunately we can't." Olivia chewed on her lip, thoughtful. She glanced at me tentatively and weighed her words carefully before speaking. "There are a lot of legends in our world. Some true, some not. I think this poem refers to one of them, or is maybe foreshadowing something." I had a feeling she knew a lot more than she was telling us. And whatever she was hiding had something to do with why she'd decided to help us. I didn't trust her as far as I could throw her, but we still needed her help. I glanced down at the second stanza. It appeared to be instructions.

anchor off her shore
whilst shifting currents slew
cease the tidal surge
and arrive her sprites to woo

"So we anchor off shore. That makes sense. But what does the second line mean?" I spread jelly on another piece of toast.

"I think it means high tide. Which we think is confirmed by the third line." Willow pointed at the paper.

"So we anchor off shore at high tide and calm the waves?" I guessed. An uneasy feeling pushed its way into my throat and the anxiety in my heart became overwhelming. We had to calm the waves. That meant either I or Carmen would have to do it. I didn't know if I could do it again, especially without Finn. And with so much at stake.

"That's what we're thinking." Willow touched my arm with compassion.

"I don't even want to know what the fourth line means, do I?" I closed my eyes.

"We think the water sprites are the ones who decide who enters the islands and who doesn't." Olivia sighed.

"And how does one go about wooing a sprite?" I asked, exasperated. This was getting more and more complicated by the minute. What if we couldn't figure it out? What would happen to Kira?

"We haven't gotten that far yet." Willow shook her head, clearly frustrated. Thankfully I had learned about sprites last week in class. They could breathe both air and water, but lived mostly in the sea. They were all female and the color of the sea, so it was very difficult to see them unless you knew what you were looking for. They were harmless unless provoked, but that didn't do much to calm my nerves, which were completely frayed by that point. How was I supposed to woo a sprite? Tell her how beautiful she was? Sing her a love song? I sighed and stood up.

"Hey guys! Guys! Come down here! Quick!" Phoebe yelled to us from the stairs. We ran to see what had her all excited. She just shuffled us down to the first level and out to the deck.

"Look!" She pointed over the side of the yacht. I peeked over the side, not sure what to expect, and saw an entire school of dolphins swimming on both sides of us. Jumping and darting back and forth, I could almost feel their excitement. No, I could feel their excitement. It was like a thousand buzzing bees flying through my veins; tiny vibrations shooting through me all at once. It felt like I'd drunk a gallon of espresso in one sitting. My whole body was jittery and my head began to spin, so I sat down on one of the seats and pinched my nose. I tried to concentrate on just one dolphin, thinking maybe that would block out the rest of them. I zeroed in on one of the smaller dolphins closer to the boat. It was a darker gray then the others and very, very fast. Eventually my head stopped spinning and the buzzing in my body lessened to only a light tickle. I glanced up and met the piercing gaze of Olivia watching me intently. She narrowed her eyes momentarily, but then looked away.

"Dolphins are good luck, you know." Phoebe launched into a lesson about dolphins and their symbolism. I did feel somewhat comforted by the ocean we were gliding over. As weird as it sounded, I felt like we were being trailed by more than just dolphins.

Since we had been going full speed for almost twelve hours, we decided to anchor the boat for the night so all of us could get some sleep. The high-tech weather system on the yacht told us there were no storms brewing or even a chance of rain, so I wasn't too worried. Willow spent two hours in the kitchen making us a dinner of roasted chicken with potatoes and artichokes on a bed of kale, and I was amazed at what she could do with the modest ingredients we had available to us on the yacht. After dinner, everyone piled onto the leather couches on the second level to watch a couple of movies. After an overwhelming veto of Phoebe's first movie choice, The Perfect Storm, we decided to watch Sweet Home Alabama first.

It started tugging at me about halfway through the movie. That familiar pull. Slightly different than the sea turtles and no singing involved – just a slight urge to go to the back of the boat. A little apprehensive, I tried to determine if it felt friendly or threatening. It was hard to trust anything right now. I excused myself, saying I had to go to the bathroom. I made sure none of the girls followed, then quietly snuck out to the back deck.

The night was warm and clear, with only a slight breeze swirling through my blond hair, and the only sounds I heard were the waves lapping at the sides of the yacht. Thousands of stars sparkled above, but the moon was nowhere in sight. The ocean resembled black tar; rolling and extending into the darkness. I couldn't figure out where the pull was coming from. The only thing on the deck was me. As I continued towards the back of the boat, it grew stronger. I gazed down at the dark water and saw nothing but my own perplexed expression staring back at me.

"I'm here," I whispered, instantly feeling ridiculous. Why was I talking to the water? Did I expect it to talk back? I laughed softly at myself and perched on the back of the boat; allowing my legs to dangle toward the water. Every fiber of my being wanted to slide into the comfort of its arms below. It was tantalizingly close; like a part of my soul speaking to me from the deep, longing to be reunited. It took every ounce of restraint I had not to oblige. We were in the middle of the ocean! But at the same time, the boat was anchored. It wasn't going anywhere. After a couple more minutes of deliberating, I looked over my shoulder to make sure the coast was clear. Quickly stripping off my clothes so I wouldn't get them wet, I was left standing in my bra and underwear. I looked over my shoulder one more time and stepped up onto the railing of the yacht. I climbed over, leaned against the top bar and balanced myself with the backs of my legs. Once again I was reminded of Rose in Titanic right before Jack talked her out of plummeting to her death. Fortunately, there was no Jack on this voyage to rescue me from myself. I reeled with sweet anticipation and dove in head first.

Trying not to over think it, I forced myself to take a deep breath of water. I got a huge rush of adrenaline as the water expanded in my lungs and my eyes became acclimated to the darkness. Instead of being in the ocean, I felt like I was actually a part of it. The fine line between my body and the water surrounding it quivered and blurred, and I relinquished all control as the salt water caressed my skin...then instinctively dove deeper.

The pull was stronger than ever, and it wanted me to go down farther. I did. I stopped and looked down. I couldn't see the ocean floor and an odd fear of heights suddenly hit me. I'd never been afraid of heights before, but the black abyss below my feet was pretty scary. Although my vision was much sharper in the water, there was still nothingness all around me. I didn't see any fish, animals, or anything else for that matter. It was very disorienting, but I squelched the anxiety building in my chest. Just when I was about to give up and swim back to the surface, I saw something floating up all around me. Silently and steadily they continued up; surrounding me. I felt like I was caught in an upside down snow storm, because they were all I could see in every direction. Upon further inspection, I identified my new friends - hundreds of seahorses. With so many around me I was hit with a strong sense of purity. Their spirit was innocent and playful as it wrapped around me and made me smile. They responded to my happiness instantly. Looking at the whole, it appeared they were vibrating, but looking at just one I could tell they were simply propelling themselves faster with their coiled tails. I reached my hand out to touch one and it stopped hopping around and drifted in my direction. It watched me for a second and slowly floated downward; touching down on my palm softly.

A tiny electrical shock went through my hand when it landed. It was the same sensation I'd felt with the sea turtles, but that didn't make sense. I had an affinity for sea turtles, not seahorses. Or dolphins. I thought back to my earlier experience with the dolphins. How many affinities could one person have? A suffocating fear abruptly hit me from every direction. How could I be afraid of seahorses? Then I realized what was happening. I was actually feeling the seahorses' emotions! And they were downright terrified. They darted off in every direction and I spun around to look for the source of their fear, but all I could see was infinite blackness. Then I felt a shadow pass above me. I looked up and my eyes fell onto something much more terrifying than a simple shadow. A massive great white shark emerged from the darkness, and it paralyzed me with the same fear I felt in the seahorses. But this time it was my own terror slicing through my heart. I was locked in its cold, dark eyes as it bore down on me at warp speed.

I stayed as still as humanly possible while it circled me, and I tried to make myself relax. I didn't know if they could smell fear like dogs, but I didn't want to find out. After several deep breaths and three minor heart attacks, my heart slowed and a new feeling took hold of me. The shark. I could feel her. It was definitely a she, and she was happy, almost excited. She radiated a staggering amount of wisdom and confidence, and the feeling I got from her was actually calming. She wasn't there to tear me to pieces or take a chunk out of my leg. She just wanted to meet me! In a momentary lapse of sanity, I did something no normal person should ever do. I moved closer and touched her side.

Her skin was rubbery beneath my fingers and I actually felt her shiver beneath my touch. Everything I felt from her before was amplified and my heart sang with renewed strength. With a flip of her tail, she disappeared from sight. Something off to the right caught my attention, but when I looked, nothing was there. A prickle of fear ran down my spine and I actually wanted the shark to come back.

Out of nowhere a strong arm wrapped around my throat; cutting off my breathing. An enchanting sound filled my ears and wrapped around me. It was so beautiful, I instantly relaxed and listened. It filled my senses and I felt like I was floating, then reality came crashing back to me. One word played over and over in my mind. Siren. She was singing. Just like at the candlelight vigil, I concentrated as much as I could with my airway blocked and tried to push the sound out of my mind. It was easier than I expected, and once I could think again, I bit down on her arm until I tasted blood. Her grip lessened slightly, which allowed me to twist around. I came face to face with a beautiful woman I didn't recognize. She had dark brown hair and blue eyes that broadcasted her total shock. Apparently she hadn't expected me to overcome her song. I narrowed my eyes at her, and with all of my strength, kicked her in the stomach. She winced in pain and flew backwards, just as a dark ominous shape appeared nearby.

I felt her anger, sensed her urge to kill and froze, as I watched the shark barreling towards me. Before I could move or uselessly try to defend myself, her enormous body shot past me in a fit of rage that overwhelmed my nervous system. My skin sizzled with her anger as she barely missed me and attacked the Siren. Never having a chance against the massive killing machine, the Siren was caught in her massive jaws full of razor sharp teeth. I turned away as they disappeared into the deep, and then someone grabbed my arms from behind.

"Get off me!" I screamed and struggled to get out of their grip, but they just held on tighter and locked my arms behind me. "Let. Me. Go."

Maybe it was the leftover shark rage or adrenaline, but suddenly I was able to release myself from the grip easily. I swung my arm around and made contact with Olivia's cheek. Unfortunately it didn't seem to hurt her. She glared at me, pointed up and I followed her to the surface.

"What the hell were you doing?" I yelled at her as we swam toward the yacht. Surprisingly it was only a couple feet away.

"What was I doing?!" Olivia lifted herself up the ladder, ignored the towel Willow held out for her and turned to face me as I climbed up. "What were you doing?! Are you trying to get yourself killed?"

"No. I was trying to go for a swim. The sea was calling to me."

"The sea was calling to you," she said dryly and rolled her eyes. "Drop the Lifetime movie bullshit, Stasia. You can't just go for a swim in the middle of the ocean at night by yourself because you feel like it!! You almost got killed! If it wasn't for me, you'd be dead right now!" She stepped closer to me as I tried to dry off. I handed the towel to Phoebe and stood up straight, meeting her dark eyes as they flashed with anger.

"You didn't do a damn thing, Olivia! The shark saved me! Whoever that was is definitely dead! I felt what the shark was feeling, and she knew exactly what she was doing!" I saw Phoebe and Carmen's jaws drop.

"I'm done looking out for your ass," she mumbled as she stomped off. I followed her into the yacht, up the stairs and into the living room with my roommates trailing us.

"Looking out for me?! Seriously?! Nobody asked you to look out for me. I don't need a babysitter! Especially not you!"

"Obviously you do," she said in a deadpan voice and turned to face me again.

"Why do you even care?"

"Open your eyes, Anastasia." She put emphasis on my name and smirked at me. "I'm beginning to think Mom was wrong about you."

"Mom?"

"My mom." She raised her chin with indignation. "My full name is Olivia Noel Campbell."

My jaw dropped. Olivia was Dr. Campbell's daughter? That couldn't possibly be true! Dr. Campbell was so caring and understanding. Olivia was so...not. Speechless, I sat down in one of the oversized leather chairs facing the couch. Phoebe, Carmen and Willow all sat down too, completely engrossed in our conversation. Olivia remained standing and glared down at me. I looked up at her in shock.

"Dr. Campbell's your mom?" I saw Phoebe ask Carmen who Dr. Campbell was, but she just shrugged her shoulders and they kept listening intently.

"She told me to look out for you, and believe me I've tried. But if you are so hell bent on getting yourself killed, then who am I to stop you?" She counted off on her fingers. "Almost drowning, saving some dumb sea turtle eggs in the middle of a hurricane, swimming alone with Finn Morrison in the middle of the night - who is the last person you should be hanging out with - and now swimming alone with sharks at midnight?!" She threw her arms up in frustration and I stood up, suddenly irate.

"You've been spying on me!?" I was so angry my hands were shaking, and I felt tears burning my eyes. All those times I felt like I was being watched... "Why won't you just leave me alone!?"

Instead of yelling back, she pointed at me and said, "I'd love to. Unfortunately everyone thinks you're part of that stupid legend. And if that's true, which I'm beginning to seriously doubt, every Siren on the planet will want you dead before your eighteenth birthday. So don't come crying to me when the shit hits the fan." She waved her hand at me like I was a piece of gum she'd pulled off her shoe and headed for the stairs. "I'm done."

I was too stunned to produce a comeback for her rant. Legend? That woman in the water was definitely a Siren. I sat back down on the leather chair and stared blankly at my roommates.

"Will someone please tell me what she was rambling about?" I asked them wearily. They exchanged looks and their eyes hit the floor in shame. Willow spoke first.

"We didn't want to tell you yet. We didn't want to scare you."

"I didn't want you to freak out and leave," Phoebe whispered.

"Plus, we have no way of knowing if it's true yet." Carmen shrugged her shoulders and looked back down at her feet. I rubbed my temples and tried to figure out what was going on. I didn't understand why everything had to be such a secret. Finn wouldn't answer any of my questions, no one told me what to expect at Lorelei, and now my roommates were keeping things from me. Who was I supposed to trust? I let out a loud sigh and tried to rein in my anger.

"Just tell me." I pinched the bridge of my nose, but my head was already pounding.

"There's a legend. A very old legend," Willow began hesitantly. "Back in the day, the leader of the Nereids, Thetis, was destined to bear only one son. That son would be stronger and more gifted then the father. Neither Zeus nor Poseidon wanted a son that would eventually overpower them, so they forced Thetis to marry a mortal. They had a baby boy, Achilles, and in an effort to make him immortal, she dipped him in the River Styx by his heel. Then he was killed in the Trojan War when an arrow pierced his heel; the only unprotected part of his body. Thetis was so distraught, she vowed never to have another child. This is where the legend comes in. Thetis had the ability of foresight, just like her father Nereus. It is said that when she foresaw her own death, she knew she would give birth to a baby girl who would take her place as the leader of the Nereids. The girl would grow to be stronger than her father, like Achilles was, but also stronger than her mother, Thetis. Her name was destined to be Anastasia."

Thirty-one

At least that explained the weird looks when I'd introduced myself at school. A smile crept across my face and I chuckled with relief. "Well I can clear everything up real quick. I chose 'Anastasia' when I came to Lorelei because of a dream I had, and I thought it was a pretty name. The state of Georgia gave me my previous name, Hannah. I never knew the true name given to me by my parents, so the chances of me being The Anastasia are pretty slim. Problem solved." I left out the part about the woman I saw crying in my dreams who called out to an Anastasia. I pushed that from my mind.

"There's more." Willow gave me a harsh look and continued. "When you told us you could breathe underwater, I started to do more research so we could be sure you were the one. I found other things associated with the legend that I'd never heard before. Like, Thetis's daughter would have the same abilities as her mother and more – foresight, an affinity for all sea creatures – which goes along with breathing underwater - and manipulating not just the ocean, but also the shore and wind."

Phoebe looked at me, hopeful. "So…from what we know so far, you definitely have foresight, an affinity for sea turtles and it sounds like sharks? Have you 'felt' any other animals?"

"Maybe seahorses…and the dolphins," I said and shrugged; running my hand over my trace.

"Seahorses?" Carmen said in disbelief. "Okay, so that means the ones we can check off are foresight, an affinity for all sea animals-"

"Not necessarily – I mean four isn't really a good judge of the hundreds of animals and fish out there," I tried to convince her, but it didn't work.

"Anyway." She raised an eyebrow at me. "You've got foresight, an affinity for all animals, we know you can breathe underwater and manipulate the ocean. Have you ever tried to manipulate sand or wind?"

"Of course not. Look, you guys are on crack. This legend or whatever could just be a story somebody made up. It doesn't mean anything." Deep down I didn't really believe what I was saying, but I wanted to think about this on my own. I didn't want anyone else dissecting me and telling me who I was. I got up and went to find Olivia while they continued to pick me apart. I found her outside on the back deck.

"What do you want?" She didn't look up from the magazine she was reading.

"I want to apologize," I said and sat down beside her. "I shouldn't have yelled at you."

"I'm touched, really, but I'm not taking back the things I said. I meant every word." She kept reading. She was the most stubborn person I'd ever met.

"I'm not taking back what I said either, I'm just saying I shouldn't have yelled them at you."

"Maybe next time you could try hand signals." I saw a ghost of a smile on her face. "I'm really good at those." She flipped me off and kept reading.

"I'm better at smoke signals, but I know a few hand signals too. Apparently I need to work on the whole punching-thing." This got me a full grin. She didn't have a bruise or scratch on her. I was a miserable fighter. She set her magazine down and looked at me.

"Fine. You're forgiven. Happy now?"

"Almost."

"What else do you want?" She sighed and turned towards me.

"Willow explained the legend you were talking about, but it can't mean I'm that Anastasia. I chose my name when I came to Lorelei-" I stopped abruptly as a memory surfaced and something in my mind clicked. I scratched my head. "I met your mom when I was still going by 'Hannah'. Why would she have thought I was part of the legend before I chose the name 'Anastasia'?"

"She didn't care about your name, even though she thought it was pretty ironic you chose Anastasia when you got to school. But what proved it to her was your trace." She pointed down at my wrist and raised her eyebrows at me.

"But no one knows what my trace means."

"My mom does."

"How would your mom know?"

"She was part of Thetis's personal council," she said proudly, then looked me up and down and smirked. "She said you're the spitting image of her. I find that hard to believe too."

I gave her a look and continued, "Willow also said if I was her daughter, I'd have all of her abilities. Is that true?"

"All her abilities and more. The legend says you would be more powerful than her once all your abilities surface. But that's honestly all I know."

"Did she tell you what my trace means?" I asked, hopeful.

"Nope, she wouldn't tell me. She said there were some things you would have to find out on your own. Whatever that means." She shrugged.

"Have you really been following me around?"

"Somebody had to make sure you didn't do anything stupid." She rolled her eyes at me.

"I always felt like somebody was watching me, but I never saw you..." I narrowed my eyes at her accusingly. I still didn't like the fact that she had been following me around.

"I'm a concealer. It's what I do," she said nonchalantly.

"A what?"

"A concealer. I'm descended from Calypso. I can match myself to whatever environment I happen to be in at the time."

"Sort of like camouflage?" I guessed.

"Exactly like camouflage." She grinned wickedly at me, and then suddenly she disappeared. I looked closer and could actually see the outline of her body, but she took on the colors of the seat she was in. Then she moved and I really could see her.

"You're like a chameleon!" I said, completely fascinated. She reappeared, narrowed her eyes at me and crossed her arms.

"I am not a cold-blooded scaly, slimy lizard," she hissed at me; sounding exactly like a lizard. And I wouldn't be surprised if she was cold blooded. I giggled at my own thoughts, which only made her madder. "What are you laughing at?"

"I was wondering if you had a forked tongue." I smirked at her, still laughing. The corners of her mouth were twitching and I could tell she was trying not to laugh too. She stuck her tongue out at me, which only made me laugh harder.

"Whatever. You're just jealous." She flipped her dark hair and stood up.

"You're right, being a lizard has been a dream of mine for years," I said sarcastically, trying to make her laugh. It almost worked.

"Keep dreaming, blondie. You'll never be this awesome." She actually smiled at me this time. "I'm going to bed." She started to walk back inside.

"Wait!" Something dawned on me. She turned around. "Did you help get the Siren off of me? Were you concealing yourself?"

"I jump at any chance to kick a Siren's ass." She winked at me and closed the door.

Maybe she wasn't that bad after all. I looked out over the dark water, thoughtful. A part of me actually wanted the legend to be true. And it would also tell me who my parents were and who I was. I wanted that more than anything. But if Thetis was really my mother, who was my father? And why would they abandon me? The more I thought about it the more I wanted to know for sure. Either way, I would be a little closer to finding out who I was and where I came from. Carmen was right; I could do almost all of the things Thetis could. I knew I had foresight and could manipulate the ocean. I knew I could breathe underwater, but I still wasn't sure about having an affinity for every single animal in the ocean. That seemed like a tall order. And manipulating the wind and shore? Seriously? Maybe the next day before we made it to the Isles I could test out some of the theories. Could I really be destined to be the leader of the Tydes? And what about Keto? No wonder the Sirens didn't like me. That would also explain Isadora and Priscilla's aversion to me. As I felt the weight of the world fall onto my shoulders, I walked back inside and decided to get some sleep.

The next day brought abundant sunshine and clear blue skies, and we expected to make it to the Fortunate Isle by late afternoon. We had obviously been followed by one

Siren, so it was entirely possible there were more where she came from. We hadn't seen any other visitors since, and I had a feeling it had everything to do with the three great white sharks trailing the yacht. They kept a reasonable distance but they were always there. Not having Finn there, three sharks the size of school buses was just as good.

We gathered on the third level to eat lunch and to dissect Nicolet's poem for the hundredth time. We tried to come up with a good plan but weren't getting very far, so Willow read the third stanza out loud one more time.

hidden amongst the mangroves

beyond the blue lagoon

stands the house of Thetis

seen only by those deemed true

"So is Kira at Thetis's house?" Phoebe's brow furrowed in thought as she picked at the rest of her ham sandwich.

"That's what we're hoping, but I think we should just get on the island first and then go off of Stasia's vision," Willow suggested. She had way too much faith in me.

"But I don't know exactly where I went in the woods. The beach is just one big circle; we could be wandering around for hours. Plus, we don't know for sure that she'll still be where she was in my vision by the time we get there." I didn't want to depend too much on my vision; there were too many unknowns. Willow nodded and read the last stanza, which made me the most uneasy.

she whispers to the creatures

and answers to the blue

the heart of the Isle rejoices

its soul to be renewed.

"It's definitely talking about Stasia," Olivia said absently as she turned on the cruise control from her seat at the controls. Her assumption was exactly why I didn't like the last stanza. I just wanted to save Kira, not renew an entire island's soul.

"I honestly think we should just concentrate on getting admittance to the island. Once we figure that out, we can regroup and go from there," I tried to convince them as much as myself.

"I don't know if playing it by ear is really the best idea." Carmen scrunched her nose. And although I understood her opinion, I just didn't think we had much of a choice.

"Stasia's right." I silently thanked Willow; always the voice of reason. "We don't have enough information to make any hard, fast plans once we're on the island. We could sit around all day coming up with a million scenarios that may or may not happen. The best thing to do is jump in with both feet and hit the ground running." Everyone reluctantly nodded their heads in agreement. None of us felt completely comfortable with what we were about to embark upon, but Kira was depending on us and I wasn't going to let her down. I stood up.

"So...." I shrugged my shoulders innocently and smiled shyly. "I was thinking about going outside to figure out if I'm the direct descendant of the most powerful sea Goddess to ever live. Anybody wanna come?"

"Yes!" They all cheered and gave me warm smiles. Phoebe was so excited, she almost knocked over the coffee table trying to stand up. They followed me downstairs to the back deck while Captain Olivia manned the controls.

I had to find out if I could manipulate sand and wind, but being nowhere near a shore, sand would have to wait. I had no idea how to manipulate wind, but I was going to give it a try. With the yacht moving at full speed, there was only one area on the deck that wasn't windy.

"See if you can make the wind blow around Phoebe," Carmen suggested.

"Why do I have to be the guinea pig?" Phoebe whined.

"Do I really have to answer that?" Carmen smirked at her.

"Nobody has to be the guinea pig," I stood at the corner of the deck where an extension from the body of the yacht stretched out; shielding me from the wind. "I'll just see if I can make the wind blow around my body first." I briefly took inventory of myself. My hair wasn't blowing around, nor was my clothes. Taking a wild guess, I closed my eyes and put my hands up. I tried to channel my emotions like Finn taught me in the ocean. I calmed myself and imagined the air compressing and swirling around me. After a couple of minutes I didn't feel a thing, so I hesitantly peeked out one eye. No wind. Not even a slight breeze around me.

"Try blowing air out of your mouth. Maybe you have to give it a little motivational push," Phoebe suggested with an encouraging smile. Carmen snickered at her, but I closed my eyes again and forced air out of my lungs. I tried over and over to no avail. It only made me lightheaded.

"Maybe hold your arms out and move your hands around like you're stirring it." Willow shrugged her shoulders. We were throwing shots in the dark, but I figured it was worth a try. I held my arms out to the side and did small circles. Beginning to feel really stupid, I felt something shock my left forearm right before something landed on it. My eyes flew open and I looked directly into the eyes of a curious seagull perched on my arm. It squawked at me and I heard Phoebe gasp and Carmen laugh. If I couldn't make wind blow, maybe I could test if I had an affinity for seagulls. I instantly wished I'd had a chance to question Kira more about her ability.

The spark it caused on my skin was a good sign, though. I blocked out everything except the bird and tried to 'feel' it. It cocked its head at me and squawked again as I brought my arm in front of me. Suddenly, anxiety hit me and a slight buzzing slid through my veins. I could tell immediately he was under a great deal of stress.

"Are you okay?" I whispered to him. He turned his head, looked at me through his other eye and adjusted his feathers. He let out a heartbreaking soft squawk. It was almost a whine, but it was so sad it brought tears to my eyes. That's when something slammed into the boat.

Thirty-two

All four of us were thrown forward violently; landing hard against the yacht's exterior. Carmen fell into the door of the cabin and broke the hinges off as she slid halfway down the hallway. Phoebe ended up on top of me, and Willow was crumbled in the same corner I had just been standing in.

"Are you okay?" I asked Phoebe as she untangled herself from me.

"I think so." She looked herself over and glanced at Willow. "Willow! Are you okay?"

"Yeah, ow - my arm just hurts." She attempted to sit up carefully.

"Carmen?" I looked down the hallway and saw her rubbing her head. Then my stomach dropped to the floor. Phoebe and I stared at each other in panic.

"Olivia," we said at the same time. Running down the hall, we climbed the stairs to the third level in record time.

"Olivia! Olivia?" I looked around frantically and found her lying on the floor against the bottom of the front console. I could already see a cut running the length of her arm. "Olivia!" I shook her gently and she slowly opened her eyes. When her memory caught up with her, they flew the whole way open and she jumped to her feet.

"What happened? Are ya'll okay? Is anybody hurt?" I took her hand to calm her down.

"Everybody's fine, we're okay. You didn't see what happened either?" We searched out the front window for

271

any sign of what hit us, but there was only water surrounding us. I looked out the side window. Still nothing.

"The front of the boat looks fine, but how's that possible? We had to have run into something." Olivia peered out the front windows at the bow of the yacht. I crossed the room to the other windows and stopped dead in my tracks; my heart squeezing in my chest.

"Uh, guys?" I pointed toward the windows. Phoebe and Olivia ran over to see what stunned me. They glanced at each other and back at me.

"What?" Phoebe walked to the window and looked out both ways.

"Right there." I pointed again. "You don't see it?"

"See what?" Olivia looked at me like I'd gone completely insane. I blinked several times, but it was still there. My feet started moving, taking me down the stairs, through the first level hall and out to the back deck. They walked to the side railing and I held on tight to steady myself. Stretched out before me was a picturesque island with long white beaches backed by towering mountains. Even from this far away, I knew without a doubt it was the Fortunate Isle. I could feel it. I knew behind those mountains stood a lush forest surrounding a beautiful lagoon, and a ribbon of golden happiness made its way into my soul.

"Stasia?" I turned towards Willow and noticed the tears swimming in my eyes. I wiped them away quickly. "What are you doing?"

"You don't see it either?" She followed my gaze and shook her head solemnly.

"I just see water. What is it?" She placed her hand on my shoulder; sending tingles of numbness down my arm, relaxing my muscles.

"We're here. We made it." I smiled at her. Olivia, Carmen and Phoebe walked outside. Olivia's arm was bandaged up and she frowned at the broken door, but didn't say anything. They gathered around me, looking concerned. I pointed at the island again.

"It's the Fortunate Isle. We must have hit the shield surrounding the island," I told them. Willow looked at everyone.

"Can anyone else see it?" Everyone shook their heads. I had a bad feeling about this. If they couldn't even see the island, how were they going to gain admittance? I couldn't do this by myself!

Several minutes later we dropped anchor. Thankfully the shield hadn't damaged the yacht, only our bodies. I had a couple of bruises on my side and Phoebe had a scratch down her leg. Willow had a knot on her head and Carmen's shoulder was banged up pretty bad, as well as Olivia's bandaged arm. We were a mess. Luckily, we also had our own personal healer. Willow went around and healed each person, one by one. I could tell it was draining for her, but she vehemently refused to stop when we told her we'd be fine.

For whatever reason, I had a hard time not constantly staring at the island with longing. To look away was almost painful. I wanted nothing more than to jump in the ocean and swim ashore, but I knew that wasn't possible. According to Willow, high tide was still a couple hours away. We were stuck for a while.

"Next?" Willow walked up behind me and gave me a quick hug as I tried to tear my eyes away from the island again. She placed her hands on my side and started to work her magic. I was becoming accustomed to the tingles and numbness that flowed from her hands.

"Hey Willow?" She stepped around to face me; keeping her hands on my side and raising her eyebrows in response. "Do you think I'll have to go alone?" I wanted her to tell me no. I wanted her to tell me not to worry about anything, that everything was going to be okay. But I knew she wouldn't lie to me.

"I think that might be a very good possibility." She smiled encouragingly. "But we would just slow you down anyway. You're really amazing, Stasia. I know you'll find her and bring her home." Once again she had more faith in my abilities than I did.

"What if I can't?"

"What-ifs are kind of like ex-boyfriends." Carmen appeared on my other side. "The more attention you give 'em, the more likely they are to stalk you and show up in your bedroom closet when you're getting out of the shower." Willow and I looked at each other and started laughing.

"What? It's true – I'm not making it up. I read it in Cosmo." It felt so good to laugh, I couldn't stop. Some of the stress from the last couple of days fell away and my shoulders felt slightly lighter.

"Um, you guys?" Olivia's face was white and her eyes were wide with fear. "I think we have company." She looked towards the back of the boat. I stood up and saw them instantly. Apparently everyone else did too, because I heard several gasps behind me. As Olivia slowly stepped backwards, I stepped forward; my eyes locked on the water and its newest inhabitants.

Three pairs of large, crystal blue eyes stared back at me. Each had long, straight hair the color of the sky framing their pale blue faces. They were the personification of the ocean; glistening with reverence. The sprites were much smaller than I would have expected; about the size of a small child. I eventually summoned up enough courage to speak.

"I need to gain admittance to the island. Our friend has been kidnapped." The sprites began chattering at each other, and their voices sounded like wind chimes blowing in a summer breeze. I didn't know how I was supposed to woo creatures that didn't speak my language, but before I could say anything else, two of them sank beneath the water. The one in the middle remained. She glowed with a quiet dignity and her blue eyes emanated wisdom. When she smiled I felt a cool breeze swirling around me that smelled of sea grass.

"Come." It was only one word, but it wasn't what she said that had my pulse quickening, it was how she said it. She was speaking into my mind.

"I need my friends to come too," I told her out loud.

"Only you." My skin prickled. She nodded her head at me respectfully and then joined her sisters beneath the waves.

"She wants me to go with them." I blinked at my friends.

"What about us?" Phoebe squeaked, and wrapped her arms around herself.

"She said I was the only one that could go," I answered blankly; glancing at the island in the distance.

"How do you know?" Olivia sounded more skeptical than she probably intended.

"She...talked to me. I heard her in my head." They stared back at me with a shock I felt mirrored on my own face. My nerves were standing on end and every muscle in my body was tensed with anticipation.

"Where are they going to take you?" Phoebe asked; tears rolling down her cheeks.

"I don't know." I was trying to make my body move, but it was frozen on the boards of the deck. Willow ran to me and hugged me tightly. Carmen and Phoebe followed.

"Please be careful." They held on to me tightly. I finally turned toward the back of the boat.

"Wait." I turned to see a red-faced Olivia; her dark eyes frightened. She stepped forward and hugged me. "Good luck, Stasia. You'll do great."

"We wouldn't have gotten this far if it wasn't for you. It means a lot." I tried to smile with courage I didn't feel. I made my legs step up onto the railing like I had the night before, only this time, the water didn't feel warm and inviting; it held mysteries and secrets I would have to face alone. I had no idea what I was getting myself into. Kira's beaten and bloodied face flashed in my mind and a renewed sense of purpose washed over me. I glanced back one more time, took several deep breaths to steady myself and dove in.

THIRTY-THREE

"The island's essence wanes. You have arrived just in time." My skin prickled again at the ominous tone of her voice sounding in my mind. The other two were still quiet, so I assumed the one speaking held some sort of status. I had no clue what she was talking about, but since these sprites were my ticket onto the island, I was willing to say or do anything to ensure that happened. I tried to focus on the reason I was there...Kira. I needed to find her.

"I need to find Kira. She's in trouble," I told them.

"As you wish." Face to face with me, I saw how magnificent she really was. Her entire body sparkled from the sunlight streaming through the water above, while her skin was almost translucent; shimmering lightly. She touched my shoulder and the world turned to a blur. As the water rushed by me the only thing I could see were her sparkling eyes full of exuberance. In less than thirty seconds, the world was still again. She nodded her head at me respectfully and smiled widely.

"Welcome to the Fortunate Isle, Anastasia." Before I could ask her how she knew my name, she disappeared and I was alone. I kicked to the surface. The sprite had taken me to some kind of cave. I pulled myself up onto a smooth ledge and looked around. I wasn't claustrophobic, but if I stayed in that dark, menacing cave much longer, I would be. I sensed I was actually beneath the island. Jagged stalactites hung above and more water trickled down the walls. The eerie echo of my every move sent chills down my spine. I searched for an exit, but had trouble seeing anything distinct in the low light. I saw a small tunnel hidden in the shadows that looked tall enough for me to walk through. I crept along slowly, expecting vampire bats or giant rats to eat me alive at any moment. Thankfully, the only thing I heard was my own ragged breathing as I stumbled through the thick blackness. After about twenty yards of steady incline, a ray of sunlight up ahead had me picking up my pace.

I emerged from the tunnel and my senses were immediately assaulted by a litany of sights, smells and sounds. I was suddenly soaked in the sun's rays; warming my skin and drying my wet shorts and tank top. The smell of mangos and oranges cleared my head and I took a deep breath; cherishing their fruity aroma. I was standing at the edge of the forest, facing the beach. Just like in the ocean, everything had a surreal quality to it. Each color was more vivid than the last, the flowers and trees appeared to be dotted with diamonds, and the water itself felt magical. A collage of blues swirled and crashed toward the beach.

As I stepped onto the sand, a low hum began flowing through my veins. It increased with each step and became so overwhelming I had to sit down and close my eyes. It was similar to the sensation I got from the dolphins, but much more intense. Remembering how I had blocked it out on the boat, I focused my attention on my own thoughts and feelings and slowly the humming fizzled; slowing my heartbeat and allowing me to think clearly again. I slowly ran my hands over the velvety white sand beneath me. The lagoon from my vision stretched out in front of me. The same white beaches and lush forest circled it, all of it preserved by the jagged mountains protecting the island. I felt the wind blowing through my hair and the sun bronzing my skin. There was a distinct vibration of energy flowing through everything, connecting it all together. I knew from the lightness that filled my heart, the same energy flowed through me. I was just as much a part of the island as the trees growing from its soil.

Across the lagoon I could just make out the small wooden canoe, which told me I was on the wrong side of the island. I decided the best course of action would be to find the little-big house, because I knew for a fact Isadora would bring Kira there at some point. I just hoped I wouldn't be too late. Unfortunately I had a long way to go if I was going to make it there before dark. I skirted the forest and hid in its shadows as I walked. After several hours, my stomach began to growl and my throat became parched. Thankfully there was more food growing on the island than one person could ever eat. Glimpsing over my shoulder every few seconds to memorize my path, I maneuvered through the forest looking for fruits or berries. I could immediately tell something was wrong. Not only did I not hear any birds, but most of the flowers had shriveled and several trees were dying; their branches bare. An all-consuming sadness weighed on my heart and I walked farther and farther looking for food. Finally I came upon an orange tree. Plucking several ripe oranges, I peeled them and devoured their sweetness in minutes. The tangy juice soothed my dry throat and gave me much needed energy.

I sat down on a flat, sturdy stone while I ate and rested my legs. That's when I noticed it wasn't just one stone. It extended out on both sides. A wall. Almost completely covered with thick green moss, it was made of sandstone and only stood about four feet tall. I abandoned the oranges and followed it through the forest, dodging low hanging trees and overgrown sage bushes. I recognized the trees as willows; their cascading branches hanging down gracefully and silently blowing in the wind. The tiny leaves tickled my skin as I parted its curtain and made my way through. The wall brought me to a large iron gate rusted by time and weather. It, too, had succumbed to the dense forest. It was covered in thick vines that coiled tightly around its intricate patterns. Past the gate was a rolling meadow of yellow, purple and blue wildflowers. I was inspecting the gate for a lock when I saw something that would change my life forever.

Amongst the twists and turns of the iron was a small upside down triangle, with one spiral extending from each corner. I'd only seen one other design like that...my trace. Was it just a coincidence? The voice in the back of my head told me what I already knew. No - it wasn't a coincidence. Utterly stunned, I forced my body to move. I stepped closer and traced the spirals with my fingers, just as I'd done so many times to the ones decorating my left wrist. A searing heat beneath my fingers made me pull my hand away and I watched as the iron design actually started to glow. My trace burned too, and began to pulse with a light blue color. Astonished by this turn of events, I definitely wasn't expecting what happened next. A bolt of lightning struck the middle of the meadow and I automatically dropped to my knees and covered my head. I didn't hear any accompanying thunder, so I peeked through my hands but didn't see anything amiss. Hoping I was just hallucinating, I stood slowly and cautiously glanced around. Time stopped, along with my pounding heart, when my eyes scanned the meadow. Or what used to be a meadow.

A majestic, sprawling estate had appeared out of nowhere; the meadow replaced with gardens and acres of Bermuda grass. The manor itself was constructed of sandstone and just like the wall, was aged and worn by the elements. It could have belonged in medieval England with its high walls and regal turrets. Although the house was absolutely magnificent, the overgrown gardens and wilted trees dampened its grandeur. It was obvious the estate had lost its owners, and along with them, maintenance of the grounds. I felt like I was seeing an empty shell; the forgotten leftovers of a once prosperous and glorious paradise hidden beneath the imposing dark green mangrove trees. Something tickled at my memory. The third stanza of Nicolet's poem. Hidden amongst the mangroves. Seen only by those deemed true. This was it. This was the house of Thetis. As I thought it, I knew it to be the truth. Tugging at my heart strings, I felt the manor calling to me.

I tentatively pushed the gate open, which gave way easily and led to a worn stone path. As I stepped onto the grounds, the humming vibration returned to my veins and waves of energy pulsed through me. It was exhilarating! Instead of fighting it, I closed my eyes and welcomed the thrumming sensations coursing through every fiber of my body. Eventually it centered in my chest; swirling and leaving me breathless. I felt a warming on my skin and realized I was still wearing the aquamarine necklace Finn had given me. The stone was very warm to the touch. Instead of the normal tingle, a warm glow spread from the pendant throughout my limbs; renewing my tired body and strengthening my weary mind. I closed my eyes and silently thanked him again for the necklace. Not just a gleaming stone, it must have some kind of healing quality.

I opened my eyes and tried to figure out what I was looking at. If this was the house of Thetis, then whose house did I see in my vision? Is this where they were keeping Kira? Either way, I knew I had to find out. As I approached the rustic, wooden carriage doors of the manor entrance, they creaked open of their own accord. To say I was freaked out would have been an understatement. I glanced around and waited for someone to appear, but the only thing that greeted me was the dank smell of the abandoned interior. I peered through the doorway into a dark, murky foyer full of dust and cobwebs. I took a step inside.

I started to take another step when a slight breeze blew across my arms, giving me chill bumps. The breeze swirled around the rest of my body, lifted my hair and tousled my clothes. It became so strong I had to brace myself against the door frame. But the second my hands touched the worn paint, a gale force wind blew into the house. If I hadn't have been holding on, I would have been thrown across the room. It stopped abruptly and I regained my balance and brushed the hair out of my face. I glanced down at my clothes to make sure they were still intact, and then noticed the floor. My gaze shifted upward, my breath caught in my chest and my jaw dropped open.

The dreary interior had been completely transformed to its former glory. The dust and cobwebs were magically swept away, leaving clean surfaces and the faint smell of lavender. The foyer where I stood opened up to a grand parlor of epic proportions. The slate tile floor beneath my feet met walls of stone that extended to the cathedral ceilings above. Skylights of stained glass scattered the sunlight across the room in spectacular fashion. A stone fireplace dominated the right side of the room, and a grand staircase of mahogany opened its arms to me at the opposite side of the room. Rich blue carpet blanketed the stairs as they split halfway up and led to opposite sides of the manor. An immense wrought iron chandelier hung above the middle landing; strings of crystals hanging delicately from its arms. The crystals sent prisms of sparkling light into every corner of the room.

The most impressive feature was at the parlor's center. An elegant stone fountain rose from the floor, surrounded by a small, pristine pool of water. The fountain itself was a sculpture of a man kneeling and pouring water from a large bowl. He was adorned in a long robe and gladiator sandals. The water fell over the sides of the pail and created a gushing waterfall. I smiled when I realized who it was. Aquarius. I walked closer and became mesmerized as I peered down into the pool encircling him. The fountain was merely the top of a massive underwater cavern; the small pool around the fountain acting as the entrance. It gave a whole new meaning to the term 'indoor pool'. Portraits of men and women I didn't recognize, as well as vast, awe inspiring landscapes decorated the walls. I froze when my eyes found the portrait hanging above the fireplace. With legs full of bricks, I walked over to get a closer look. It was the portrait of a gorgeous young woman dressed in a long, flowing dress of silver and blue. An ethereal glow emanated from her thick blond hair and bright blue eyes. Upon closer inspection I saw that they weren't just blue. They were a teal or aqua. Exactly like mine. If my heart skipped a beat at her eyes, it stopped completely when I saw the necklace around her neck. A brilliant aquamarine stone encased in a swirling pendant, hanging on a dark metal chain. My necklace. Finn gave me Thetis's necklace. My mother's necklace.

A terrifying scream coming from outside broke my thoughts and I immediately ran to the door and down the stone path to the gate. Once outside the grounds, I looked from side to side, trying to find the source. I hesitated when I glanced over my shoulder and saw the estate had disappeared, replaced once again by the rolling meadow of wild flowers. I turned to run but at the same moment, my head exploded in pain and everything went dark.

Thirty-four

The good news was that I found Kira. The bad news was that I found Kira.

"Like a moth to a flame," Isadora literally cackled at me, once I'd woken up from the blow to my head. "You made it way too easy. Really Anastasia, it's pathetic." She looked at me with mock sympathy. My hands and feet were both bound in chains and I was leaning up against a tree at the edge of the beach. The chains themselves pulsed with a silvery glow, and I knew Isadora had enchanted them somehow. Kira was a couple yards away in a similar position. Her mouth was taped, but I still saw the panic in her green eyes as the sun began to sink below the horizon. Her face was beaten and bloody, just as I'd seen in my vision. I clenched my teeth.

"Why are you doing this? What do you want?" I growled at Isadora.

"Oh, if it were only that easy." She smiled down at me, shook her head and continued pacing between Kira and me. Her dark hair fell down her back in waves and her long black skirt dragged in the sand as she walked. I got the feeling we were waiting for something or someone, I just didn't know what or who that was. After several minutes passed, Isadora strolled over and kneeled down in front of me. Her bright green eyes burned into mine.

"This isn't about what I want. This is about what never should have been. And you, dear Anastasia," she squeezed my cheeks hard with her fingers, "never should have been born." I tried to wrench myself free of her grip, but failed miserably as her fingernails dug into my skin. "But don't worry; we'll be rectifying that situation very soon."

"You don't know anything about me!" I yelled at her through squished cheeks. She turned my head side to side as if inspecting my face and laughed. Her breath smelled like stale coffee.

"I know everything about you. You are the one who's clueless, child." She pressed my head up against the tree. "What a waste. So much power hidden in that scrawny little body of yours, and Mommy Dearest was never around to teach you how to use it." She shook her head and tsked. "She thought she was being so careful, so smart by blending you in with the humans. Make no mistake, she is the reason you're about to die. It's her fault you are in this situation." I didn't want to believe what she was saying, but unfortunately it was true. If Thetis was my mother, she had given me away instead of preparing me. She hid me instead of teaching me about this world. How could she leave me so vulnerable? She took the cowardly way out. And now I was the one who would have to pay for her decisions. In the hands of Isadora I was at a distinct disadvantage. I didn't know if I was angrier at Isadora or Thetis. And what about my father? Where was he in all of this? Was he still alive?

"What does any of this have to do with Kira? Let her go!" I demanded through her hand. My cheeks were beginning to ache and I tasted blood as my teeth dug into the sides of my mouth.

"Patience, patience. No need to fear for her life, she was just the bait. And what an excellent bait she turned out to be." She turned and cast an appreciative glance at Kira, who stared daggers at her.

"Then let her go!" I yelled. Isadora let go of my cheeks and wrapped her hand around my throat. Her frigid green eyes were suddenly blazing with hysteria, and her nails sliced into my skin.

"Silence!" She squeezed harder and my breaths were suddenly much harder to come by. She quickly composed herself and the emotion slid off her face. She smiled so coldly at me, frostbite started to form on my heart. "She is still extremely useful to us. You'll see." She winked at me and I wanted nothing more than to tear out of my bindings and rip her head off. She stood and began pacing again.

"You see, Kira has been more helpful to us than Nicolet ever was. Nicolet had so many good theories, so many good ideas. She was closer to the truth than anyone else. But unfortunately for her, she wore out her welcome and we had to get rid of her. A pity, really." I saw Kira's eyes widen at what I already knew. Nicolet was murdered. But I still didn't know why. Did Nicolet know about me somehow?

"You killed her because of me." I decided to throw out my own bait to see what information she was willing to divulge. She shook her head at me and a malicious grin slithered across her beautiful face.

"Oh you poor dear, don't flatter yourself. You're just an orphan. Your own parents dismissed you; abandoned you like a fleeting memory." She turned and pointed at me. "You. Are. Nothing." I felt tears burning my eyes at her harsh words, but unfortunately I had no way of challenging them. "Your mother, on the other hand, she had everything. She was the most powerful Nereid and she wasted it! All of it! Her status! Her power! She was a fool!" Part of the puzzle suddenly clicked in my mind and a savage storm began to boil inside me. I narrowed my eyes at her.

"You murdered her." It was a statement - not a question - and by her expression I knew I'd hit the truth on the dot. Behind Isadora I saw tears running down Kira's bruised cheeks.

Isadora's eyes turned frigid. "So much power and she wouldn't use it against us. Virtue is a weakness, Anastasia. The merciless will always prevail. Your father, however, was much easier to deal with. So weak. So pathetic. You remind me of him."

I stared back at her as a burning anger centered in my soul; simmering and hardening into bitter resolve. This woman had taken my parents from me. She deprived me of the family I so desperately needed. Even if they had given me away, at least I could have found them...tried to reconnect with them. But now that was impossible. I'd finally found my true home, but there was nothing to come back to. Most importantly, there was no one to come back to.

"You will pay for this." The venom in my voice was palpable. Isadora laughed.

"Enough!" I could tell the booming voice caught her by surprise, too. Panic swam in Isadora's eyes and she swiveled around in one quick movement. Priscilla glided out of the shadows of the forest, looking ravishing in a long red dress; her collection of sapphire jewelry shining brightly. Her piercing blue eyes and grim face were locked on Isadora. "I don't have time for this. Get the ring."

"Yes, Priscilla." Isadora produced a velvet pouch from a small bag in the sand. The pouch was peculiarly similar to the one my necklace came in. She opened it and handed the contents to Priscilla.

"We need to make sure you're the true Anastasia before we go about killing you, now don't we?" She sauntered toward me as her blonde hair blew in the ocean breeze; giving her an unearthly quality. I didn't understand how someone so beautiful could be so corrupt. She wrapped her long, skinny fingers around my left hand and slid the ring on my finger. It held a stone shaped like a teardrop in a black metal setting. An aquamarine. It reminded me of a drop of pristine water the color of my eyes. It took my breath away and matched my necklace perfectly. I examined Priscilla's face, unsure as to why she would give this to me now. She stared intently at the ring as if waiting for something to happen. Confused, I glanced back down too. The large aquamarine stone sparkled brightly and the skin beneath warmed and slowly grew hotter. The heat spread up my hand and wrapped around my wrist to my trace. The heat turned to a burning fire and I watched in awe as the trace on my wrist began to expand. From the three spirals the seaweed began to creep and twist outward; creating a beautiful design in and of itself. It wound back around my wrist and up toward the ring. Finally, it encircled my finger and stopped. I looked up at Priscilla in shock. She leered at me with wicked excitement.

"Excellent." She slowly walked back to Isadora. I stared at my newly elaborated trace with bewilderment and looked over at Kira, who was now crying so hard, her whole body shook. The fiery resolve cloaked my heart once more.

"Why are you doing this!?" I challenged Priscilla. She twisted around, appalled at my outburst. I thought I heard her hiss.

"You are in our way. You are the only thing that stands between the Sirens and complete and absolute power of all Tydes. Keto is our true leader now, and nothing," her approaching steps were menacing as she stared daggers at me, "nothing is going to stand in her way."

"You can't kill me. Everyone will be looking for me. They'll figure out what you've done," I informed her calmly.

"We're already two steps ahead of you, sweet Anastasia. We won't be killing you tonight. Your precious Kira will do the honors." She smiled at Kira, who was now screaming and struggling against her bindings. Isadora opened her mouth and began to sing, and Kira's body went limp as she stared dumbfounded at Isadora. I immediately blocked out the song; not allowing it to enter my conscious. Priscilla smiled at me knowingly and slowly bent over Kira to undo her bindings. She ripped the tape off her mouth but Kira didn't even flinch. She continued to look fixedly at

Isadora. Priscilla handed her something I recognized from a previous vision. A long, silver dagger.

"No! You can't do this!" I screamed at Priscilla.

"Of course I can." She smiled at me innocently, then allowed the evil to drip down her face. She radiated darkness. And not the good, comforting kind like Finn. This darkness was all-consuming and devoured anything in its path. She stepped aside as Kira got to her feet; grasping the dagger tightly. Kira's gaze shifted to me and I noticed that her usually warm green eyes had turned into hollow black holes. Panic started to build in my chest as I watched her slowly slink towards me. I had to concentrate. I had to think. I was the direct descendant of Thetis! I had her essence running through my veins. I was destined to be stronger than any other Tyde or Nereid...but I didn't know what to do. My essence was useless if I couldn't figure out how to use it. I let my resolve turn back into unadulterated rage, and handed it over willingly to my heart and soul. I relaxed and allowed it to engulf me; strengthen me. I felt my necklace and ring warm as the inner glow spread outwards again and drenched every cell in my body with energy. Wind, sea and shore. Wind, sea and shore.

As she stepped closer and closer, I concentrated on the sand around me. I planted both of my feet firmly and drew a circle with my eyes. My imaginary circle in the sand began to tremble and I waited for Kira to step inside. She still stared at me blankly with the blade drawn and pointed directly at me. The moment her back foot breached the circle, I raised my bound hands and a wall of sand shot up around us; blocking out the rest of the world, as well as Isadora's poisonous song. Kira was instantly released from her trance and looked around, confused. She gawked at the knife she held, then at me, and threw it down in disgust. She ran to me in a panic.

"Stasia! Oh my God! What was I about to do!?" The waterworks started up again.

"It was Isadora, not you. Listen to me, Kira." She tried her best to hold in her sobs and took a deep shaky breath. "I need you to untie my bindings." She nodded and frantically unfastened the bindings around my legs and hands. I could tell this had been an incredibly traumatic experience for her already, and I wished there was a way I could protect her from the reality of our situation. Unfortunately, that wasn't possible.

I let the sand cocoon collapse and it came crashing back to the ground with the force of an avalanche. I immediately assessed our situation. Both Isadora and Priscilla appeared to be in shock; still trying to figure out what had just happened. The instant they realized I was free from the bindings and Kira was out of her trance, they both began to cantillate. Unable to block them out, Kira once again fell under the guise of their songs. Even for me, it took a great deal of effort to block them out. It felt like several hundred pounds of pressure weighing down on my entire body, threatening to crush me. In my fight to withstand the onslaught, I didn't see Kira retrieve the dagger from the sand.

With Kira bearing down on me again, I decided to try out my other supposed abilities. I started channeling every morsel of red hot rage that had culminated inside of me. I took a deep breath and as I projected outward, a gust of wind exploded out from around my body; pinning Isadora against a tall palm tree. The force of her body hitting the dense bark of the tree broke her song, and I quickly dodged Kira's strike; easily knocking the knife out of her hand and into the sand. Priscilla appeared in front of me, wrapped her hand around my neck and swiftly lifted me off the ground. She tossed me like a rag doll against a jagged rock, effectively slicing my arm open and knocking the wind out of me. I watched helplessly as she charged Kira and threw her to the ground in a heap. Then she lunged for the knife lying in the sand and advanced on me. I tried to move but the pain in my abdomen wouldn't allow it. She picked me up by my hair and flung me down in the sand. While I struggled between the need to fight and the excruciating pain, she jumped on top of me, held me down by my throat and lifted the knife in the air with a sickening smile. Squelching the pain, I channeled it into my arms instead and pushed her body off of me. She flew off and crumpled on the sand beside me. I scrambled back to my feet, ready to defend myself, but she was unconscious.

Free of her wind prison and eyes burning with hatred, Isadora now began attacking me and wrestling me to the ground. She pulled a second knife from her clothing and swung it down towards my chest. In an instant, she was ripped off of me and thrown against a tree by an unseen force. I rolled over and got to my feet; sweeping the beach with my eyes. Priscilla was nowhere to be seen, and Kira was lying motionless in the sand. Someone stepped out from the forest and I snatched the other knife from the sand, ready to attack. Her straight black hair and piercing blue eyes caught me off guard, but she held up her hands to let me know she wouldn't hurt me.

"Natasha?" I squinted at her and tried to figure out if it was really her. Her eyes widened.

"Stasia, move!" she yelled. I rolled to the right, just in time to see Isadora bring a dagger down in the sand where I had just been. In the same instant, an axe came out of nowhere; hitting her directly in the chest. She collapsed in the sand beside me and I watched in horror as the life drained from her flawless face. I tore my eyes away and ran to Kira, desperate to make sure she was still alive. Her leg was drooped over at an odd angle and her face was pale, but she was still breathing.

"Kira!" I called out to her. "Kira!" Her eyelids fluttered and slowly opened. They widened in panic and she pulled me down on top of her in a tight hug. I felt a hand on my shoulder.

"Stasia, we need to go. Priscilla is still nearby," Natasha urged me. I inspected Kira's leg.

"What about Kira? There's no way she can walk," I told her frantically.

"Of course I ca-" She let out an ear-splitting scream as she tried to move her leg. I reached out to comfort her when a familiar voice caressed my ears.

"I'll carry her, but we need to move, Stasia." He lifted her in his arms with lightning speed and his deep blue eyes took me in. A blanket of security instantly wrapped around me.

"Finn," I whispered. I was so happy to see him I wanted to cry. Instead, I stood and smiled at him.

"Cease this disturbance!" The accompanying shockwave was unlike anything I'd ever experienced before. A whole fleet of trucks couldn't hold a candle to the force that shook my body in that moment. I felt myself fly backwards, hit the ground, and heard the sickening sound of breaking bones. Dazed, I painstakingly turned my head to look around for the others. Finn stood in the same spot untouched, but Kira had been ripped from his arms. She was lying a few feet away from me, unconscious. Natasha was stirring to my left, slowly trying to lift herself up off the ground. I tried to sit up too, but my body wasn't responding. A sharp pain coursed through my left side; leaving me breathless. A pool of thick, wet liquid was already collecting beneath me, and a sudden onslaught of dizziness had me closing my eyes. I tried straightening my legs, but they refused to work as well. I leaned my head to the right as someone walked out of the shroud of the dark beach.

She was terrifyingly beautiful; the most incredible contradiction I'd ever laid eyes on. She had a commanding presence that claimed the attention of every living being. The plants seemed to falter amidst her power and the sand glistened beneath her feet. Glittering silver and green scales covered both sides of her body, extending from her face down her neck, arms and legs. What could only be described as a dress of dark green kelp was draped haphazardly around her voluptuous figure; trailing behind her. Long black and dark green hair fell around her shoulders and accentuated her cat-like, bright green eyes. Keto. She glided to a stop in front of Finn and he bowed his head ever so slightly to her.

"We meet again, Scion." An amused grin twitched on her lips and I actually saw Finn's entire body tense in preparation for a fight. Her voice hardened. "What is the meaning of this dissension?"

"Your daughters have conspired to take matters into their own hands." I heard the hatred seething from his voice. At this, Priscilla emerged from the forest, her blue eyes wide with panic. She dropped to her knees. Keto looked down at her lovingly.

"Stand before me, daughter," she commanded her. Priscilla stood and raised her chin with pride. Keto's eyes lasered across to Kira, Natasha, and finally settled on me. My skin prickled. "The child has returned," she declared with annoyance.

"You knew about her?!" Priscilla gawked at Keto in surprise.

"Of course. Thetis was my sister. I knew this day would come."

"And you let her come back? Why haven't you done something about it?" Priscilla was near madness.

"Do not question my actions, daughter." Her tone was so steely, the hair on my unmoving arms rose. She shifted her attention to Finn. "She is not yet immortal. Has she not taken the journey to the river?" I spent the next couple of minutes wondering if I'd heard her right. As the blood continued to pool around me, my senses became increasingly muted and I wasn't sure of anything anymore.

"She will!" he boomed with fervor. "And she will prevail. She is the rightful leader, not you." Keto just smiled at him, but the malice behind it was obvious.

"I will not challenge a lesser being. Once she has made the journey, the time will come." She looked back at Priscilla. "Return to Lorelei. It is not your place to interfere with the destiny of the Nereids." Priscilla shrank beneath the weight of her reprimand. Keto looked directly into my now hazy eyes, and my thoughts halted under her glare.

"We will meet again, Anastasia," she threatened straight to my mind. A trickle of fear ran through me, followed swiftly by another bout of rage. Her dress of kelp swirled around her in a dramatic fashion as she turned to leave, and she disappeared back into the darkness of the beach. Finn immediately turned and unexpectedly stopped beside Natasha first to make sure she was okay. I found that odd, since she was sitting up while Kira and I were both immobile, but I didn't question it at the time. She was pretty dazed and badly bruised, but appeared to be fine. He crouched down beside me next.

"It's okay, Pasha. I'm going to take care of you," he tried to comfort me. All I could do was look up at him. I felt the energy literally draining from my body, and I was getting weaker by the minute. He glanced up at Natasha with something I'd never seen on his dark, handsome face. Fear.

"Mom, we need to hurry. She's... It's not good." Mom...Mom... My mind whirled at the word. My mom had a name now. I knew who she was. I smiled inwardly at the thought and closed my eyes. But what about my dad...Dad...Mom...

"Take her to the estuary. I'll take care of Kira," Natasha instructed Finn. Everything started to get fuzzy, and all I could think about was going to sleep. Even breathing had become an incredibly difficult task. I had the vague sense of being carried and I heard a low voice in the distance, but the all-consuming blackness was so comforting, I blocked everything else out. A numbness settled over my mind and I let it overcome me; becoming lost in its endless depths.

Thirty-Five

The next thing I remembered was breathing water. It was so cold and it hurt as it expanded in my lungs. However, with each labored breath, the darkness receded.

"Come on, Stasia, breathe. Come on." Finn. His voice was far away, but so comforting and strong. The tenor vibrated in my consciousness like an echo; making me dizzy. As the water began to circulate within my body, I was able to breathe easier and the pain in my side started to fade. It dawned on me that I was lying down and something was rubbing my hair. I tentatively opened my eyes. Finn's face swam in my vision momentarily before clearing.

"Hey there." He smiled down at me and my heart melted for the zillionth time. I wondered if I would ever get used to his presence. I hoped not.

"Hey," I croaked. My body was growing stronger, but I could tell it would be very sore. How was I healing so fast? I looked around, feeling completely out of sorts. I was in an underwater cave. The water felt…soft. Almost like a bubble bath without the bubbles. All around me a beautiful forest of sea grass, vines and kelp reached up from the bottom, while flowering plants blanketed the stone walls; creating a colorful, serene oasis. Rays of light filtered through the water from all directions, which gave the whole cave an ethereal ambiance. I was lying on a suspended hammock filled with pillows that hung from the ceiling high above. Also above me, I saw a small circle of light, and I could tell it led to the outside world. The pool! Finn must have brought me back to Thetis's house. We were in the underwater cavern I'd seen earlier.

"What kind of water is this?" I asked him.

"This connects to the lagoon, but its water has many purposes - healing being one of them."

"That's convenient." I smiled and he chuckled at me. I cast an accusing glare in his direction as I remembered something he said earlier.

"Oh, and thanks for telling me I'd be buying my dress from your mother." I raised my eyebrows at him expecting an explanation, but couldn't stop the grin fighting its way onto my lips.

"Must have slipped my mind." He shrugged his shoulders innocently and ran his fingers through my hair as his face softened. "We used to live here. On the island."

"You did?" I finally had enough strength to sit up.

"We did..." he clarified. "Not being able to talk to you about any of this...it's been so hard. We would have grown up together, Stasia." He shook his head and crushing sadness hit me with force. My eyes burned with tears, even as the water washed them away.

"Why, Finn?" I began to sob in earnest. "Why did they give me away?"

"To protect you," he said softly, and wrapped his arms around me. I put my head on his shoulder and let myself cry. I cried for the life I never had. I cried for the parents I would never know. I cried for myself; for the life of pain I endured for so many years. "They would have killed you, just like they killed them. No one knew you had been born except for a select few, and Thetis wanted to keep it that way. But she loved you so much and talked about you all the time. It tore her apart...she cried every day."

"But she didn't protect me, Finn. She gave me away to people almost as evil as Keto. Why didn't she save me? Why didn't she do something?"

"She didn't know. She only knew what I told her from your brief appearances to me. It broke her heart that you weren't able to appear to her. Only after she died was she able to see you."

One of my previous reveries came back to the forefront of my mind. The woman on the water. I looked wide-eyed at Finn.

"It was her. She was there in my first vision. Right before I saw you and Nicolet, I was on the beach and she was in the water. I could hear her, too." I couldn't hide my excitement about this newest revelation. "She called my name. She's the reason I chose the name 'Anastasia' when I came to Lorelei!"

"She was ecstatic about that." He smiled down at me.

"How did she know if she was dead? Wait - how could you know she was happy about it?" His face froze when he realized he'd said something he shouldn't have.

"You'll know everything in time. But first, I have something to give to you." He cupped my cheek. "It's from your mother." He took my hand and we swam up toward the fountain. My body was now completely healed...even the soreness had disappeared. It was miraculous.

He helped me out of the fountain and gave me a fluffy robe to put over my wet clothes. His shorts and t-shirt were soaked as well, but he didn't seem to mind. The house was just as immaculate as the first time I'd seen it, except for one thing. Now I knew this really was my home. Or would have been. As we walked up the grand staircase, I glanced over my shoulder at Thetis's portrait hanging above the fireplace. Just as I suspected, she not only wore the same necklace in the portrait, but also the same ring.

"Finn?" I stopped at the landing. He turned to face me with concern in his eyes. "What does this mean?" I held up my hand to show him the ring and expanded trace. He simply smiled and took my hand again.

"It means you're one step closer," he said simply. I furrowed my brow at him, not happy with his vague answer, and then followed him up the stairs and into one of the many doors in the main hall. My hand went to my mouth as I gasped, and Finn put his hands on my waist to steady me. It was a good thing too, because my legs were about to give out. Stark white carpet supported my bare feet and the walls around us were painted a bright silver. A white wicker crib stood in the middle of the room, shielded by a white lace curtain hanging from a hook in the ceiling. The lace was wrapped around the crib to thwart any light from reaching a sleeping baby's eyes. I walked closer and ran my hands along the sides. In one corner of the room sat a single rocking chair. I recognized it from one of my dreams. A large antique wardrobe stood against one wall with a smaller chest of drawers beside it. The opposite wall had been painted to resemble the ocean; white, blue and silver paint swirled to create crashing waves. I was completely speechless. Above the window, lined up on a shelf, perched rustic letters that spelled out one word: Anastasia.

"This was my room," I whispered the words aloud, testing them on my lips.

"She would sit in here for hours at a time." A faraway look changed his features and tears formed in his eyes. I suddenly realized that all this time, I'd only thought about myself. I turned to face him.

"You miss her," I said softly. His tears spilled over and he nodded.

"Yes. Very much. I didn't know your father very well, but Thetis...she was an amazing Goddess. She taught me so much. You're like her in so many ways. I don't know what I would have done if I'd lost you. You stopped breathing. I thought..." His sadness meshed with my own and I felt my heavy heart lighten. I stood on my tiptoes and kissed each tear as they slid down his cheeks. He hugged me close. We stood that way for several minutes, sharing in each other's grief; comforting one another. I'd never felt so loved. He leaned back to look in my eyes, and the storm of emotion I saw on his face caught me by surprise. He gently wiped away a tear that escaped down my cheek and met my eyes again. In his deep blue ones were whispers of tenderness floating within, layered with desperation. And something else…something much more powerful…

"I love you, Anastasia." He whispered it so softly I almost didn't hear him, but once it registered, I got chills and my soul danced. I knew then that I loved him, too. I'd never been so sure of something in my entire life. He'd been with me through everything and had never once doubted my strength and courage. He had become the sturdy bridge between the old me and this brand new world of the unexpected. He knew me better than I knew myself, and was willing to give me something I'd never had before: unconditional love. There was no one else I would entrust my heart to.

"I love you, too." His dark features lit up and the joy in his smile threatened to sweep me off my feet. It was his kiss that sent me over the edge. The mixture of our salty tears and newly professed love for each other blossomed down deep in my soul; planting the seed that would glow within me forever. The depth of his feelings played out on his soft, tender lips as his strong arms held me close. I lost all track of time, letting the power of that one moment take hold of us; binding us together.

Eventually he took my hand again and led me out to the hall. We turned down yet another hallway and entered a large wooden door with pointed rustic hinges. Mahogany shelves covered every wall and ran from floor to ceiling. Each shelf overflowed with old books and manuscripts. There was even one of those ladders that ran along the walls on wheels, so you could reach the books on the top shelves. The whole room smelled of worn leather and firewood. A large mahogany desk sat facing a fireplace that hadn't been used in a very long time. Finn produced a small skeleton key from his pocket and unlocked one of the drawers in the desk. He pulled out a large wooden box. Sitting it on top of the desk, he took a deep breath and looked up at me with a weighted gaze.

"This was Thetis's study." He slid the box across the desk to me. "It's time."

I inspected it carefully. A large engraving dominated the top of the box; an upside down triangle with three swirls extending from the corners. I ran my fingers over it lightly and the lock clicked; catching me off guard. I looked up hesitantly at Finn, suddenly terrified by the possibility of its contents. I knew the box didn't contain anything dangerous or harmful, but I knew it held something much more potent: Answers. Was I ready for this? Could I handle what was inside? He smiled at me encouragingly and pulled the chair out from behind the desk.

"Maybe you should sit down first." I walked around the table with shaking legs and lowered myself down into the leather chair. I ran my hands over the soft, worn arms. My mother sat there, in that very seat, at that very desk. I smiled, and my hesitation turned to eagerness as I reached for the box in front of me. I opened the lid and the smell of lavender wafted around me. I breathed in deeply; cherishing the smell that I'd always loved. A flat velvety box was the first treasure to show itself. Bracelets, necklaces and earrings filled every inch of it. All the jewelry had one single thing in common; different sizes and shapes of aquamarine. I looked up at Finn.

"Turquoise represents the Tydes, but aquamarine represented Thetis." He grinned knowingly at me. "And now you." I instinctively touched my necklace.

"All this time, I just thought aquamarine held a special meaning for you…" I said to him with wonder.

"Anything connected to you holds a special meaning for me." He winked at me. A separate velvet drawstring bag tumbled out as I closed the box. I hadn't seen it among the rest of the jewelry. I untied the strings and reached inside. It was another necklace with a pendant made of the same dark metal, but I knew this one was meant for only me. The pendant was the exact shape of my trace, a triangle shaped aquamarine set in its middle. It was breathtaking. Finn gently unhooked the necklace currently around my neck and replaced it with my new one. It felt as if it belonged against my skin, and it warmed slightly when I touched it with my finger. A small slip of paper fell out of the bag as I placed it back in the box. It read:

Triskelion (Tri-Goddess): Sea, Wind, Shore

I turned my wrist over to inspect my trace. So that was what the three spirals stood for. Three spirals, three major abilities.

"You're a Tri-Goddess, Stasia." My eyebrows went up in disbelief. "The seaweed that makes up your trace is another symbol of Thetis. She had a strong connection with sea grass. As do you." His eyes were laughing at me, along with a smirk he didn't try to hide.

"It still shouldn't have attacked me," I mumbled and jabbed him in the ribs. Next, I pulled out a brown sheath with the feel of something substantial inside. Unbuckling the strap twisted around it, the leather folded back to reveal a jewel encrusted handle. It was five or six inches long and fit my hand perfectly. Aquamarine, diamonds and fresh water pearls made up the entire handle, from the bottom to the guard. Carefully, I pulled the knife from its sheath. The blade itself was silver and around six inches long. It was utterly deadly and incredibly beautiful. I had to admit, the dagger felt good in my hand. Finn gently took it from me and held it up; admiring it.

"Wow. This is amazing," he said, awe-struck. As he drooled over my new weapon, I pulled out a curious assortment of items that didn't seem to have anything to do with each other. A two-inch piece of rope, a conch shell, a large smooth black stone, a gorgeous antique compass that didn't appear to work, and a ring of three skeleton keys. Each key was a different metal: bronze, silver, and gold.

The last thing in the box was a very old leather bound book. Upon closer inspection, I saw that it was more of a journal, but it was massive; more the size of a scrapbook, it held a collection of various maps, directions, drawings, and information. I couldn't imagine the invaluable information hidden within its seams, and I couldn't wait to devour every last bit of it. As I held it in my hand, I felt a piece of paper that was attached to the back. I retrieved it carefully and unfolded the delicate stationary. A letter. I felt the blood drain from my face.

My Dearest Pasha,

I shot a skeptical look at Finn. "What does 'Pasha' really mean?" He averted his eyes sheepishly.

"It means 'princess'. It was her nickname for you." My heart warmed and I gave him a wide smile and kept reading.

My Dearest Pasha,

If you have received this letter, it means you have found your way back to our sacred home. And for that, the entire island shall rejoice. I cannot tell you how much it saddens me that I will not be there to welcome you. Destiny brought you into this wicked world because I am destined to leave it. Any anger towards me is warranted and equally justified. I know that to save you, I have to let you go. I will never forgive myself, but I hope there comes a day when you are able to forgive me. Until then, know that I love you with all of my heart. Not a minute has gone by when I didn't think about you. Not a day has gone by that I didn't cry for you. You truly are my everything.

It is important for you to know I have seen my own demise, as well as your father's. They will steal us both from you. He will be taken any day now. He is human and therefore more vulnerable than I. I have not told him of my knowledge. As you will learn, some things are better left unknown. As half human, you are also vulnerable to the hands of our enemies. Before you can fulfill your destiny, you alone must complete your essence by journeying to the River Styx before the age of eighteen. Know that we will live on through you, my daughter. You are the future, Anastasia. You will carry on the legacy and lead with dignity and grace. This is your destiny. This is why you have been Chosen.

The valise contains everything you will need and more. Be strong, my child. You will endure. Goddess blood runs through your veins and a glorious Goddess you shall be.

With all my love,

Mother

My tears flowed freely as I read the letter again and again. The simple fact that these were her own words made my heart sing. She loved me. She was depending on me. I couldn't let her down. I wouldn't let her down. With a renewed confidence in myself, I met Finn's eyes to see he was watching me with unabated patience and love. I set down the letter and took in all of the contents of the box, or valise, as she had called it.

"What do I have to do?" I asked, with as much courage as I could manage. His dark blue eyes turned stormy, but his smile brightened the room.

"The River Styx is one of the five rivers of the Underworld. Without your parents, it's the only way to complete your essence."

"So...I have to go to the Underworld." It sounded simple....right?

"Not exactly. Your soul has to go to the Underworld. Your body will remain in this realm."

"So that means....?"

He stepped closer and his features darkened completely.

"If your soul makes it back to this world and therefore your body, you will have succeeded. But to get there...you have to die."

To be continued...

Want more? Read on to catch a sneak peek at the prologue for the second book in the Daughters of the Sea Series!

Awaken (Daughters of the Sea #2)

PROLOGUE

The familiar call of seagulls diving for fish amongst the crashing waves pulled him from his restless slumber. His tired, bloodshot eyes opened and gazed upon that same weathered stone ceiling looming above. As they roamed down the sloped wall where he kept count, he pushed back the agonizing hopelessness encasing his heart. Another long night behind him simply meant another long day before him. He swung his legs over the side of his cot and gently placed his worn feet on the stone floor. It was always bitterly cold in the morning. He shivered as he glanced down at his too-skinny legs and the dirt that clung to his calloused feet. His ragged, cotton shorts now hung low around his emaciated waist, and his faded blue shirt had been discarded long ago; traded for a sunken-in, bare chest. He smoothed down his gray hair and thick beard; wondering if today would be the day.

Sighing, he stood and collected the conch shell he kept hidden within a crack in his counting wall. He found the last mark and bent down to add yet another. He never counted days, only nights. The darkness always brought out his worst nightmares, and he was continually amazed he had made it through so many. Thousands of marks littered the wall before him; a diary of solitude and sheer will captured forever in stone.

As he did every morning, he padded over to the window and looked out over the rolling sea. The lone window of his small room faced east, which allowed him one pleasure amidst the hell that had become his life.

Sunrise. At first, each sunrise brought only tears to his eyes while the slow ache in his chest grew; threatening to wrack his body with a sadness no man should bear. What those brilliant colors dancing across the sky stood for only served as a reminder to his unending loss. Another night bereft of her loving arms. Another day without her magical presence. Over the years the pain had receded, but her memory never faded. Neither did the seed of hope she planted so long ago. It grew every day; branching out and becoming the only thing that kept him alive. Many nights he peered out of his window at the white sand far below. He thought of how easy it would be to end this torture and return to her. But he knew he had a bigger purpose and he would not let her down. He would endure and wait until his heart beat no more.

Once a week he was allowed to stroll along the beach and speak to the others. But it was only a brief illusion of freedom. They could feel the eyes that watched their every move. The others had become his only companions. For years there had only been seven. But a couple of months ago, a newcomer had arrived. He heard her anguished cries at night and her deep despair was evident in the scratches along her arms; the victims of her own fingernails. She, too, finally succumbed to the seclusion and hopelessness; becoming void of emotion and as hollow as the rest of them. His thoughts moved back to the present and to the brilliant ball of light inching its way above the horizon. This was when he felt closest to her. He closed his eyes and called upon the memory of her ever gentle, loving eyes.

"My love, I have lived to see yet another dawn cast its light upon this retched spit of land. Thankfully, this dawn brings new hope for my weary soul. You appeared to me in my dreams once again last night, but for the first time I heard the sweet melody of your voice. You spoke to me and breathed life back into my withered heart. You told me to be

307

patient; to remain steadfast. You assured me the hour is growing near and I know the words you speak are true. Indeed, it is almost time."

The Daughters of the Sea Series

About the Author

Kristen Day is a native North Carolinian who, in true southern fashion, is addicted to sweet tea, baked goods and football. She graduated from Appalachian State University and bleeds black and gold. When she's not kayaking or making jewelry, she writes paranormal romance and urban fantasy novels. Forsaken is the first novel in the captivating and addictive Daughters of the Sea series.

Made in the USA
San Bernardino, CA
15 May 2015